Guillaume Musso is one of the most popular authors in France today. To date he has had seven novels published. His novel *Afterwards* has been made into a film starring John Malkovich. He lives in the south of France.

Anna Brown translates from French. She lives in Hertfordshire with her husband and two young children.

Anna Aitken studies French and German at St Peter's College, Oxford.

Where Would I Be Without You?

Guillaume Musso

Translated by Anna Brown
and Anna Aitken

Gallic Books
London

Where Would I Be Without You?

A Gallic Book

First published in France as Que serais-je sans toi?
by XO Éditions
Copyright © XO Éditions, 2009

English translation copyright © Gallic Books, 2011

First published in Great Britain in 2011 by Gallic Books
134 Lots Road, London, SW10 0RJ

A CIP record for this book is available from the British Library
ISBN 978-1-906040-34-5

Typeset by Gallic Books in Helvetica
Printed and bound by CPI Bookmarque, Croydon CR0 4TD

This edition printed as part of an Evening Standard promotion.

For Ingrid,
this story written in the painful wonder of that winter

I have always preferred the folly of passion to the wisdom of indifference.
Anatole France

We have all known it …
The solitude that sometimes consumes us.
That blights our sleep and plagues our mornings.

It's the sadness that comes on that first day of school.
It's when you see him kissing a prettier girl in the
playground.
It's Orly, or the Gare de l'Est at the end of a love affair.
It's the child that we'll never have together.

Sometimes it's me.
Sometimes it's you.

But sometimes, a chance meeting is enough …

1

THAT SUMMER

Our first love is always our last
Tahar Ben Jelloun

San Francisco, summer 1995

Gabrielle, a twenty-year-old American student
That summer she was in her third year at Berkeley and often wore faded jeans, a white shirt and a leather jacket. With her long straight hair and her green eyes flecked with gold she looked like Françoise Hardy in the photos taken by Jean-Marie Périer in the sixties.

That summer she divided her time between the campus library and the fire station on California Street where she volunteered as a firefighter.

That summer she had her first serious love affair.

Martin, a twenty-one-year-old Frenchman
That summer he had just completed his law degree at the Sorbonne, he was in the States to improve his English and explore the continent. As he didn't have a penny to his name he took odd jobs, working more than seventy hours a week as a waiter, ice-cream seller and gardener.

That summer, with his shoulder-length dark hair, he looked like the young Al Pacino.

That summer, he had his last serious love affair.

Berkeley cafeteria

'Hey, Gabrielle, you've got a letter!',

The girl sat at a table reading. She looked up from her book. 'What?'

'You've got a letter, honey!' repeated Carlito, the cafeteria manager, as he put a cream envelope beside her cup of tea.

Gabrielle frowned. 'Who from?'

'From Martin, the French boy. He's not working here any more but he came by this morning to leave this for you.'

Gabrielle looked at the envelope in puzzlement and slipped it into her pocket before leaving the café.

The immense lush campus, dominated by the clock tower, was bathed in summer sunshine. Gabrielle wandered along the paths and walkways of the park until she came to an empty bench in the shade of some ancient trees. Then, in the peace and quiet, she opened the letter with a mixture of apprehension and curiosity.

26 August 1995

Dear Gabrielle,

I just wanted to tell you that I am going back to France tomorrow.

I wanted you to know how much the time we spent together meant to me. Those moments in the campus cafeteria discussing books, movies, music and generally putting the world to rights meant more to me than anything else I experienced in my time in California.

When I was with you, I often wished I was a character in a novel. Because a character in a novel, or a film, wouldn't have been so awkward about telling the heroine how much he adored her, how he loved talking to her, and what a magical feeling he had when he looked at her. It was a painful, sweet and intense feeling. An amazing feeling that I've never felt before. A feeling that I wouldn't have believed possible.

That afternoon when the rain took us by surprise in the park and we sheltered in the library porch, I felt, and I think you did too, such fierce attraction that I was momentarily shocked. I know that we almost kissed then. I held back because you had told me about your boyfriend who was travelling around Europe, and who you could not cheat on. And I didn't want to be one of those blokes you despised who hit on you without knowing whether their advances were welcome.

I do know though that had we kissed, I would have been in seventh heaven, not caring whether it was raining or not, because it would have shown that I meant something to you. I know that the kiss would have stayed with me for a long time, like a glorious memory to hold on to when I felt alone. But actually some people say that the most beautiful love affairs are the ones that don't get *the chance to develop. So perhaps it's the same for the kisses that don't actually happen.*

When I look at you, I'm reminded of a film's twenty-four frames a second. With you, the first twenty-three frames are light and luminous, but the twenty-fourth reveals a real sadness, which is such a contrast to the inner radiance you seem to have. It's like a subliminal image, a hairline crack: a tiny flaw that defines you more surely than all your qualities and achievements. I often wondered what was making you sad. I often hoped you would tell me, but you never did.

Please take care of yourself, and try not to give way to melancholy. Don't let that twenty-fourth frame take over. Don't let the demon have the upper hand.

I want you to know that I found you as magnificent as the sun. But I know you have people telling you that all the time, so I am just like all the others after all.

I'll never forget you.
Martin

Gabrielle looked up. Her heart was racing. It was so unexpected.

From the very first lines, she'd realised that the letter was special. Of course, she knew what had happened between them, but not how Martin felt. She looked around her, worried that her face was betraying her emotion. When she felt tears coming, she left the campus and took the subway back to downtown San Francisco. She had planned to stay longer at the library, but she knew that she would be incapable of doing so now.

Sitting in the carriage, she alternated between surprise at Martin's letter and the painful pleasure she took in reading it. It wasn't every day that someone paid her that kind of attention. And usually when it happened it was because of her looks, not her personality.

Everyone thought she was strong and outgoing, when in fact she was fragile and still a little bit lost in the contradictions of being a young woman. People who had known her for years weren't aware of her distress. But he'd sensed this in her and had understood everything in just a few weeks.

That summer, the heat had overwhelmed the Californian coast – even San Francisco with its microclimate. In the carriage the passengers seemed lifeless, as if stunned by the summer torpor. But Gabrielle was not among them. She had suddenly become a medieval heroine, transported to an age of chivalry: an age in which courtly love made its first appearance. Chrétien de Troyes had just sent her a missive and he was resolved to transform her friendship for him.

She read and reread her letter, which did her good, but was also painful.

No, Martin Beaumont, you're not like the other guys.

She felt happy, desperate and undecided.

So undecided that she missed her stop. Now she had an extra station to go through in the heat to get back to her place.

Nice one, she said to herself. She obviously wasn't much good at being a heroine!

The next day, San Francisco International Airport
9 a.m.

It was raining.

Still half asleep, Martin stifled a yawn and gripped the bus's handrail as it lurched round a bend on its worn-out suspension. He'd flung a moleskin coat over his shoulders, and wore ripped jeans, battered trainers and a T-shirt with the image of a rock band on the front.

That summer, all the kids were crazy about Kurt Cobain. His head was full of memories of his two months in the US. He'd seen so much and felt so much. California had taken him so far away from Évry and the Parisian suburbs. At the start of the summer, he'd envisaged doing the exams to become a police officer, but the trip to the USA, a rite-of-passage journey, had changed all that. The kid from the estates had gained in self-confidence, in the country where life was just as tough as anywhere else, but where people still had the hope and ambition to fulfil their dreams.

And his own dream was to write stories – stories that would reach out to people, stories about ordinary people to whom extraordinary things happened. Reality wasn't enough for him, and fiction had always been a part of his life. Since he was a child, his favourite heroes had so often drawn him out of his misery, comforted him in his disappointments and his sorrows. They'd fed his imagination, honed his emotions so that he could see life through a prism that made it tolerable.

The shuttle from Powell Street dropped its passengers off in front of the international terminal. In the scramble,

18

Martin got his guitar caught in the baggage rack. Weighed down like a mule, he was the last to get off the bus. He rummaged through his pocket for his ticket, and distractedly tried to work out which way to go through the urban maze.

He didn't see her straight away.

She had double-parked her car. The engine was still running.

Gabrielle.

She was drenched from the rain. She was cold. She was shivering a little.

They spotted each other at the same moment. They ran towards each other.

They hugged, their hearts hammering. The way you do the first time, when you still believe in it.

Then she smiled and teased him. 'So, Martin Beaumont, do you really think that the kisses you never get are the most intense?'

They kissed.

Their mouths sought each other, their breathing merged, their wet hair became entangled. He had his hand on the nape of her neck, she had her hand on his cheek. In the urgency of it all, they exchanged clumsy words of love.

She said, 'Stay a bit longer!'

Stay a bit longer!

He didn't realise it, but that was to be the most precious moment of his life. There would be nothing purer, more radiant or more intense than Gabrielle's green eyes shining in the rain on that summer's morning.

And her voice imploring him: Stay a bit longer!

28 August – 7 September 1995, San Francisco

By paying an extra hundred dollars, Martin had been able to postpone the date of his departure. That one hundred dollars allowed him to experience the ten most important days of his life.

They loved each other.

In the bookshops on the streets of Berkeley, where a little of the old bohemian atmosphere still lingered.

In the cinema on Reid Street, where they were so engrossed in one another they didn't see much of the film *Leaving Las Vegas*.

In a little restaurant, over an enormous hamburger, Hawaiian-style with pineapple, and a bottle of Sonoma.

They loved each other.

They goofed about, played like kids, held each other's hand tight as they ran along the beach.

They loved each other.

In a university bedroom, where he improvised a totally new version of Jacques Brel's 'La Valse à Mille Temps' for her on his guitar. She danced for him, languorously at first, then faster and faster, twirling round and round, arms outstretched, palms up, like a whirling dervish.

He dropped his instrument and joined her in her trance. Together they became a spinning top, finally sinking to the ground where …

… they loved each other.

They floated, they flew.

They were God, they were angels, they were alone.

Around them, the world receded and became nothing more than a theatrical backdrop where they were the only actors.

20

They loved each other.

With a love that ran in the blood.

With a constant euphoria.

In the moment and for eternity.

And at the same time, fear was all around.

Fear of an absence.

Fear of finding oneself without oxygen.

Their love was so obvious, so confusing.

It was both a bolt of lightning and annihilation.

The most beautiful of springtimes, the most violent of storms.

And yet, they loved each other.

*

She loved him.

In the middle of the night.

In her car that she'd parked in a parking lot in Tenderloin, the dodgy area of the city. The car stereo throbbed to the sound of gangsta rap and 'Smells Like Teen Spirit'.

It was the thrill of danger, the other's body rising and falling amid the sudden glare of headlights, with the ever-present threat of being attacked by gangs or caught by the cops.

This time, it wasn't a 'bouquet of roses' kind of love, a 'whispering sweet nothings' love. It was a red-hot love, where you grabbed more than you gave. That night, between them, it was all about getting a hit, getting a fix, feeling the buzz, like a junkie. She wanted to show him that side of her, the less polished part behind the romantic image: the fault line, the twenty-fourth frame. She wanted to see if he would follow her onto this terrain, or leave her by the wayside.

That night, she was no longer his sweetheart – she was his lover.

*

He loved her.

Tenderly.

On the beach, in the small hours.

She'd fallen asleep on his coat. He'd rested his head on her stomach.

Two young lovers enveloped by the warm breeze in the pink light of a Californian sky.

Their bodies at rest, their hearts as one, entwined, while a little portable radio placed on the sand played an old ballad.

8 September 1995, San Francisco International Airport 9 a.m.

End of the dream.

They held each other on the concourse of the airport, amid the crowds and the noise.

Reality had finally beaten the illusion of a love that was timeless.

And it was brutal. And it hurt.

Martin sought Gabrielle's gaze. This morning, the glints of gold had disappeared from her eyes. They didn't know what to say any more. So they hugged each other, they clung to each other, each trying to find in the other the strength he or she was lacking. In this game, Gabrielle was stronger than he was. Those past days of happiness, she'd known she was snatching them from life, while he'd thought they would last for ever.

But she was the one who was cold. So he took off his moleskin coat and draped it over her shoulders. To begin with, she refused the coat, making out that she was OK, but he insisted because he could clearly see that she was shivering. In turn, she removed her silver chain with the small Southern Cross pendant. She slipped it into his hand.

Final call. They were forced to part.

For the umpteenth time, he asked her, 'This boyfriend of yours travelling around Europe, do you love him?'

But, as always, she put a finger to his lips and looked down.

Then they parted and he went through to the departure lounge, never taking his eyes off her.

9 September, Paris, Charles de Gaulle Airport

After two stopovers and numerous delays, towards the end of the afternoon, the Aer Lingus flight landed at Roissy. In San Francisco, it had still been summer. In Paris, it was already autumn. The sky was dark and dirty.

A little disoriented, his eyes red from lack of sleep, Martin waited for his luggage. On a TV screen, a plastic-looking blonde was belting out 'Dieu m'a donné la foi'. That morning he had left Clinton's America, this evening he was back in Chirac's France. And he hated his country because his country was not Gabrielle's country.

23

He retrieved his case and his guitar then began his trek back home: first the RER to Châtelet-Les Halles, then another train to Évry, and finally the bus to the Pyramides housing estate. He wanted to cut himself off from everyone with some music, but the batteries in his Walkman had given up the ghost a long time ago. He was in a state of confusion, bewildered, as if his heart had been injected with poison. Then he realised that tears were trickling down his face and that the little jerks from his estate were watching and taking the piss out of him. He tried to pull himself together: it didn't do to show signs of weakness in Évry, on a bus heading for Les Pyramides. So he turned his head, but realised for the first time that he wouldn't be sleeping next to her that night.

And the tears started flowing again.

The next day
Martin left the tiny bedroom that he had in his grandparents' council flat.

Lift wasn't working. Nine floors on foot. Letterboxes torn out, arguments in the stairways. Nothing had changed.

For half an hour, he looked for a telephone box that hadn't been vandalised. He slid his fifty-unit card into the slot, and dialled a transatlantic number.

*

Some seven thousand miles away, it was twelve thirty in the afternoon in San Francisco. The telephone in the Berkeley campus cafeteria started to ring …

49, 48, 47 …

His stomach in knots, he closed his eyes and simply said, 'It's me, Gabrielle. I'm phoning as arranged.'

Initially, she laughed because she was so surprised and because she was happy, then she burst into tears because it was too tough not to be together any more.

… 38, 37, 36 …

He told her that he was missing her so much, that he adored her, that he didn't know how to live without her …

… She told him how much she wished she were there with him, to be near him, to sleep with him, to kiss him, to caress him, to bite him, to kill him with love.

… 25, 24, 23 …

He listened to her voice and everything came back to him: the texture of her skin, the smell of the sand, the wind in her hair, her 'lots of love' …

… his 'lots of love', his hand clasped round the back of her neck, his eyes searching for hers, the violence and the tenderness of their embraces.

… 20, 19, 18 …

He stared in terror at the liquid crystal display on the phone box. It was torture to see the units on his card tick away so fast.

… 11, 10, 9 …

Then they had nothing more to say, because their voices became choked.

They just listened to the thudding of their hearts, beating in concert, and the softness of their breathing which merged, despite the damned phone.

… 3, 2, 1, 0 …

Back then, nobody yet really knew about the Internet, email, Skype or instant messaging.

Back then, love letters sent from France took ten days to reach California.

Back then, when you wrote 'I love you', you had to wait three weeks for the reply.

And having to wait three weeks for an 'I love you' back is unbearable when you're twenty.

*

Then, gradually, Gabrielle's letters became more and more intermittent until eventually they stopped altogether.

Then she hardly ever answered the phone, either in the cafeteria, or in her university room, leaving her room-mate to take messages for her.

One night, in a fury, Martin ripped out the phone handset and smashed it against the glass walls of the phone box. Rage drove him to do what he'd always condemned others for doing. He'd become like one of those people he detested: people who wrecked public property, who needed to knock back a six-pack of beer before going to bed, who smoked joints all day because they didn't give a damn: about life, about happiness, about sorrow, about yesterday, about tomorrow.

In total turmoil, he regretted having encountered love because right now he no longer knew how to keep going. Each day, he convinced himself that tomorrow it would all be better, that time would heal everything, but the next day things just went from bad to worse.

*

Eventually, Martin told himself that the only way to win Gabrielle back was by putting all his heart into it. Through action, he found the strength to regroup. He went back to university and got a job as a warehouseman at the Carrefour hypermarket in the Évry 2 mall. At night, he worked as a security guard in a car park and he began to save every penny.

It was at this point that he could have done with an older brother, a father, a mother, or a best friend, someone to tell him never to 'give all his heart'. Because when you did, you ran the risk of never being able to love again afterwards.

But Martin had no one to listen to, he could only follow his own reckless instincts.

*

10 December 1995

Gabrielle, my love,

Let me call you that even if it is for the last time.
I'm not kidding myself any more – I know that you're drifting away from me.
For my part, the absence between us has only served to strengthen my feelings and I hope that you do still miss me a little.

27

I am there, Gabrielle, with you.

Closer to you than I've ever been.

At the moment we're like two people making signs at each other, each on opposite sides of a river. Sometimes, they meet up briefly in the middle of the bridge, spend a short time together sheltered from the ill winds, then each goes back to his or her side, expecting to meet again later, for longer. Because when I close my eyes and imagine us in ten years' time I see in my head pictures of happiness which don't seem unrealistic to me: sunshine, children's laughter, the intimate glances of a couple who are still in love.

And I don't want that opportunity to pass me by.

I'm there, Gabrielle, on the other side of the river.

I'm waiting for you.

The bridge that separates us may seem in bad repair, but it's a solid bridge, built with logs from trees that have withstood many storms.

I understand that you're afraid to cross it.

And I know that perhaps you'll never cross it.

But give me some hope.

I'm not asking you for a promise, for a reply, for a commitment.

I just want some sign from you.

And there's a very easy way to give me that sign. You'll find in this letter a special Christmas gift: a plane ticket for New York on 24 December. I'll be in Manhattan that day, and I'll wait for you all day at the Café DeLalo, at the foot of the Empire State Building. Come and meet me there if you believe that we've got a future together.

Lots of love,
Martin

24 December 1995, New York
9 a.m.

Martin's footsteps crunched on the fresh snow. There was an arctic chill, but the sky was clear blue, barely disturbed by a light breeze that sent a few snowflakes spinning.

New Yorkers were clearing their sidewalks in good spirits, buoyed up by the Christmas decorations and the carols ringing out from even the smallest store.

Martin pushed open the door to Café DeLalo. He removed his gloves, hat and scarf and rubbed his hands together to warm up. He hadn't slept for two days and felt feverish, excited, as if drip-fed with caffeine.

The place was warm and exuded Christmas good cheer, weighed down with garlands, sugar angels and gingerbread men, all hanging overhead. The scent of cinnamon, cardamom and banana pancakes mingled in the air. On the radio in the background, Christmas melodies alternated with the latest pop music. That winter, the Oasis craze was in full swing, and 'Wonderwall' played constantly on the radio.

Martin ordered a hot chocolate sprinkled with mini marshmallows before sitting at a table next to the window.

Gabrielle would come, he was sure of it.

At 10 a.m., he checked for the thousandth time the schedule of the ticket he had sent her.

Departure: 23 December 22.55 San Francisco (SFO)
Arrival: 24 December 07.15 New York (JFK)

He wasn't worried: with the snow, the flights would be hours late. On the other side of the window, a human tide

29

spilt onto the sidewalk, like some peaceable army that had traded its weapons for paper cups with plastic lids.

At 11 a.m., Martin glanced through the *USA Today* that another customer had left on a table. In its pages, the debate still raged on about O. J. Simpson's acquittal, the soaring value of the stock market and about *ER*, the new TV series that had taken the US by storm. That winter, Bill Clinton hadn't yet met Monica Lewinsky and was valiantly confronting Congress in defence of his social policies.

Gabrielle would come.

At midday, Martin put on his Walkman headphones. Staring into space, he walked with Bruce Springsteen along the 'Streets of Philadelphia'.

She would come.

At 1 p.m., he went to buy a hot dog from a street vendor, all the while never taking his eyes off the door to the café, just in case she …

She was going to come.

At 2 p.m., he started *The Catcher in the Rye*, the book he'd bought at the airport.

One hour later, and he'd only read four pages …

Surely she would come.

At 4 p.m., he got out his Game Boy and lost five rounds of Tetris in less than ten minutes.

Perhaps she would come.

At 5 p.m., the staff at the café started to look at him a bit strangely.

One-in-two chance that she'd come.

At 6 p.m., the café closed. He was the last customer to leave.

Even once outside, he still believed it would happen. And yet …

San Francisco
3 p.m.
Heavy-hearted, Gabrielle walked along the sand, the ocean before her. The weather mirrored her mood: the Golden Gate Bridge was wreathed in fog, dense clouds shrouded the island of Alcatraz and the wind blew wildly. To keep out the cold, she had wrapped herself up in Martin's coat.

She sat down cross-legged on the beach and took the sheaf of letters that he had written her out of her bag. She reread certain excerpts. *Thinking of you makes my heart beat faster. I wish you were here, in the middle of my night. I wish I could close my eyes and open them to find you.* She fished out of an envelope the little gifts that he'd sent her: a four-leaf clover, an edelweiss flower, an old black-and-white photo of Jean Seberg and Jean-Paul Belmondo in *Breathless*.

She knew that something unusual was happening between them. It was an extremely strong bond that she wasn't sure she'd ever find again. She imagined him waiting for her in New York, in the café where he'd arranged to meet her. She imagined him and she wept.

*

In New York, the café had been closed for half an hour, but Martin was still waiting outside, immobile and frozen.

At that moment, he had no idea what Gabrielle's real feelings were. He didn't know how much good their relationship had done her, how much she'd needed it, how lost and adrift she'd felt before him. He didn't know that he had stopped her from losing her footing at a very sensitive time in her life.

*

Rain began to fall on the sand in San Francisco. The mournful wailing of the Wave Organ, vibrating to the sound of the waves surging through its stone pipes, could be heard in the distance. Gabrielle stood up to take the cable car back up the steep slope of Fillmore Street. She made the journey on auto-pilot as it took her two blocks behind Grace Cathedral to Lenox Hospital.

Huddled in Martin's coat, she went through the sliding doors one by one. Despite its festive decorations, the hospital entrance hall was dull and dreary.

Next to a drinks machine, Dr Elliott Cooper recognised her face and guessed that she'd been crying.

'Hello, Gabrielle,' he said, trying to give her a reassuring smile.

'Hello, Doctor.'

*

Martin waited for her until 11 p.m., alone in the biting-cold night. He felt empty-hearted and ashamed. Ashamed of having gone to the frontline without protecting himself, with his heart on his sleeve, with his youthful enthusiasm and his naiveté.

He had gambled it all and he had lost it all.

So he roamed the streets: 42nd Street, the bars, the cafés, the alcohol, the encounters that were so obviously bad news. That winter, New York was still New York. It was no longer the city of Warhol or the Velvet Underground, but neither was it yet the sanitised city that it was to become. It was a New York that was still edgy and dangerous for those who were ready to let in its demons.

That night, for the first time, Martin's eyes took on a look of severity and gloom.

He would never be a writer. He'd be a *flic*, he'd be a hunter.

That night, not only did he lose love.

He also lost hope.

*

There it is – this is just an everyday story.

It's the story of a man and a woman who run towards each other.

Everything began with a first kiss, one summer's morning, under the San Francisco sky.

Everything nearly ended one Christmas night, in a New York bar and a Californian clinic.

Then the years went by …

PART ONE

UNDER PARISIAN SKIES

2

THE GREATEST THIEF
OF ALL

*One hates a person for the same reason
one loves him.*
Russell Banks

**Paris, Left Bank of the Seine, 29 July 2008
3 a.m.
The thief**

Paris was shrouded in the darkness of a midsummer's night. On the rooftops of the Musée d'Orsay, a furtive shadow slipped behind a column then appeared again in the halo of the half-moon.

Dressed all in black, Archibald McLean tied two climbing ropes to a harness round his waist. He adjusted the black woollen hat that came down to his glistening eyes, the only part of his blackened face that was visible. The thief fastened his backpack and paused to look down at the city spread out before him. The roof of the famous museum afforded him an impressive view of the buildings on the Right Bank: the massive Palais du Louvre with its abundance of sculptures, the meringue-like basilica of the

37

Sacré-Cœur, the dome of the Grand Palais, the Ferris wheel in the Tuileries Gardens and the green and gold dome of the Opéra Garnier. In the gloom, the city had a timeless air – it was the Paris of Arsène Lupin, of *The Phantom of the Opera*.

Archibald pulled on his climbing gloves, steadied himself, and then uncoiled the rope down the side of the stone wall. Tonight's escapade would be difficult and dangerous, but that was exactly why it was so enticing.

The *flic*

'He must be mad!'

Hiding out in his car, police captain Martin Beaumont trained his binoculars on the man he'd been pursuing for over three years: Archibald McLean, the most famous art thief of modern times.

The young *flic* was feverish with excitement. That night, he was going to arrest a famous thief, the kind a *flic* comes across once in his career. He had waited a long time for this moment and he'd replayed the scene over and over in his head. Interpol would be green with envy, as would all the private detectives hired by the millionaires Archibald had robbed.

Martin focused his binoculars to get a clearer image. Finally, Archibald's elusive shadow emerged from the darkness. Martin's heart raced as he watched him let down his rope and slide down the wall of the museum until he reached one of the two huge clock faces that overlooked the Seine.

For a moment, the *flic* thought he might catch a glimpse of his quarry's face, but Archibald was too far away and had his back to him. It seemed incredible that in his twenty-five-year career as a thief, nobody had ever seen Archibald McLean's face.

*

Archibald paused at the bottom of the glass clock face that radiated a pale light. It measured over twenty feet across, and as he stood squeezed up against it Archibald found it difficult not to feel somewhat pressed for time. He knew he might be spotted at any moment, but still his eyes darted towards the street. The banks of the Seine were quiet, but not empty: an occasional taxi drove by and a few nocturnal strollers were about, while others were making their way home after a long night out.

Without hurrying, the thief leant against the stone ledge and unhooked a diamond-tipped glass cutter from his belt. With a quick, bold sweeping movement he ran the cutter over the glass surface where the brass struts framed the clock's sixth hour. As he expected, the wheel only scratched the surface of the glass, marking out an area the size of a small hoop. Archibald fixed a three-headed suction cup onto the circle of glass then took hold of an aluminium tube the size of a torch. It emitted a beam which he ran back and forth round the score line with dexterity and assurance. The laser cut through the glass like cheese wire, allowing him to make a fine, deep fissure. The fracture quickly opened up along the line of incision. Just as the glass was about to give way, Archibald pressed on the suction cup. The heavy slab of glass broke away all in one piece, without splintering or smashing, and came to rest gently on the ground, leaving a circular hole as sharp as a guillotine. With the agility of an acrobat, Archibald slipped through the opening into one of the world's most magnificent museums. He now had thirty seconds before the alarm went off.

*

His nose pressed up against the window of his car, Martin could scarcely believe his eyes. Archibald had just made the most spectacular entry into the museum. But surely the alarm would go off at any moment. Security at the Musée d'Orsay had been heavily reinforced after a group of drunken individuals had broken in the year before by battering down one of the fire-exit doors. The revellers had wandered around the rooms for several minutes before being stopped. Time enough to slash a famous Monet painting, *Le Pont d'Argenteuil*.

The incident had caused uproar. The Minister of Culture had said that it was totally unacceptable for people to be able to get into the Orsay so easily. As a result, the museum's lack of security had come under careful scrutiny. As a member of the OCBC (the central agency set up to combat the trafficking of cultural treasures) Martin Beaumont had been asked to list and secure all possible points of access. The Orsay's famous Impressionist rooms were now supposedly impregnable. But in that case why wasn't the sodding alarm going off?

*

Archibald landed on one of the cafeteria tables. The huge glass clock was situated directly above the Café des Hauteurs, on the museum's top floor, near the rooms dedicated to the Impressionists. The thief glanced at his watch: he had twenty seconds left. He leapt onto the floor and ran up the few steps leading to the galleries. The infrared security lights formed an invisible network of long-range beams that could detect movement anywhere along the 150-foot-long corridors. He found the housing for the alarm and unscrewed the protective plate in order to plug the alarm into a tiny computer scarcely bigger than an iPod. The screen flashed a series of numbers at dizzying speed. The two cameras fitted with heat detectors on the ceiling would go off any moment now. Only ten seconds left …

*

Unable to stand it any longer, Martin climbed out of the car and stretched. He'd been confined for four hours and was beginning to get pins and needles in his legs. He was out of practice. Early on in his career he would spend whole nights hiding in impossible places: car boots, rubbish bins, false ceilings. There was a sudden gust of wind. He shivered and buttoned up his leather jacket. He had goosebumps, which felt quite pleasant on this hot summer's night. He hadn't felt such exhilaration in all the time he'd been working for the OCBC. His last adrenalin rushes had been five years ago, in the drugs squad. It had

41

been a rotten job associated with a difficult period in his life, and he'd been glad to put it behind him. He preferred his current job of 'culture cop'. It was unique and allowed him to combine his love of paintings and his commitment to the police force.

There were only thirty-odd people in France who'd finished the advanced training course provided by the École du Louvre, which allowed them to join this specialist unit. Even though he now carried out his investigations in the hushed surroundings of museums and auction rooms, mixing with antique dealers and curators rather than drug dealers or rapists, he was still first and foremost a policeman. And a very busy one at that. With more than three thousand thefts a year, France was a favourite target for 'heritage stealers', whose activities generated revenues comparable to those made in the drug or arms trades.

Martin despised the thugs who stole from village chapels, making off with chalices and statues of angels or the Holy Virgin. He detested the stupidity of vandals who took pleasure in defacing sculptures in parks. And, most of all, he loathed the thieves who were hired to steal for private collectors or crooked antique dealers. Because, contrary to popular belief, people who stole art weren't gentlemen thieves. Most of them were in cahoots with the toughest organised crime rings which laundered stolen paintings by arranging their exit from the country.

Leaning against the bonnet of his old Audi, Martin lit a cigarette, his eyes glued to the front of the museum. Through his binoculars he could see the gaping hole in the glass clock. No alarm had gone off yet, but he knew that it was only a matter of seconds before a piercing wail broke the silence of the night.

*

Three seconds.

Two seconds.

One sec—

A glimmer of relief lit up Archibald's face when he saw the six figures fixed on the tiny computer screen. Then the winning combination flashed, disabling the motion sensors. Exactly as he had planned. One day, possibly, he'd make a mistake. One day, he might commit a burglary too far. But not tonight. He had the all-clear. The show could begin.

3

MY BROTHER IN SOLITUDE

There are two types of people. Those who live, play and die. And those who only ever manage to stay balanced on the knife-edge of life. There are actors and tightrope walkers.
Maxence Fermine

Martin lit another cigarette but it did nothing to calm his nerves. Something had gone wrong, he was sure of it. The alarm should have gone off ages ago. Deep down, the young man was quite pleased. Wasn't that what he had been secretly hoping for – to nab Archibald on his own, without the help of the security guards or the Police Judiciaire, so that he could enjoy a private confrontation with him?

Martin was aware that quite a few of his colleagues were fascinated by Archibald's 'exploits' and enjoyed the thrill of hunting down a criminal of his calibre. It was true that McLean was no ordinary thief. For over twenty years he'd been causing museum directors to break out in a cold sweat and had made a laughing stock of police forces the world over. He loved making a grand gesture and the brilliance and originality of each of his thefts had turned burglary into an art form. He had never resorted to violence, fired a single bullet or spilt a single drop of blood. His only weapons were cunning and bravery yet he hadn't hesitated to rob dangerous men like the mafia boss Oleg Mordhorov or the drug baron Carlos Orteg – even if it meant being hunted by the Russian mafia or having a contract taken out on his life by the Latin American cartels. Martin was frequently exasperated by the way the media reported the thief's crimes. Journalists portrayed Archibald in a favourable light, more like an artist than a criminal.

Paradoxically, the police knew almost nothing about Archibald McLean – neither his nationality, nor his age, nor his DNA. The man never left any fingerprints behind. His face was rarely captured on CCTV and, if it was, he was such a master of disguise that it always looked different. No matter how big a reward the FBI offered for information leading to his arrest, all they got was contradictory reports. Archibald was a veritable chameleon, capable of changing his physical appearance and getting into character like an actor. All of which suggested that Archibald worked on his own and for himself.

Unlike his colleagues and the press, Martin had not allowed himself to romanticise the man. Despite his bravura, McLean was nothing but a common criminal.

As far as Martin was concerned, the theft of a cultural treasure couldn't be compared to the theft of any other object. Quite apart from its market value, every work of art contained something sacred and contributed to the transmission of centuries of accumulated cultural heritage.

45

The theft of a work of art was therefore a serious attack on the values and the foundations of our civilisation. And those who took part in it deserved no leniency.

*

The museum was eerily calm. Silent as the grave. Not a squeak. Not another living soul. Archibald walked into the galleries with the same reverence as if he were entering a church. The emerald-green and cobalt-blue tones of the museum's night lights gave the rooms the atmosphere of a haunted castle. Archibald absorbed the ambiance. He had always imagined museums catching their breath at night in the silence and the gloom, far from the chattering crowds and the flash of tourists' cameras. In our zeal to expose the beauty of these works didn't we end up compromising their integrity and, in the long run, destroying them? Each canvas was now exposed to as much light in a year as it had been in fifty years in times past! Paintings exhibited in this way gradually lost their sparkle, their vigour and their life.

He entered the first of the rooms, devoted to Paul Cézanne. Archibald had 'visited' dozens of museums in the last twenty years or so and had handled some of the greatest works of art, and yet he always experienced the same excitement, the same emotion, when he found himself face to face with genius. Some of the most beautiful works by Cézanne were hanging in this room: *Les Baigneurs*, *Les Joueurs de cartes*, *Mont Sainte-Victoire*.

The thief had to tear himself away from them. He plucked a small titanium rod from his belt and screwed it firmly into the section of wall which separated the gallery he was in from the one next door. Because Archibald had not come for Paul Cézanne.

*

Martin crushed his cigarette butt under the heel of his boot before getting back in the car. He couldn't risk being seen. If there was one thing he'd learnt in ten years of being in the force it was that even the cleverest criminals end up making a mistake. It was human nature. Sooner or later they became overconfident and let their guard down. And when they let their guard down they made a mistake that, however small, was enough to get them arrested. And it was a fact that over the past few months Archibald had pulled off more and more remarkable feats in a series of spectacular thefts the like of which the art world had never known. He'd stolen treasures such as Matisse's *La Danse* from the Hermitage in St Petersburg, a priceless original handwritten score of Mozart's symphonies from the Morgan Library in New York and a sublime nude by Modigliani from London. While he was spending the weekend on his yacht three months ago, the Russian billionaire Ivan Volynski had received a nasty shock when he discovered that he'd been relieved of the famous *No. 666* by Jackson Pollock, which he'd bought at Sotheby's for nearly 90 million dollars. The oligarch had been particularly incensed by this robbery because he'd bought it, supposedly, for his new young girlfriend.

Martin turned on the car's interior light and pulled from his pocket the small moleskin notebook where he'd listed Archibald's latest thefts.

47

Date of theft	Work of art	Artist	Date of artist's death
3 Nov	La Danse	MATISSE	3 Nov 1954
5 Dec	Original MS	MOZART	5 Dec 1791
24 Jan	Female nude	MODIGLIANI	24 Jan 1920
6 Feb	Portrait of Adèle	KLIMT	6 Feb 1918
8 April	The Beggar	PICASSO	8 April 1973
16 April	The Nude Maja	GOYA	16 April 1828
28 April	Triptych	BACON	28 April 1992

There were too many similarities for him to believe they were simply coincidences. Archibald McLean didn't strike at random. He had a distinct modus operandi, like a serial killer. He appeared to plan his thefts according to the anniversaries of the deaths of his favourite artists – as though paying homage to them! As a supreme show of arrogance or another way of poking fun at the police and creating his own myth, he always left his calling card emblazoned with a Southern Cross at the scene of the theft. Archibald was undeniably in a class of his own.

The first thing Martin had done after working out the thief's method was to go over Interpol's files with a fine-tooth comb, but he'd found nothing which reflected his deductions. It seemed he was the only investigator in the world to have made the connection between the dates of the thefts and the artists' deaths. The young policeman had been reluctant to inform his superior, Lieutenant-Colonel Loiseaux, head of the OCBC, and in the end he had chosen to keep the information to himself and to act alone. The sin of pride? Probably, but it was also a question of character. Martin was a lone wolf. He felt uneasy working in a team and when he did he never performed well. He was at his best when he was able to work the way he wanted. And that was what he was going to do that night: serve Archibald's head up to the OCBC on a platter. As always, Colonel Loiseaux and his colleagues would be quick to take all the credit but there was nothing Martin could do about that. He hadn't joined the police force in search of glory and rewards.

He wound down the window of his old coupé. The night was electric, full of danger and promise. Very high up, through the museum's front windows, you could catch a glimpse of the massive chandeliers bearing witness to the splendour of yesteryear. He glanced at his watch, an Omega Speedmaster, a present from an ex-girlfriend who had long since ceased to be part of his life.

It was early morning on 29 July.

The anniversary of Vincent Van Gogh's death.

*

'Happy birthday, Vincent,' said Archibald as he entered the next room, the one containing some of Van Gogh's most famous works: *The Siesta*, *Portrait of Dr Gachet* and *The Church at Auvers-sur-Oise*.

He took a few steps into the room and stopped in front of the artist's best-known self-portrait. Surrounded by a mysterious shimmering halo, the painting possessed a ghostly quality with its turquoise and absinthe-green tones glowing in the semi-darkness.

From within his gilded wooden frame, Van Gogh gave him a penetrating and disturbing sidelong glance. His eyes seemed to follow him and avoid him at the same time. A series of hatched brushstrokes portrayed his hard, emaciated features. The painter's orangey hair and fiery

49

beard engulfed his face like flames while wild arabesques swirled in the background.

Archibald stared intensely at the canvas.

Like Rembrandt and Picasso, Van Gogh had often used himself as a model. In his inimitable style he had striven, through his paintings, to find himself. More than forty of Van Gogh's self-portraits existed: ruthless mirrors following the course of his illness and his inner turmoil. But this painting was known to be the one Vincent was most fond of. Perhaps because he had painted it while he was in the asylum at Saint-Rémy-de-Provence, less than a year before he killed himself during one of the most productive but also the most painful periods of his life.

Looking at the tortured face, Archibald experienced a real feeling of sympathy. He felt the canvas was projecting the image of a brother in solitude. He could have stolen this painting ten or twenty years ago. But he had preferred to wait until tonight, which would be the pinnacle of his career.

Archibald could hear footsteps on the floor below but was unable to tear his eyes from those of the Dutch painter, mesmerised by his genius, which in a certain sense had triumphed over his madness.

The questions raised by Van Gogh through his self-portraits reminded Archibald of the questions he asked himself about his own life. Who was he really? Had he made the right decisions at critical moments? What was he going to do for the rest of his life? And, above all else, would he one day have the courage to take a step towards Her, the only woman who really meant anything to him, in order to ask her forgiveness.

'So, shall we go then, Vincent?' he asked.

A trick of the light made Van Gogh's eyes appear to shine more brightly. Archibald decided to take this as a sign of assent.

'All right, fasten your seatbelt. This promises to be a bumpy ride!' he warned as he made to grab the painting off its rail.

Instantly, the alarm went off and a piercing wail echoed through the museum.

*

The clamour of the alarm could be heard in the street.

Already on the alert, Martin reacted immediately. He opened the car door and stepped onto the pavement after grabbing his service gun from the glove compartment – a semi-automatic Sig Sauer 9mm pistol now carried by most French policemen. He checked the cartridge containing fifteen bullets and jammed the gun into its holster.

Hopefully I won't need to use it.

He was out of practice. He hadn't fired a single shot since his transfer to the OCBC, whereas in the drugs squad he'd used his weapon regularly.

Martin crossed both lanes of the *quai* and took up position on the museum concourse, his back to the Seine. Rue de la Légion-d'Honneur was empty except for a couple of homeless people asleep in their sleeping bags at the entrance to the underpass leading down to the RER. The young *flic* slipped behind an advertising column and kept watch from his new observation post. His head tilted up towards the rooftops, he could see through his binoculars another rope hanging down the museum's east-facing wall, allowing access to one of the first-floor balconies.

He felt his heart beating faster.

Don't be too long, Archie. I'm here. I'm waiting for you.

*

As soon as Archibald unhooked the painting, the security gates came down at a dizzying speed on both sides of the room in order to trap the thief and prevent his escape. The same security system was used in most of the world's largest museums nowadays: the idea was not to stop the criminals from entering the buildings but to make sure that they couldn't get out.

In a matter of seconds, a troop of security guards had blocked off the upper floor of the museum.

'There he is, room 34!' cried the head of security as he entered the corridor leading to the galleries.

Archibald stayed calm. He slipped on a breathing mask, put on a small pair of blue safety glasses and pulled his escape plan from his bag.

The squad moved in, filing swiftly through the Impressionist galleries. When the guards reached the steel gates, they were met by three grenades, which had just been thrown onto the parquet floor, their safety pins removed. Panic-stricken, the guards froze. The projectiles exploded, releasing a purplish gas. The room was immediately filled with a thick pungent smoke, plunging it into a fog that reeked of burning plastic.

'The bastard! He's smoking us out!' cried the man in charge, stepping back a few paces.

The smoke detectors didn't take long to react and this time it was the fire alarm that went off, adding to the general mayhem. A curtain of metallic slats instantly appeared all around the room, protecting the paintings from the automatic fire extinguishers, which would go off as soon as the temperature in the room became too hot.

*

At that moment, the police station in the seventh *arrondissement* received live digital images from the cameras installed at the Musée d'Orsay. The museum's security system was linked to the police station and the alarm had been known to go off by mistake, but this time it was taken seriously and almost immediately three police cars drove off, sirens wailing, towards the famous museum on the Left Bank.

*

'I don't understand what he's playing at!' muttered the head of security, holding a handkerchief over his face to protect himself from the fumes.

He grabbed his walkie-talkie and barked orders to the control room: 'Send some lads up the back stairs. I don't want to lose sight of him!'

All he could see through the bars of the gate was an amorphous shadow moving in the Van Gogh room. Before it became completely filled with smoke, he studied the room through his infrared glasses. On the face of it, there was no danger of the thief getting away: as far as he could see, the metal bars on the other side of the room had also gone down, making any escape impossible. *The cops'll be able to grab him as soon as we open the exits*, he thought, completely relaxed.

What he hadn't noticed was the fine titanium rod that had blocked the gate a foot and a half from the floor.

*

A little smile lit up Archibald's face as he crawled under the portcullis before leaving the museum the way he had come in. The whole operation had taken no more than five minutes.

Five minutes that had been time enough for him to take a priceless painting off the wall.

4

TWO MEN IN THE CITY

*Only enemies speak the truth; friends and lovers lie
endlessly, caught in the web of regard.*
Stephen King

After running across the rooftop, Archibald grabbed the
rope so he could fasten it to his karabiner before lowering
himself down as far as the balcony. Without pausing
for breath, he jumped over the balustrade and onto the
thick glass roof which jutted out over the entrance to the
museum. Then, with catlike agility, he leapt several yards
and landed by the museum's front entrance.

Not a bad little acrobatic number there, thought Martin,
still concealed behind his advertising column. The young
flic pulled out his gun, ready to intervene. At last, he was
going to get him! For reasons he didn't really understand,
the notorious thief had become an obsession. He had
vowed to be the first to solve the mystery. Despite the
lack of information on McLean, he had tried to build up a
psychological profile, forcing himself to think like him in
order to understand and anticipate his logic. It wasn't just
fascination. It was something else. It was an insatiable

curiosity coupled with an invisible thread of the kind that links two chess players. A duo like Broussard and Mesrine, Roger Borniche and Émile Buisson, Clarice Starling and Hannibal Lecter …

Right, stop fantasising. Leave the comfort of your hiding place and nab him!

And yet, despite spurring himself on, Martin stood motionless, a passive spectator of a film in which he was not the hero. Just when his pursuit was about to pay off, he felt a peculiar emptiness inside. What was he waiting for? Why this unhealthy desire to play cat and mouse?

To draw out the pleasure?

As for Archibald, he wasted no time. As quick as a flash, he disappeared behind a newspaper kiosk on Rue de la Légion-d'Honneur only to emerge a moment later transformed. He had exchanged his camouflage clothes for a light-coloured jacket and a pair of linen trousers.

He really is a master of disguise, thought Martin. More than the actual new clothes, it was the thief's whole appearance that looked different: he was heavier, more stooped, as though in a matter of seconds Archibald had aged ten years.

But the most amazing thing was yet to come.

I don't believe it!

By the light of the streetlamps, the young *flic* watched the thief as he mounted a Vélib: one of the twenty thousand bicycles that the city council had made available for tourists and Parisians. In the space of a few months, the bulky shape of the mousy-grey two-wheeler had established itself as one of the iconic sights of the city.

Even as a chorus of sirens heralded the arrival of the *flics* of the seventh *arrondissement*, Archibald was already well on his way to Quai Anatole-France. Martin considered taking his car then decided against it. With the young captain on his trail, Archibald rode along the Seine, his back to the Assemblée Nationale, and pedalled towards Île de la Cité. The three police cars stopped on Place Henry-de-Montherlant, right in front of the museum entrance, and ten or so uniformed policemen piled out and rushed as one through the main doors.

Not for a second did they imagine that the cyclist they had passed a few moments before was the man they had come to arrest.

*

Taken completely by surprise, Martin was wondering what to do next. Archibald had mounted the riverside pavement and was pedalling at a leisurely pace against the traffic. Not once did he turn round to see whether he was being followed. On the opposite pavement, Martin was not letting him out of his sight. Fortunately, the Vélib was highly visible, with the reflective strips on its wheels and bright lights at the front and back making it easy to keep tabs on him. Moreover, the bike's heavy frame, encasing the brakes and the cables, must have weighed a ton and put people off trying to emulate Lance Armstrong.

A strong wind had risen, causing the cluster of tricolours above the Caisse des Dépôts to flap about. Martin felt tense, but the situation was under his control. Even if

Archibald did spot him, he couldn't escape. He was too close. Martin went for a long run almost every day, pushing himself to the point of exhaustion to increase his stamina. If Archibald attempted to speed up he wouldn't let him pull away. But he had to be careful; he mustn't let him get too far ahead.

The two men went past Pont Royal, with its humpback and curved arches, which joined Rue de Beaune to the Pavillon de Flore.

Archibald appeared to be enjoying his ride, pedalling nonchalantly and breathing in the night air like a tourist on a trip. At the front of his bicycle, two bars supported a metal basket and in it Archibald had placed a khaki kit bag straight out of an army surplus store. A bag that contained a Van Gogh worth a hundred million euros.

On Quai Voltaire, he indulged himself by slowing down even more and idling in front of the galleries, art bookshops and smart antique shops.

That's right, play the tourist! Martin said to himself, exasperated.

And yet, almost in spite of himself, the *flic* was seduced by the elegance of the area. At night, Quai Voltaire appeared timeless and it was easy to imagine oneself transported back to the past. Back to a time when Ingres and Delacroix had their studios there, or Baudelaire was composing *Les Fleurs du Mal* in a nearby hotel.

A gaudy hoarding on a bus shelter brought Martin sharply back to reality. Archibald was now riding past the metal boxes belonging to the booksellers. Some had been newly tagged with graffiti and the tenor of the messages was not exactly elevated: *I love Djamila*; *Régis is stupid*; *Sarko is a fascist*; *Ségo is to politics what Paris Hilton is to culture.*

Just after Pont du Carrousel, the thief lingered like a connoisseur outside the Sennelier art shop, Les Couleurs du Quai, which had supplied oils and canvases to Cézanne as well as Modigliani and Picasso. Next door, a couple of guards on duty outside ex-President Chirac's apartment block were enjoying a chat. Archibald rode past them smiling.

Then the thief grew bored of playing the tourist and began pedalling faster. Not fast enough to worry Martin though. There were plenty of streetlamps along that section of the street. As the metal Pont des Arts footbridge appeared in the distance, the traffic seemed to come to life when several taxis bombed down the bus lane. Next to the Seine, two street cleaners were sweeping the deck of a long barge that had been turned into a restaurant. A green and white vehicle marked 'Paris Cleaning Service' was parked up on the pavement with its engine on and its warning lights flashing, but its driver had vanished.

Archibald was now pedalling flat out. He flew past the dome of the Académie Française, obliging Martin to break into a sprint. The young policeman didn't know what to do. Should he arrest McLean now or trail him as far as he could? Because even with Archibald behind bars, there was no guarantee that they would be able to unearth his breathtaking haul and recover the dozens of paintings he had stolen. An image flashed through the young policeman's mind, that of l'Aiguille, the hollow needle rock in the cliffs at Étretat – Arsène Lupin's legendary hiding place where he had kept his treasure: the *Mona Lisa*, Botticelli's masterpieces and Rembrandt's darkest offerings. No doubt McLean's grotto would be every bit as illustrious.

I'm the one who worked it out. I'm better than him. I can arrest him whenever I want.

Beneath the leafy trees on Quai de Conti, Archibald slowed down again, to Martin's relief. A police car was patrolling the quayside, not far from the fire brigade's launch, but it was hunting down homeless people rather than burglars. Archibald didn't bat an eyelid and continued riding towards Île de la Cité.

When he saw Pont Neuf silhouetted against the sky, a worrying thought occurred to Martin for the first time. What role was he playing? The hunter or the quarry?

*

On Quai des Grands-Augustins, the thief left his bicycle at the foot of the Wallace fountain, where four caryatids gracefully held aloft a cast-iron basin decorated with dolphins and water gods.

Archibald picked up his kit bag and hoisted it onto his shoulder before walking across Pont Neuf. Taken by surprise, Martin instinctively drew his gun for the second time, though he had no choice but to break cover and follow close behind Archibald on the same pavement.

With its semicircular balconies and the hundreds of gothic faces decorating its cornices, the oldest bridge in Paris was also the most bewitching. Its twelve arches crossed the two branches of the Seine, tracing an elegant broken line the middle of which crossed the far end of Île de la Cité.

Buffeted by a sharp wind, the bridge was strangely deserted. Archibald the chameleon had rediscovered his agility and his stamina. The way he ran had nothing in common with the leisurely pedalling of the sedate cyclist whom Martin had been following up until then. In the space of a few seconds he had passed the first two semicircular balconies overlooking the cornices.

Suddenly, the young *flic* felt a flash of panic. He was out of breath and sweating, his weapon angled downwards. What if there was a car waiting for Archibald on the other side of the bridge? Perhaps he had an accomplice. This time, the risk of losing Archibald was too great for him to continue the chase. Martin released the safety catch on his gun, and barked, 'Police, stop!'

The thief slowed down sharply.

'Stop or I'll shoot!' Martin went on, taking advantage of the element of surprise.

This time Archibald stopped dead in his tracks.

'Hands up and turn round slowly!'

Archibald obeyed, and for the first time Martin saw the thief's face.

Archibald was a well-preserved man of about sixty. His brown hair streaked with silver and his clipped beard both shone in the dark. His pleasant face, lit by intensely pale, almost laughing green eyes, still bore a few traces of black camouflage cream. Nothing in his expression suggested

61

fear or surprise. On the contrary, everything about him exuded an air of calm amusement.

'Hello, Martin, lovely night, isn't it?'

The young *flic* felt his blood run cold.

How the hell does he know my name?

… But he tried not to let his surprise show.

'Shut up and put your bag down on the ground!'

Archibald let go of the bag and it dropped at his feet. Martin noticed the Royal Air Force badge sewn onto the canvas.

'If you really wanted to arrest me, you should have done so in front of the museum, Martin.'

How did he know … ?

'You had your chance and you blew it,' concluded the thief.

He had a deep voice and a lingering Scottish accent with lightly rolling 'r's. Martin thought of Sean Connery, who had proudly hung on to the accent of his homeland, regardless of the nationality of the character he was playing.

'Hold your hands out!' yelled Martin, taking a pair of handcuffs from his jacket pocket.

This time the Scot didn't comply.

'You only made one mistake, but it's the worst one of all. You gave yourself the chance of losing when you could have won. Always a fatal error.'

Martin was paralysed by this sudden switching of roles.

Archibald went on: 'Losers are always defeated by themselves, not by their enemies. But I think you know that already.'

The wind was blowing harder. A gust blew up a cloud of dust, forcing Martin to cover his face.

Unflustered, McLean continued. 'Sometimes it's easier to lose than to pay the price of winning, don't you agree?'

As Martin didn't reply, Archibald went on. 'At least admit that you've asked yourself the question!'

'What question?' asked Martin, in spite of himself.

'"If I arrest McLean today, what meaning will my life have tomorrow?"'

'No need to speculate now as I'm arresting you today. This minute.'

'Come on, kid, admit it, I'm all you have in life.'

'I'm not your kid, OK?'

'You have no wife or children, haven't had a steady girlfriend in years. Both your parents are dead. Your colleagues? You despise most of them. Your superiors? You don't think they appreciate your work.'

Despite being threatened by a gun, McLean was astonishingly calm. Martin was armed and Archibald's only weapons were words. And yet, right then, words were proving more intimidating than an automatic.

Archibald's eyes sparkled as if to lend weight to his words. He looked both rugged and refined.

'For a moment there, you overestimated your strength, laddie.'

'I don't think so,' Martin lied.

He tried to reassure himself by clutching his gun tighter, but the weapon felt like it weighed a ton. His hands were clammy and despite the grips round the handle the Sig Sauer was slipping from his grasp.

'You ought to have called your colleagues in tonight,' the Scot pressed on.

He picked up the canvas bag lying at his feet as though the time had come for him to leave and he pulled out the Van Gogh self-portrait, waving it about in mid-air.

'It's the painting or me!' he warned, making as if to hurl it into the river.

Martin felt his panic get the better of him. His eyes were fixed on the painting whose intense blue colour formed a mesmerising halo.

Something was wrong. As far as he knew, Archibald was an aesthete, a true connoisseur. Not the kind of man to destroy a painting, not even to ensure his escape. Admittedly, the year before, he'd distinguished himself by sabotaging a polemical exhibition by Jeff Koons at Versailles. The homemade bomb he had planted beneath a giant lobster hanging in one of the rooms had demolished the modern artist's sculpture. But Jeff Koons wasn't Vincent Van Gogh.

'Don't be stupid, McLean!'

'Not an easy choice, is it?'

'You wouldn't dare!' Martin challenged him. 'I know you better than you think.'

'In that case … *hasta la vista*, kid!' cried Archibald as he flung the painting as far as he could into the river's murky depths.

Panic-stricken, Martin clambered onto the edge of the balcony overlooking the cornice. The wind had whipped the Seine into waves. Martin had always loathed the water and hadn't set foot in a swimming pool since almost failing that part of his lieutenant's exam. But tonight what choice did he have?

He took a deep breath and jumped into the black water. Van Gogh's life was in his hands.

*

Archibald crossed the second branch of the Seine and walked down towards Port du Louvre where a vintage English car was parked. He got behind the wheel and drove onto Quai François-Mitterrand before vanishing into the night.

5

THE LOVERS OF PONT NEUF

I wish I had been born with two hearts, one unfeeling, the other constantly in love; I would have entrusted the latter to those who made it beat, and with the other I would have lived happily.
Amin Maalouf

Quai Saint-Bernard
3.20 a.m
'Let's go, boys, we're needed at Pont Neuf!'

Captain Karine Agneli walked into the staff room at the headquarters of the Paris river police.

'Diaz and Capella, you're coming with me. A guy's just thrown himself into the water.'

The two lieutenants fell in behind their boss and several seconds later the three police officers climbed into the *Cormorant*, one of the patrol boats used to police Paris's river.

The boat seemed to glide over the smooth waves that reflected the liquid gold spilling from the streetlights.

'Suicides piss me off!' grumbled Diaz. 'This is the fourth one this week.'

'Yeah, why can't they just throw themselves in front of trains instead!' agreed Capella.

'Guys, give it a rest!' barked Karine.

Whatever the season, the bridges of Paris attracted those in despair, and the river police, who prevented over one hundred suicides a year, would be called out. But during the summer, when the banks overflowed with people, the number of incidents increased significantly. Between the idiotic end-of-evening wagers and the devotees of 'Paris Plage', more and more people ran the risk of falling head first into the river. However, despite the promises of a former mayor, it was still forbidden to swim in the Seine. Because of all the traffic out on the river, the danger of being hit by a boat was a very real one, not to mention the risk of contracting Weil's disease, a bacterial infection spread by rats' urine. A nasty disease, which often left people paralysed and could even be fatal.

The boat carried on down the river, passing Quai d'Orléans, Port Saint-Michel and Quai des Orfèvres, before slowing down just before Pont Neuf.

'Do you see anything?' asked Capella.

'Bloody hell, where is the idiot?' replied Diaz.

Looking intently through her binoculars, Karine Agneli tried to stay calm. Her boys were nervous at the moment. The week before, at the end of Quai de la Tournelle, a *bateau-mouche* had crashed into a launch hired by some tourists. Pinned against the pier of the bridge, the rented boat had immediately sunk to the bottom. The river police had moved quickly, but not quickly enough to pull one of the children out of the water, a three-year-old who had drowned. None of the officers in the river police had made the slightest error, but that made no difference: the loss of the child had been a traumatic experience for those involved.

'There he is!' shouted Karine, pointing towards Square du Vert-Galant.

The boat slowly approached the riverbank.

'I'll go,' she decided, zipping up her wet suit and putting on her mask.

Before either of the men could object, she had already dived in. With her long body, supple legs and graceful arm movements it took her just a few seconds to come to the aid of the man who was trying to swim to the bank.

When she drew level with him, she noticed that he was hanging on to a painting as if it were a raft.

*

'You're not professionals – you're nothing but a bunch of amateurs!' The Interior Minister pointed threateningly in turn at the curator of the museum, his head of security, the head of the Police Judiciaire and the head of the OCBC. Within half an hour, a crisis meeting had been set up at the Musée d'Orsay itself.

'This kind of thing simply cannot happen!' thundered the minister.

As the first person from a poor immigrant background to reach this prestigious position, she had been overexposed in the press to the point where she had become an icon of the Republic. Intelligent and ambitious, she symbolised both an openness to the Left and cultural diversity. She was known for being a straight talker and for her unfaltering loyalty to the President of the Republic, who sometimes referred to her as 'the French Condoleezza Rice'.

'You're useless, that's what you are!'

In a grey Paul Smith suit and a white agnès b. shirt, she had been pacing around the Van Gogh room for five minutes, unleashing her wrath on those she deemed responsible for this latest theft. Her ebony hair fell in smooth locks and framed her kohl-darkened eyes, which were as cold and sharp as crystal. Standing next to her, her opposite number at the Ministry of Culture didn't dare intervene.

'One would almost think that you actually enjoy being made to look ridiculous by this thief!' she shouted, indicating the card that Archibald had pinned to the wall, in the space once occupied by Van Gogh's self-portrait.

The long corridor dedicated to Impressionism was now swarming with policemen and had been turned into a small police station. The steel barriers had been lifted and excessively bright lamps replaced the soft bluish light that was normally used at night. In the Renoir room, detectives were interviewing the security staff. In the Monet room, other officers were scrutinising a screen filled with images provided by the security cameras, while a police forensic team went all *CSI* in the Van Gogh room.

'This painting must be recovered as soon as possible,' said the minister decisively. 'Your careers are on the line.'

*

A beautiful silver DB5 travelled up Voie Georges-Pompidou. The car was from another era, the 1960s, the golden age of Aston Martin. At the wheel, Archibald felt as if he were part of another world. The car was a remnant of a bygone age, an age of real British luxury: elegant but not ostentatious, athletic but not coarse, refined yet still masculine. The car resembled the driver.

Slowly, he accelerated, passing Quai de la Rapée and Pont de Bercy, and turned onto the ring road. For a collector's item, the old DB5 drove extremely well. Counting cars as works of art as he did, meant that Archibald only drove the rarest models. And this one had rather a unique history as it had appeared in the first James Bond films, *Thunderball* and *Goldfinger.* Built in an age when films had not yet been ruined by digital special effects, the car still had its arsenal of gadgets, which had been kept in good condition by successive owners: there were machine guns concealed in the indicators, rotating number plates, a smoke-screen system, a bulletproof windscreen, a mechanism that poured oil or nails onto the road and retractable blades to slash the tyres of any pursuing cars that got too close.

Two years ago, at a huge, highly publicised auction, the car had been sold for over two million dollars to a mysterious Scottish businessman.

*

'Martin Beaumont!' exclaimed Karine Agneli in surprise, still in the water.

Diaz and Capella, the two river police officers who had stayed on the boat, hauled Martin on board and offered him a blanket.

'What the hell were you doing in the Seine in the middle of the night using a painting as a life raft?' asked the young woman, grabbing the hand of one of her lieutenants to pull herself back onto the boat.

His teeth chattering, the young *flic* wrapped himself in the blanket. He squinted in the direction of the familiar voice addressing him.

With her short light hair, faint freckles and athletic, slender frame Karine Agneli hadn't changed a bit. She had always been a good-looking girl, enthusiastic, with a sunny disposition. His polar opposite, in fact. For two years, they had worked together in the drugs squad. She had been his partner on several undercover operations. At the time, fieldwork was their life. There was nothing separating their work and their hearts. It had been at once a wonderful and a terrible experience. Being an undercover agent showed you facets of your personality that you would perhaps rather not have known about, and forced you to go places from which no one emerged unscathed. To keep from going under, they had fallen in love. Or, rather, had become dependent on each other. It was a relationship with occasional moments of beauty, but one that had never found its balance.

Briefly, painful memories resurfaced, unbidden. Their time together had been full of highs and lows, like dope.

In the glow of the streetlamps, Karine looked at Martin. Water streamed from his hair, and dripped into his stubble. She thought he looked drawn and tired, even if his face still had something childlike about it.

Sensing that he was being observed, Martin teased her. 'Do you know how sexy you look in that wet suit?'

71

In response she threw a towel in his face, which he used to delicately dab the Van Gogh self-portrait.

Karine was as beautiful as a siren and seemed radiant. Like him, she had left the drugs squad for a less self-destructive field. Most people saw the river police more as lifeguards than real police, which made them considerably more popular.

'Is that painting the original?' she asked, sitting down next to him.

Moving at the speed of a pleasure boat, the police launch had just passed Île Saint-Louis and was preparing to draw alongside Port Saint-Bernard. Martin smiled.

'Does the name Archibald McLean mean anything to you?'

'The thief? Of course.'

'I had him at gunpoint,' fumed Martin.

'Was it him that pushed you into the water?'

'That's one way of putting it.'

'How odd, because ...' Karine looked troubled.

'Because what?'

'The guy that phoned headquarters to report your fall said his name was Archibald.'

*

The smooth, streamlined shape of the Aston Martin cut through the night at full speed. In the driver's seat, Archibald took in the smell of the expensive wood and the pure wool of the carpet. Next to him, on the soft leather of the passenger seat, he had placed the bag with the RAF insignia, which he had kept from his days in the air force.

Earlier, on Pont Neuf, in front of the young policeman, he had felt a sudden surge of adrenalin, an unexpected feeling that he couldn't explain. Beneath the ambitious façade, there was something rather endearing about the young man. Above all, it was the way he had looked at him that Archibald remembered: like a sad and lonely child, who still had everything to learn.

As soon as he rejoined the A6 – the famous Autoroute du Soleil – Archibald revved up the six-cylinder engine, unleashing its 280 horsepower. He loved speed, and he loved feeling alive.

*

Together, Karine and Martin leapt onto the bank of Port Saint-Bernard.

'You have to take me back to the Musée d'Orsay,' he said.

'Change your clothes first; you're soaked. Capella will find you something to wear while I go and get the car.'

Martin followed the lieutenant into the long, narrow building beside the river. When he came out again, he felt very oddly dressed in the eighties outfit the lieutenant had lent him. It was really more of a disguise than a police uniform, consisting of a royal-blue polo neck, navy polyester trousers and an extra-large windcheater.

A Land Rover pick-up truck equipped with cattle bars and a winch pulled up next to him.

'Get in,' said Karine, opening the passenger door. 'Looking good.'

'Oh, spare me the jokes please.'

The 4 x 4 sped off, tyres screeching.

Although there was hardly any traffic, the area surrounding the museum was completely closed off. Place Henry-de-Montherlant was full of the Renault Scenics and the 307s of the police force, government vehicles and reporters' cars.

'Go play the hero then,' laughed Karine, stopping the car just before the square.

Martin thanked her. As he was about to get out, she stopped him. 'You still wear the watch,' she said, pointing at the silver Speedmaster that she had given him five years earlier.

'And you still wear the ring,' he replied.

The young woman drummed her fingers on the steering wheel and the three interwoven rings of the Trinity sparkled in the early-morning light: pink gold, white gold and yellow gold.

It had been an exchange of gifts that was far too extravagant for their meagre police salary. At the time they had spent all of their bonus – and more – on those gifts. A gesture that neither of them had regretted.

In just a few seconds, the idea resurfaced that perhaps their story was not quite finished. It seemed that these strange circumstances had brought them together again. Perhaps it was a sign. Perhaps not.

Then the moment was gone. Martin opened the car door, taking the portrait with him. He turned round one last time to look at the Land Rover before crossing the street. Karine rolled down her window and gave him a smile.

'Take care of your pretty little self, Martin, and learn to swim. I won't always be there to save you, you know!'

*

'A bunch of idiots, that's what you are!'

As Martin approached the Van Gogh room, he recognised the shrill tones of the Interior Minister. He stopped on the threshold of the room where you could have heard a pin drop in between the hurled insults.

'A bunch of losers. An utter waste of space.'

Martin spotted the familiar profile of his boss, Lieutenant-Colonel Loiseaux, as well as the tense expression of the head of the Police Judiciaire, whom he had come across several times while working at Quai des Orfèvres. To their right stood Charles Rivière, the director of the Orsay.

'A pack of useless good-for-nothings!'

All three men looked sheepish, and none of them dared look her in the eye. To get to their current positions, they had all done their fair share of boot-licking and had learnt to weather the insults without flinching.

'Come on! Get moving and find this bloody—'

'This bloody painting is here, Madame,' Martin cut in, walking towards her.

Immediately all eyes turned to him.

Standing in the middle of the room, he brandished the portrait in her face, just as Archibald had done on the bridge.

Taken aback, the Interior Minister frowned and scrutinised the painting.

'And who are you then?' she asked finally.

'Captain Martin Beaumont, from the OCBC.'

Charles Rivière had already rushed forward to snatch the painting from him.

Martin, who had decided to tell the whole truth, began his account, relating how he had managed to work out McLean's modus operandi, which had led to him staking out the museum in the hope of catching the criminal in the act. The young policeman was not naïve, and did not expect to be congratulated for his efforts. He had not been able to arrest Archibald, but, for the first time, the thief had been held in check.

When he had finished his account, there was a moment of uncertainty in the room. The Interior Minister looked at Loiseaux, who, to save face, could think of nothing better to do than unleash his anger.

'We would have been able to corner McLean if you had called us in time, Beaumont! But, no, you preferred to work alone! Always so damned condescending towards your colleagues!'

'Without me, the painting would have disappeared.' Martin tried to defend himself.

'Don't think you can get away with it that easily, Captain!'

The Interior Minister lifted her hand and shot Loiseaux a look to silence his tirade. All this internal arguing didn't interest her at all. In fact, she could see a way of turning the whole incident to her advantage. She somehow had to pass this young *flic* off as a hero to the press. The French police had recovered the painting in record time. It was this aspect of the story which had to be highlighted, not the malfunctioning of a public service. There was no need to lie. She would simply not tell the whole truth. It was just a matter of being political. Moreover, Martin was rather handsome and the press would adore him. Basically, the police's failure to arrest Archibald McLean could be transformed into a bit of good publicity for the force and, therefore, for her too. If everything went according to plan, she might even get a photo shoot in *Paris Match*, in jeans and a nice leather jacket, surrounded by the painting and all the policemen looking like sports stars.

This appealing idea was suddenly wiped out when the director of the museum, sounding alarmed, announced, 'Sorry, Beaumont, but you've been completely had by this fellow.'

'What do you mean?' Martin asked worriedly.

'It's a very good imitation, but the painting is a fake.'

'But that's impossible. I saw him take it out of his bag, and I never took my eyes off him.'

'Come and see for yourself; look at the signature.'

'The signature? What signature?'

Van Gogh never signed any of his self-portraits.

Martin bent over the painting, which was laid flat on a trestle. Van Gogh had signed very few of his works – fewer than one in seven – and when he did, for example on *Sunflowers*, it was with his first name. Now, on the painting in front of him, it was not the name 'Vincent' that was spelt out in separate little characters but another signature, in mocking handwriting:

Archibald

77

The Aston Martin left the motorway following signs to Fontainebleau and turned onto the B road leading to Barbizon. Archibald looked at his watch and couldn't help smiling as he imagined the kid's expression when he became aware of Archibald's little trick. Carefully, he opened the canvas bag on the seat next to him to uncover the top part of the self-portrait – the real one this time – and continue his imaginary conversation with the painter.

'So, Vincent, what did you think of our little joke? Not bad, eh?'

The light from the streetlamps made the painter's tormented expression glow. Archibald had a complicated relationship with the masterpieces that he stole. He had never really felt that he was the owner of a work. In truth, the paintings did not belong to him; rather, he belonged to the paintings. Even if he did not like to admit it, stealing had become like a drug for him. He needed a hit at regular intervals. His body and his brain craved a new work, a new adventure, a new danger.

On the radio, a classical music station was playing a Glenn Gould recording of the 'Goldberg Variations'. The thief forced himself to slow down so as not to arrive at his destination too quickly, and thus cut short the special moment he was experiencing. A moonlit drive with Van Gogh and Bach: could anyone imagine better company?

To complete his enjoyment, he reached into the inside pocket of his raincoat for a silver flask that contained a forty-year-old Scotch whisky.

'Here's to you, Vincent!' he said, savouring a mouthful of the amber-coloured nectar.

The alcohol burnt his gullet deliciously as he tasted the various flavours – roasted almonds, dark chocolate and a hint of cardamom.

Then he turned his attention back to the road, coming off the B road at the Bois-Dormant and speeding down a narrow country lane. After a few miles he reached a walled property, at the edge of the Fontainebleau and Malesherbes forest. With one click of the remote control, Archibald opened the electric gates and the car swept up the drive that cut through the park and led to a beautiful nineteenth-century stone house, covered in ivy and surrounded by chestnut trees that had been there for over a hundred years. All the house's shutters were closed but the building was far from abandoned; the hedges had all recently been trimmed and the lawns had just been mown.

He parked the Aston Martin in what had once been the stables, now transformed into an enormous warehouse that currently housed an all-terrain motorbike, an old military Jeep and a pre-war sidecar, as well as a stripped-down Bugatti. But most of the space was occupied by the latest Colibri helicopter in burgundy and black. Archibald inspected the machine, checked the fuel level and brought it out of the hangar with the help of the helicopter tow tug. Once in the cockpit, he put on a helmet, started the engine and gently twisted the throttle. He had positioned the helicopter so that it was facing into the wind, and so had to do nothing more than pull up on the collective lever to lift off.

'Keep your eyes wide open, Vincent! I'm sure you're going to love seeing things from up high.'

6

PARIS AWAKES

The Eiffel Tower feels a chill,
The Arc de Triomphe has been revived,
Aggravated people arise,
It's time for me to go to bed,
It's five o'clock,
Paris is waking up,
It's five o'clock,
I can't sleep.
Music by Jacques Dutronc
Lyrics by Jacques Lanzmann and Anne Ségalen

Quai Anatole-France
5.02 a.m.
'Hey, that's my car!'

Martin had barely stepped out of the museum before he discovered to his annoyance that his car was being towed away.

'What do you think you're playing at?' he yelled at the traffic warden.

'I'm sorry, sir, but you're parked in a bus lane, and the impounding of your car has already started and can't be stopped.'

81

'I'm a policeman! I was on a stakeout in my car!'

'This vehicle doesn't belong to the police,' the traffic warden pointed out. 'It would have come up on our database when we checked the car registration.'

'Well, I'm here now, so just give me back my car, OK?'

'If you're a policeman, you'll know the procedure: to stop the car being towed you have to pay a fine, as well as the cost of towing.'

Martin looked at his run-down Audi TT 98. Caught in the clutches of the towing vehicle, it looked its age more than ever, with its dented door and scruffy interior. Most of its scars came from his time on the drugs squad. Despite what it said in the rule book, he had always used his own car rather than the shitty Citroëns belonging to the police force. At the rear of the Audi, there was even a dent from a misfired bullet, the result of a dealer's violent arrest. Maybe it was time for a change. It wasn't as if he didn't want a new car; the problem was he didn't have two pennies to rub together.

'Fine, I'll pay,' he sighed.

He searched the pockets of the windcheater, but couldn't find his wallet. He had left it with his jacket back at the headquarters of the river police.

With a resigned air he took the form the officer handed him describing the state of the car and watched the towing vehicle disappear into the distance.

He went through his pockets again. He didn't even have a euro to buy a metro ticket. Never mind, it was a lovely morning for a walk across Paris.

Just one of those days.

The Colibri soared above the Normandy countryside. The helicopter was equipped with a spacious cockpit, which made for an extremely comfortable journey, and offered the pilot excellent visibility. In addition, its streamlined back rotor made it fly almost silently through the air.

Archibald activated the autopilot and took another swig of whisky. He closed his eyes to fully savour the taste. It wasn't perhaps the most sensible thing to do, but, in life, few things were sensible.

After an hour in the air, he had passed over Mont Saint-Michel and then Saint-Malo. When he had crossed the bay of Saint-Brieuc, he focused all his attention on the beauty of the northern landscapes of Finistère, which were made up of sandy beaches, little bays and fishing ports. He then located the Île de Batz just off Roscoff. His GPS sent out a signal informing him that he was less than three minutes away from his landing area. He turned off the autopilot and began his descent, facing into the westerly wind. He touched down in the wooded park of one of the island's most beautiful houses. Built into the rock face, the house was situated on the water's edge and had a landing stage and two mooring rings, as well as a garage and a slipway.

Archibald spent only a few minutes on Breton soil, just enough time to refill the fuel tank. He breathed in the sharp, invigorating air and set off in the direction of Scotland.

*

Completely exhausted, Martin walked up Boulevard Raspail. He'd had a long night, punctuated by excitement and disappointment. He'd told himself he had what it took to be a great policeman but, in reality, he didn't have the guts. McLean had toyed with him, and he had been manipulated like a rookie, a first timer, falling straight into all his traps. He had thought he could beat the system he was a part of all on his own. He had thought himself more cunning than his colleagues, but, most of all, he had underestimated his adversary: the old man wasn't just clever – he had balls too. He was a risk taker and, like an expert poker player, he could bluff. Martin had to admit it: the thief's intelligence and daring commanded admiration.

The young *flic* crossed Place Le Corbusier and reached the Lutetia hotel. The Art Deco façade of the luxury hotel in Saint-Germain-des-Prés sparkled brilliantly in the blue-tinged dawn. A porter and a valet stood waiting on the red carpet at the entrance for two rich clients who were having a discussion in front of the latest Lamborghini model and a German sedan with darkened windows. The luxury surrounding him reminded Martin of his insignificant life as a public servant, unable to pay for a new car, unable to seize the chance of a lifetime when it came along.

At the Carrefour Vavin on Boulevard du Montparnasse, Rodin's statue of Balzac, draped in its majestic monk's robes, had a ghostly air about it. Martin thought about the future of his career, which had been badly compromised by his failure that night. He wouldn't lose his job, but the next six months were going to be difficult. Loiseaux would sideline him by sending him on secondment to the

Ministry of Culture in an advisory role, thus depriving him of action in the field.

In the fourteenth *arrondissement* he came to the avant-garde building of the Fondation Cartier. The façade of completely clear glass revealed an enormous internal garden where passers-by could observe several hundred species of plant as they changed with the seasons. But this morning, Martin was not in the mood for looking at plants. He couldn't get the image of Archibald out of his head. He had closely observed his smallest movements, picked up every inflection in his voice, trying to get at some hidden truth within the man, the beginnings of an explanation. He remembered the self-confidence he had displayed, he remembered the way he had looked at him, and the way he had been able to read Martin's mind. Archibald wasn't at all how he had imagined him to be. In the three minutes during which they had confronted each other, he had learnt more about him than he had from almost four years of investigation. Now he knew his age and what he looked like. He was also convinced that all the thefts carried some hidden meaning. Money was not what truly motivated Archibald, that he was sure of. There was something else behind them, something more secret and more intimate.

By the time he reached Place Denfert-Rochereau the traffic was becoming heavier. Near the pavilion on the left, some Japanese tourists were already queuing to visit the catacombs and shudder as they passed through the underground galleries where millions of Parisian bones were kept, former 'residents' of the Cimetière des Innocents.

85

Martin stifled a yawn. He wanted a coffee, a cigarette and a long shower. His little dip in the Seine had chilled him and he was giving off a rather dubious smell.

On Avenue Reille he found the comforting contours of the Montsouris reservoir, the biggest supply of drinking water in the city, hidden behind a small hill with grassy slopes. The area was very green, almost like the countryside, but it was also protected by large numbers of surveillance cameras: the water collected here came from the rivers in south-east Paris and provided a large part of the city with its water.

When he reached Square Montsouris, he forced himself to forget the image of Archibald that was plaguing him. The image of Karine, his former colleague, quickly replaced it. He had played it cool in front of her, but seeing her again had affected him deeply. The memory of her smile and her sparkling eyes was at once both painful and soothing. It reminded him of the loneliness that had been with him since childhood. A loneliness that he often used as protection, but that would one day destroy him.

*

The helicopter flew over the northern part of the Irish Sea and approached the Scottish Highlands. Carried by a south-westerly wind, the Colibri had covered more than four hundred miles and its fuel supply was running low. Archibald spotted the immense triple-decker yacht, over 160 feet long, which flew the flag of the Cayman Islands.

Able to take on over fifteen thousand gallons of fuel, the Couach 5000 could cross the Atlantic in ten days at a speed of thirty knots. Archibald thought of the powerful boat as his sanctuary. A fortress of avant-garde design, it had been built to sail in all conditions to the furthest corners of the world. A 4 x 4 for the ocean, ready to face howling winds and the direst emergencies.

He gently landed the helicopter at the rear of the upper deck, on a vast platform that had been turned into a helipad, grabbed his bag and jumped down. The wind was blowing, but there wasn't a cloud in the sky. Brilliant sunshine flooded the deck where the crew – former naval officers who knew nothing of his real identity – greeted their boss. Archibald spoke to them briefly before climbing the stairs that led to the main deck.

'Hello, Effie.'

'Hello, Archie.'

With her hair pulled back in a chignon, her sensible clothes and her distinguished air, Miss Euphenia Wallace looked like an English governess in the grand tradition. For ten years now, this 'retired' MI6 doctor had been McLean's trusted right-hand woman and adviser. Governess, bodyguard and confidante rolled into one, she protected her employer's identity. She was the only one who knew it. Beneath her old-school exterior, this crack shot and red belt in Taekwondo was more of a bodyguard than a Mary Poppins.

'Did everything go as planned?'

'Yes, it went without a hitch.'

The glass doors opened onto a luxuriously decorated yet minimalist living room, with crystal chandeliers, a bleached mahogany floor, leather sofas and discreet furniture. An amazing picture window provided the room with a panoramic view and filled it with light, giving the impression of still being outdoors.

Archibald took the canvas out of his bag to show it to Effie. For a few moments she remained silent, gazing at the self-portrait with real emotion.

'And the young policeman?' she asked.

'He went all the way, exactly as I thought he would.'

'Good thing too.'

'Were you worried?'

'I looked over his file again. He strikes me as being unpredictable. I think you're taking too many risks with this one.'

'The whole thing was worth it though, wasn't it?' he replied, indicating the Van Gogh. 'And, anyway, we've identified all the policemen who are on my back. I'm always watching them. I know more about them than they do about me.'

'This one's different.'

'No, he's just like all the rest of them.'

'He's worked out the connection with the anniversaries of the painters' deaths,' Effie pointed out.

'Well.' Archibald shrugged his shoulders. 'Any idiot could have figured that one out.'

'He's been tracking you for three years.'

'And the FBI has been tracking me for twenty-five!'

His arms folded, the thief gazed pensively at a wide flat screen, which, thanks to an underwater camera, transmitted live images of the submarine life surrounding the vessel.

'The kid still has everything to learn.' Archibald's voice cut through the brief silence. 'He's impatient and ill at ease with himself, with flashes of arrogance and a total lack of confidence. He's far too convinced of his skills as a policeman, yet he obviously suffers from a devastating lack of self-esteem in all other areas of his life.'

'He could become dangerous.'

'To become dangerous, there are a few things he needs to learn, and in order to learn them he needs to let go of his pride.'

Archibald sat down at the glass table, where the ship's chef had just laid out one of his favourite dishes: tournedos Rossini and baby new potatoes sautéed in thyme.

Judging the conversation to be over, Effie was about to walk out in an extremely bad mood when Archibald called her back.

'This guy, Martin Beaumont ...'

'Yes?'

'I'd like to look over his file again.'

'I'll go and get it for you.'

*

Martin started walking up Square Montsouris, a steep, cobbled street that looked a little like the nicest parts of Beacon Hill, in the old quarter of Boston. The tree-lined path led past a mixture of artists' studios and middle-class houses built during the Roaring Twenties when Art Nouveau was at its height. The further he went along the street, the more sumptuous the foliage became. The fronts of the buildings were covered with ivy and the air was fragrant with the scent of wisteria, while the architecture became more baroque, with coloured half-timbering, sculpted balconies, stained-glass skylights and mosaic friezes. This green paradise was incredibly peaceful and was one of the most sought-after places to live in the city. No place for a mere *flic* who was getting by on two thousand euros a month.

Nevertheless, Martin pushed open the gate to a little garden, which led to an artist's studio with a glass roof.

The house belonged to an old Englishwoman, Violet Hudson, the muse and last wife of the American painter Henry Hudson, one of the members of the Nabi group, a collection of artists fascinated by esotericism and spirituality, who at the beginning of the twentieth century had been involved in all the struggles of the avant-garde movement. Hudson had died in 1955, and had left the majority of his works to his wife. Over the years, his popularity had soared, but Violet had always refused to be parted from the paintings, remarkable and sensual nudes, which showed her at the peak of her beauty, draped in gossamer sheets with long flowing hair; works that recalled both Klimt and Mucha.

Two years previously, in the middle of the night, the old woman had been attacked and tied up while the studio was robbed of a number of valuable paintings. The OCBC had handled the affair, and Martin, who was an ardent admirer of the artist, had thrown himself heart and soul into the investigation. The armed theft was neither a professional job, nor one ordered by a collector. It had all the hallmarks of a hasty, opportunistic attempt. Martin had bet on it being the work of a drug addict, keen to rob an old woman in order to get some easy money. With the help of several informers that he had kept in contact with from his time with the drugs squad, he had been able to follow the thief's trail easily, and managed to recover most of the works from a left-luggage locker in the Gare du Nord.

Martin had become close to Violet, whose worldliness and eccentricity appealed to him. After the investigation, the old lady had asked him to supervise the installation of a security system and to advise her on how best to protect her inheritance. At the time she had also been looking for a tenant to bring in a little more money at the end of every month, and Martin had earned her trust.

Moving noiselessly so as not to wake his landlady, he climbed the small spiral staircase that led straight to the first floor of the house – what had once been the painter's studio – where he lived. After a very long shower, he threw himself onto his bed and fell into an agitated and broken sleep.

7

THE DUELLISTS

> *I know now that what makes a fool is an inability to take even his own good advice.*
> William Faulkner

'Hello, bad boy.'

Pensively, Archibald scratched the head of the cat that was rubbing itself against his leg. The animal purred contentedly and stretched to its full extent, its ginger and black fur gleaming in the sun like tortoiseshell.

McLean got up from the table and gathered the cat up in his arms to go and lie down on a sofa. He plucked a long, thin Cohiba from the box of cigars that lay open in front of him and picked up the report on Martin Beaumont.

It had been compiled by a private agency and contained a wealth of material; stolen photographs, surveillance reports, copies of phone bills and bank statements were all there for him to study. Most importantly, the report included a copy of his professional record from police headquarters. They were all documents that had been obtained illegally, but in a time of economic crisis and a surge in private investigation, some bent *flics* were making money out of their access to supposedly secure files.

Every man has his price. What's yours? Archibald thought to himself, as he put on his glasses and began reading.

Martin Beaumont was born to an unnamed father on 5 June 1974 in Antibes in the south of France. His mother Mylène worked as a cleaner. For years she had cleaned the public library in the evenings. She often took her son to work with her and he used the time to do his homework and read.

May 1988: Mylène was killed in a car crash in Nice, near the Promenade des Anglais. Her fourteen-year-old son was seriously injured. He spent two days in a coma, but left hospital three months later without any lasting physical effects other than a couple of scars.

Martin went to live with his grandparents, modest office workers who lived on the Pyramides estate, in Évry, where he stayed until he left school, The photocopies of his school reports showed a serious and dedicated student, especially in the arts.

Yet in 1992, he chose to do a *baccalauréat scientifique* which he passed thanks to his grades in history, philosophy and French literature, having failed in maths and physics. He also won second prize at the Paris Conservatoire for the violin.

In the same year, he left his grandparents' flat, having obtained a grant and found a room in student accommodation.

1995: he completed his law degree at the Sorbonne. He then went to San Francisco for two months to perfect his English, finding work in the cafeteria at Berkeley University.

1996: he was awarded a double master's in law and history of art, for which he gained a distinction thanks to his dissertation on the collaboration between Alfred Hitchcock and the graphic designer Saul Bass.

1997–9: he passed the exam to become a police officer on his first attempt and trained at the prestigious École Nationale Supérieure in Cannes-Écluse, where he graduated third in his year.

2000: he chose to join the drugs squad in Nanterre, on the pretext that his childhood best friend had died of an overdose before his eighteenth birthday. His talents were quickly recognised by his superiors and he became one of the pillars of the squad, participating in numerous drug busts of Parisian nightclubs. Because he could blend in so easily as a student, he played a major role in putting a stop to drug dealing within the university, a project that attracted the attention of the media and resulted in the seizure of thousands of ecstasy tablets, four hundred grams of cocaine and the first samples of GHB.

2002: he followed his boss to the drugs squad in Paris. There he was faced with more delicate tasks. Three years before the Perben law even legalised such operations, he along with about ten other policemen was selected to infiltrate the drug-dealing networks in the city. He became part of an isolated world, a world outside the law, a world that knew no hierarchy. A world of 'zombies', as the group was nicknamed, a reference to their physical appearance, which allowed them to blend in with the junkies. Going undercover sometimes meant being supplied with weapons, vehicles and false papers. It meant buying and transporting dope, but it also meant accepting the odd line of coke, or shooting up, just for the sake of appearances. All this, of course, without your name ever appearing on record.

It was around this time that Martin started a relationship with a fellow undercover agent, Karine Agneli, who was the officer charged with following him from a distance and monitoring the operation.

It was a tough job, but it often proved extremely effective: several underground crystal meth labs were discovered and shut down, a convoy of three cars driving at top speed up from Barcelona on the Autoroute du Sud was intercepted, and two hundred kilos of cannabis and four kilos of cocaine were seized. It was enough to earn him promotion to captain in record time.

In 2003 things started to get complicated. All of a sudden, life as an undercover detective became too much for Martin. After a particularly difficult and sordid operation, he asked permission to leave the team – a request that was denied. His superiors thought it better to send him to the in-house psychologists, who, basing their judgements on rather vague foundations, claimed that he was 'anti-social', with a 'borderline personality disorder', or that he had 'bipolar' tendencies.

In January 2005, after a struggle lasting more than a year, he was finally able to move to the OCBC, which was the central agency set up to combat the trafficking of cultural treasures. Under the command of Colonel Loiseaux, he again became the efficient policeman he had once been, and soon had the highest success rate in the OCBC. At the same time he also took a postgraduate course at the Institut d'Études Supérieures des Arts, where he achieved impressive results. He appeared passionate about his new job. However, Beaumont's behaviour underwent a radical change during this period. He was suddenly extremely reluctant to work in a team, becoming something of a loner, and getting on the wrong side of most of his colleagues. Loiseaux was quite happy for him to do this, for the simple reason that, although he worked extremely hard, Martin also had the tact never to boast about his achievements, which left Loiseaux free to take the credit for his employee's success. The OCBC was in desperate need of good publicity, especially when it came to cases that attracted particular media attention, such as the theft of two paintings by Picasso from the Paris mansion of the artist's granddaughter. Once again it was Martin who got the vital lead that led to the arrest of the three culprits. Valued at around 50 million euros, *Maya with Doll* and *Portrait of Jacqueline* were found undamaged, and Loiseaux got his fifteen minutes of television fame.

Archibald turned the pages of the report with increasing interest.

The last section was devoted to a more personal area of the policeman's life. His name appeared twice in the Stic, a vast file of offences committed, listing the names of victims and those held for questioning. The two cases related to prostitution and both involved the same woman, a Ukrainian girl known as Nico, who plied her trade by Porte d'Asnières. The photos showing the two of them together were not the normal sordid snapshots but instead suggested something more romantic: a Sunday afternoon spent in the Luxembourg Gardens, a walk down the Champ-de-Mars, a spring evening spent on the Ferris wheel in the Tuileries Gardens, an intimate dinner in a restaurant in Place Dauphine.

There was another grey area: Martin's weekly visits to the Maison de Solenn, the clinic in the fourteenth *arrondissement*, which specialised in caring for troubled adolescents. In spite of his best efforts, the detective following him had not been able to discover the identity of the young patient Beaumont visited so often.

*

Martin felt a slobbery tongue licking his face.

'Get off, Mandoline!'

But the cocker spaniel wasn't having any of it. Martin gave in and played for a few minutes with the dog. Mandoline was the most faithful dog in the world, she couldn't stand being alone and chewed anything within reach. He had found her in the street while searching the home of a well-known dealer in Montparnasse. The guy had made a break for it several days before the search, abandoning his dog, which had been left howling on the doorstep. Martin had put her in his car and set off for the dogs' home in Orgeval. In the half-hour that it took to get there, Mandoline had managed to drool all over the passenger seat and shed hair everywhere. When they reached the car park, she had begun to sob pitifully, looking up at him with sad eyes. Martin had been won over.

The young *flic* looked at the clock: just gone midday. Wearing only his boxer shorts, Martin got out of bed and walked across the former studio to the kitchen area. Long and narrow, the room was laid out like a loft apartment and was filled with light. Without being too messy, the decor was muddled and eclectic, reflecting the personality of its inhabitant. In a bookcase made of cherry wood, manga comics rubbed shoulders with classics from the Pléiade Library, the great Russian novels stood next to collections of Sempé cartoons, whilst a model of Darth Vader brandished his light sabre at a Tintin figure straight out of *The Blue Lotus*.

In a corner of the room, at the foot of Henry Hudson's last sculpture (the ghostly spectre of a girl's face emerging from a block of marble), a PlayStation lay buried under a pile of video games. The walls were covered with posters from recent exhibitions: Modigliani at the Musée du Luxembourg, Nicolas de Staël at the Pompidou Centre, Picasso at the Grand Palais. Next to the bookcase were metal shelves lined with several hundred DVDs: all of Hitchcock, Truffaut, Lubitsch, Kubrick, Tarantino and a dozen or so American TV series that he had downloaded, as well as a few Kung Fu classics and some porn.

Martin opened the fridge and grabbed a can of Coke Zero and a pack of butter. He found some sliced bread in the cupboard and made himself two of his speciality sandwiches: half Nutella and half condensed milk. In between sugary mouthfuls he swallowed one

Effexor tablet and one Veratran: an antidepressant and tranquilliser cocktail that helped drown out the voices from his childhood, the phantoms of his past and his fear of the future. It would probably have been much better for him to put a pair of trainers on and go for a run but today he didn't feel like being virtuous. Still chewing, he turned on his iPod, which was connected to speakers, and selected an eclectic playlist.

It was a beautiful day. The dazzling sunshine that filled the garden led him out onto the balcony. Before going outside, he put on a T-shirt, covering up the 'star over the dunes', the picture tattooed below his collarbone, an image taken from the last page of *The Little Prince*, 'the saddest and most beautiful landscape in the world', the place where the Little Prince had appeared on earth and the place where he had disappeared.

He put his laptop and his can of Coke on the small metal table. Lost in thought, he turned on his Mac, going over the events of the night before in his head. His computer desktop was in need of a serious clearout. The screen was dotted with documents and downloads. Amidst the chaos, his gaze was attracted to one icon in particular that looked brighter than the others. The folder, whose icon was a Southern Cross, was simply called ARCHIBALD. He clicked on it and opened up the huge archive that contained all the information he had gathered on McLean: press articles he had scanned, statements from Interpol, detailed reports of thefts carried out on French soil, descriptions and photos of stolen works. Somewhere in the computer's innards lay Archibald McLean's secret.

All these thefts had a hidden meaning, Martin was sure of it. The 'King of Burglary's' Achilles heel was not in his technique but in the motivation behind the crimes. What was driving McLean? Martin would never be able to catch him unless he found the answer to this question.

Overwhelmed by the enormity of his task, he went back inside. He lay down on the bed and pulled two cigarette papers out of a packet, then moistened them with his tongue and stuck them together. Then he reached over for his packet of Dunhill, broke one of the cigarettes in half and emptied out the tobacco. Finally he took a small amount of cannabis wrapped in foil from his supply and with his lighter burnt one of the ends and mixed it in with the tobacco. He was just about to light the joint when a voice in his head urged him to return to the computer screen on the balcony. Archibald was stronger than weed.

Martin made some coffee then methodically started to sort through the documents that he had been over a dozen times before. In the light of his encounter with Archibald, however, he was hoping to find some clue, some lead that he had previously ignored. The thief's career spanned more than twenty-five years and was marked by various impressive feats.

1982 – Archibald carried out his first known robbery, burgling Lloyds Bank in central London, one of the largest break-ins in British history. It was also the first time he left his famous calling card at the scene of the crime, a card emblazoned with the Southern Cross.

1983 – Paris. There was a series of robberies at the most famous jewellers in Place Vendôme: Cartier, Van

Cleef and Boucheron. These were acts of disguise worthy of the quick-change artist Fregoli and provided McLean with a colossal haul.

1986 – it took the thief five minutes to snatch two Renoirs and a Watteau from Sweden's National Museum of Fine Arts.

The Guggenheim in New York was next in 1987, with the disappearance of a Kandinsky and a Mondrian.

1990 – armed with a false passport, Archibald managed to befriend an employee of a diamond bank in Anvers. The young woman gave him VIP access to all the safes, allowing him to get his hands on over thirty blue diamonds with a total value of 20 million dollars.

He was back in Paris in 1993, breaking into the town house of Pierre Berès, the most successful bookseller in the world, and leaving with the jewel of Berès's collection: the original manuscript of *Une Saison en enfer* with a dedication from the poet himself: '*à P. Verlaine, A. Rimbaud*'.

In Boston three years later he pulled off the biggest art theft in American history, raiding the Rebecca Stewart Foundation, taking two Rembrandts, a Vélasquez, a Manet, a vase from the Ming dynasty and a Rodin sculpture – a haul with an estimated value of 300 million dollars. Even now, the FBI had still not closed the case, and Boston's district attorney had vowed that he would not retire until McLean was behind bars.

2001 – he seized, from a safe in Philadelphia, the One Cent Magenta, one of the most valuable stamps in the world, dating from 1856. The philatelist's Holy Grail was just a piece of paper barely one centimetre square.

In 2005 came the theft that England would never forgive him for. McLean humiliated the royal family by breaking into Balmoral Castle and leaving with the Queen's favourite Vermeer, as well as a few Leonardo da Vinci drawings. Just to taunt Scotland Yard a bit more, Archibald even allowed himself a little joke, leaving them a message before he disappeared: 'It's up to Sherlock Holmes now!'

He turned his attention in 2007 to French billionaires. François Pinault was the first victim, robbed of an Andy Warhol at the Palazzo Grassi in Venice. Then Bernard Arnault was relieved of a fine Basquiat.

Completely absorbed by the task at hand, it took Martin several seconds to realise that someone was knocking at his door.

'Come in!' he called, looking up and sliding the joint into his pocket.

*

Archibald stepped out of the glass lift that opened straight into his bedroom. The master cabin occupied most of the upper deck. Furnished in Art Deco style, it was much more comfortable and welcoming than the living room, with its fireplace, and geometric furniture inlaid with ebony and mother-of-pearl.

Archibald sat down at the desk. Suddenly despondent, he closed his eyes and massaged his temples to banish the beginnings of a migraine. After each of his more significant thefts, he was overcome by a certain weariness.

However, this time it was different; he had never felt this exhausted and it was a struggle even to open his eyes again. In the middle of the desk, a large brown envelope had been placed for his attention. He picked up the package and felt it, unable to make up his mind whether to open it or not. Once a week for almost twenty years, he had received the same envelope: it was a report from a Californian detective, whom he had charged with an extremely sensitive and private mission.

Reluctantly he opened the envelope and began to pore over the report with a mixture of curiosity and revulsion. It contained photos of a young woman, with a detailed account of how she spent her week and all the people that she saw. There was also a transcript of all her telephone conversations and the contents of all her emails, a medical report from a doctor she had seen that week and a list of the medication he'd prescribed. The photographs had been taken in San Francisco and Sausalito, a little town on the bay. They showed a woman of about thirty, with an untamed melancholy beauty and a hard evasive gaze. It was her.

As he always did, Archibald told himself that this would be the last time he pried into his daughter's life. It was time for him to finally pluck up the courage to talk to her.

He would have to show his love and overcome his fear.

He loved her very much, but fear always got the better of him.

*

'If you keep on eating this rubbish you're going to get ill!'

Mrs Hudson walked into her tenant's den and imperiously put a tray down on the balcony table. The elderly Englishwoman had prepared her special English breakfast: toast with marmalade, kippers and a cup of tea.

'Mmm, smells good,' said Martin distractedly.

His landlady wasn't exactly a cordon bleu cook but she took good care of him and he was grateful for it. She looked after him just as he looked after her.

'I've also brought you your post, and a package that was delivered for you this morning. I didn't want to wake you, so I just signed for it myself.'

Martin thanked her. His post consisted of a bill from France Telecom, as well as a magazine his insurance company sent out every two months. He threw them away without even opening them and turned his attention to the package, which contained a small box made of inlaid sandalwood.

Martin opened the box to find a bottle of champagne bearing the label DOM PÉRIGNON ROSÉ VINTAGE 1959. Frowning, he inspected the box closely to see if the sender had attached a card. But there was nothing there.

He looked at the packaging itself; it had been posted the day before, a little before noon, from a post office in the sixth *arrondissement*. His secret admirer, whoever that might be, was certainly serious about him. Dom Pérignon was the most famous champagne in the world. A bottle from a vintage year must have cost an absolute fortune.

Something told him to return to his computer and he opened up the TREIMA programme. The OCBC photo gallery was one of a kind and contained detailed

104

descriptions and pictures of more than eighty thousand works of art stolen in France and abroad. Using this programme, any object that was found in a search could be identified and returned to its rightful owner. Martin had downloaded the database to his laptop so he could take it with him wherever he was working. He entered a few details and the software immediately came up with a response: the bottles had been stolen last year, under mysterious circumstances, just after an auction. Martin clicked on a link that led to a brief agency report about the auction.

AUCTION HISTORY MADE AFTER
RECORD SALE IN NEW YORK

On 25 April, Sotheby's held a record-breaking sale of champagne, which included two bottles of 1959 Dom Pérignon that fetched the sum of $84,700.

Although this legendary wine is considered by many to be the finest Dom Pérignon of all, only three hundred bottles were ever produced. Most of these were consumed in 1971, when high society came together to celebrate the foundation of the Persian empire.

Since then, the vintage has not been seen on the open market until this historic auction.

Martin couldn't believe his eyes; this meant the bottle he had in front of him was worth more than forty thousand dollars! He continued reading feverishly. Not much was known about the theft itself. Only one thing was clear: when the winning bidder had turned up to collect his lot, the bottles had disappeared, replaced by the most feared calling card in the art world.

For a moment Martin simply stood there, paralysed by the present he had just received.

He couldn't decide what the right thing to do was. The bottle obviously did not belong to him. It was a piece of evidence that should be returned to its owner. On the other hand though …

'Mrs Hudson, may I offer you a glass of champagne?'

'Well, I wouldn't say no,' answered the Englishwoman, sitting down on the balcony. 'It'll make a change from sherry.'

Martin went to fetch two glasses, then opened the bottle carefully, curious to see if the champagne was still fizzy after fifty years. He clinked glasses with Mrs Hudson and brought the flute to his lips. He wasn't disappointed. The flavours were sublime. It was as if he were drinking liquid gold, or the elixir of life.

As if suddenly rejuvenated, Martin raised his glass to the heavens. Looking at things philosophically, he thought to himself that a man's worth could be judged by that of his enemies. He might have lost the first battle, but the war had only just started.

*

Wearing a red polo-neck, Archibald joined Effie up on deck, at the highest point of the ship, which had been turned into an open-air gym. With a towel round her neck, the Englishwoman had been working out for over an hour, lifting weights and doing sessions on the Power Plate, punching bag and treadmill. Archibald suggested a drink, but she declined, indicating her bottle of mineral water. The thief shrugged his shoulders, unsurprised by her response. Effie lived the life of an ascetic, abstaining from several of life's pleasures.

Archibald sat down in the wicker armchair that faced out to sea. The air had cooled slightly, and the setting sun was fighting off the clouds. Purple and scarlet streams of light erupted around the sun. He reached for the bottle of champagne standing in the ice bucket next to his chair and smiled to himself as he read the label: DOM PÉRIGNON ROSÉ VINTAGE 1959. He opened the bottle with care, poured himself a glass, and raised it in the direction of the south-east.

In the direction of France.

Of Paris.

He clinked glasses with the unseen enemy to whom he had just delivered the first blow.

107

8

THE PARADISE KEY

Our life is a book that writes itself. We are just characters in the novel who do not always understand the motives of the author.
Julian Green

Five months later, 20 December, Nanterre, OCBC headquarters
7 a.m.
'This time you have to believe me, sir!'

With tangled, unkempt hair, pale, tired skin and several weeks' growth of beard, Martin laid siege to his boss's office.

Immovable on the subject, the head of the OCBC stood in the doorway, having firmly resolved not to give an inch to his subordinate.

'You shouldn't even be here, Beaumont.'

'But we have to talk about this!'

'There's nothing to talk about. You've been seconded to the Ministry of Culture until February.'

'I've had enough of their ridiculous assignments. Do you know where they're sending me today? To Rouen to train employees at the Ceramics Museum.'

'And? I imagine it's a very beautiful museum.'

'Look, stop messing me around and let me back in the field. That's where I'm most useful to you.'

The colonel lost his temper.

'You got yourself into this situation all by yourself, Captain, and at the moment I don't feel the least inclined to help you out. And what's more ...'

He paused before letting his anger completely get the better of him.

'And what's more, you can bloody well learn to dress properly. You're a police officer, for Christ's sake, not a schoolboy!'

Martin sighed. It was true that he was not exactly resplendent in his worn-out jeans, beaten-up Converses and leather jacket that he had been wearing day in, day out for almost ten years, not to mention the dark circles under his eyes that betrayed a chronic lack of sleep.

The last few months had been difficult. Despite being sidelined at work, he had continued his solo investigation, going through all the clues almost every day, dealing with the art world exactly as he had done with drugs: he let the insignificant traffickers continue as they were in order to focus his energies on finding a lead that would bring down a whole network. He had protested at the removal of his passwords, which gave him access to certain databases, but, even without being a seasoned hacker, he had managed to create a pirated password that allowed him to continue accessing confidential information so he could pursue his own investigations.

As for his evenings, they were spent in front of his computer screen, or buried in books. He had completely reviewed the entire Archibald investigation, had reread all the documents in his possession and had even travelled at his own expense to find and question potential witnesses to past events. Most importantly, he had devoured several important works on psychology and had gone back to see all the psychologists that had been such a nuisance to him during his time on the drugs squad. Officially he was going for personal reasons, but in fact he was using them to learn more about the psychology of the thief. From that point on, he had just one obsession: to put himself in Archibald's shoes, to get into his mind. He wanted, in a sense, to become Archibald.

The thief had not shown himself for five months. There were suddenly no more robberies, and no more clues. Martin had at first felt thrown off balance: he no longer had anything to work with. Then it had become obvious: after the Van Gogh, Archibald had literally run out of things to steal. He needed each new acquisition to be more challenging than the last; each new stolen work had to provoke some new emotion or create some new danger in order to provide an adrenalin rush. If no suitable opportunity presented itself, the criminal preferred to wait, and Martin was forced to do the same. Just as he was starting to lose hope, everything had suddenly changed with the arrival of a press release from Christie's, which had appeared in his mailbox in the middle of the previous night. The famous auction house had announced that an exceptional and mysterious auction was to take place in San Francisco on Christmas Eve. After a few phone calls and some further research, Martin was convinced that Archibald was about to strike again. But all this research would be for nothing if Loiseaux didn't let him go to America.

'Beaumont! You're going to miss your train for Rouen.'

Martin just shrugged. The head of the OCBC pushed money into the vending machine and handed him a paper cup.

'Just reinstate me and I'll hand you the case of your career,' promised the young officer.

Loiseaux's eyes glinted. He was good at what he did; as a forensics expert, he had been one of the main architects of the French fingerprint database, put into effect after the Guy Georges affair. He had not done at all badly as the head of the OCBC, but he had never been able to get on with Martin, because he had no particular passion for art. Loiseaux was ruled by his ambition and saw his post merely as a stepping stone to more prestigious positions.

'And what might this case be, then?'

'The arrest of Archibald McLean.'

'God, you're really obsessed, aren't you?'

'Each to their own.'

'You should have come to see me last time round. When McLean was in France.'

'Look, do you want to catch this guy or not?'

Loiseaux opened the door to his office. Martin followed him in, laptop under his arm. The room was cold and impersonal: a real 'boss's office', large and functional, furnished like a boardroom. Through the windows, there was a view of Nanterre, grey and overcast. Swathed in fog, the towers of the police district made one want to be elsewhere, anywhere but there. Martin connected his

MacBook to the screen on the wall and opened up the slideshow he had prepared.

The first image showed a bird's-eye view of San Francisco.

Loiseaux settled into his armchair.

'So what's Archibald planning on stealing this time around? The Golden Gate Bridge?'

'Better than that.'

His boss crossed his arms, frowning. 'What do you mean?'

'The Paradise Key.'

New York, Staten Island Hospital
4 p.m.

The hospital cafeteria was on the first floor and looked out over a small park that was covered in snow.

Sitting alone at a table, Archibald McLean hadn't touched his coffee. Hunched over, face etched with lines of fatigue, he felt lost and abandoned. For a few weeks now he had been suffering intense pain in his back and his abdomen. He had lost weight, his skin had become papery and yellowed, and he had no appetite for anything.

Having put off the inevitable for such a long time, he had finally resolved to make an appointment at this clinic, where he had been undergoing tests since the previous day. He had had his blood tested, his gall bladder felt, his abdomen had been scanned, and he had even had a tube inserted into his duodenum. He had been promised results and medical advice by the end of the day. He was now completely drained. He was dizzy and had a headache. He wanted to throw up.

But, most of all, he was scared.

Because it was late afternoon, the cafeteria was almost totally empty. Frozen snowflakes stuck to the windows, adding to the slightly half-hearted Christmas decorations on the walls. Over by the counter, the gravelly voice of Leonard Cohen floated from a radio and took Archibald by surprise. Overcome with emotion, he forced himself to swallow a mouthful of coffee and rubbed his eyes, closing them for a moment. The song brought back memories that he normally pushed away. Sun-kissed images, tinged with nostalgia: California at the start of the seventies. A vibrant, exciting, liberated time whose pacifism and revolutionary energy were still thrilling now.

It had been for him a magical time. He and his loved one at the wheel of a convertible.

Valentine.

A time filled with laughter, with the complicity of love and the insouciance of youth. It was the era of Pink Floyd, the Grateful Dead, of psychedelic rock and the San Francisco Sound.

Valentine, beautiful and radiant, with her irresistible French accent, and the special way she said his name.

A time of breakfasts in bed, boat trips, the passion of their bodies, and their hearts.

Valentine, her breath, her warmth, the sensation of her kisses on his mouth.

Valentine, her hair loose in the wind, her scent of lavender, the rhythm of her heartbeat, the treasure map of her beauty spots.

113

A time when they had been happy.

But then the image faded, darkened and his happiness was replaced with venom.

Archibald opened his eyes as if waking from a deep sleep. He felt oppressed, weighed down by an unbearable sadness that threatened to pull him under. It was because of this sadness that he had become 'Archibald McLean', the most wanted thief in the world. Living dangerously forced you to stay on your guard, forced you to stay alert. It was the only way he had found to escape Valentine's ghost.

All of a sudden a burning pain shot through his back and sides. He leant forward to ease the pain and almost cried out with the effort. With his right hand, he felt around for the flask of whisky in the inside pocket of his coat. He opened it and brought it to his lips.

'I wouldn't do that if I were you.'

As though caught in the act, Archibald looked up. An imposing, well-built man stared down at him, holding a file.

*

'So what is this Paradise Key?' asked Loiseaux.

'It's a diamond,' answered Martin. 'A legendary and mythical diamond, which is also said to be cursed.'

The chief's office was bathed in the greyish morning light.

Martin hit a key on the keyboard to bring up on the screen a photo of the precious stone that sparkled with reflections of deep blue and hints of silver.

'It weighs sixty-five carats and measures three centimetres,' explained the young man. 'But it's really the colour that makes it so fascinating.'

Loiseaux stared intently at the screen, as though entranced by the blue diamond.

'It's said to bring misfortune and unhappiness to its owner,' added Martin.

'Where does it come from?'

The slideshow continued, and Martin explained each picture.

'According to legend, the diamond comes from the treasure-filled mines of Golconda, in India. Set in a statue of a goddess, it was first stolen by a smuggler by the name of Jean-Baptiste Charpentier. It was a sacrilegious act and the pirate paid for it with his life.'

Loiseaux motioned for Martin to continue the story.

'Charpentier brought the jewel back to Europe, and managed to sell it to Henry IV, but one day, during a hunt, Charpentier was ripped apart by the dogs and killed. As for the king, he had the diamond cut into the shape of a heart as a gift for his sweetheart, Gabrielle d'Estrées.'

A portrait of a pretty young woman with long golden hair and a lovely figure appeared on the screen.

'Just a few days later, the king's lover, who was six months pregnant, suffered a long and painful death. Some of the court suspected that she had been poisoned, or even possessed by the Devil, because her pain was so agonising.'

'What became of the diamond?'

'It was buried with the dead woman, but reappeared mysteriously round the neck of Marie Antoinette.

115

Apparently she was wearing it in Varennes on the day of her arrest.'

'And what happened to the diamond during the Revolution?'

'Most likely it was stolen along with all the other crown jewels, but it was next seen in London, in the hands of a powerful and rich industrial dynasty, whose members all then experienced the most terrible reversals of fortune. They lost everything, with some of them driven to suicide.'

A picture of an English country manor was followed by an image of an old-fashioned rifle, a London brothel and a syringe that looked as though it might once have belonged to Sherlock Holmes.

Now Loiseaux was completely gripped. Just as with a good detective novel, he was anxious to find out what happened next, and indicated that Martin should carry on.

'The Paradise Key changed hands regularly at the beginning of the twentieth century. A European prince offered it to a girl from the Folies-Bergère who then killed him with a revolver. And when the Sultan Abdulhamid took possession of it he was overthrown just a few months later and lost the entire Ottoman Empire.'

'Are you sure that all these things really happened?' asked Loiseaux incredulously.

'I believe most of it, yes,' answered Martin. 'In the 1920s the stone fell into the hands of the jeweller Pierre Cartier, who cut it into its current oval shape before selling it to a rich banker who at the time was hopelessly in love with Isadora Duncan.'

'The dancer?'

'Yes. She had only had it for a few days before she was killed in Nice – she was strangled when her scarf became caught in the wheel of her convertible. As for her lover, he went bankrupt during the Great Depression and killed himself.'

The front pages of several well-known newspapers came up on the screen, all with headlines announcing the tragic death of the star, followed by pictures taken during the economic crisis of the 1930s, showing homeless people queuing for food and businessmen who had lost everything in the space of a few hours throwing themselves from the tops of buildings.

'What happened next?'

'The diamond then came to be owned by Joe Kennedy, who gave it to his eldest son, Joseph, as a wedding present, the son he hoped would one day become President of the United States.'

'But Joseph died in 1944 when the bomber he was flying blew up over the English Channel.'

'Exactly,' agreed Martin. 'His premature death changed for ever the political future of his younger brother, who at the time was just a rather sickly young man more interested in women and journalism than politics.'

'So did JFK really inherit the cursed jewel?'

'No one knows for certain,' Martin admitted. 'Some believe that the stone was found round Marilyn Monroe's neck on the night she died, and some even believe that it was in JFK's suit pocket when he was assassinated in Dallas. And others will swear that Carolyn Bessette was wearing it in 1999 when her husband John-John's private plane crashed into the Atlantic Ocean. But, as I said, no one really knows the truth.'

'Who owns the diamond now?'

'Stephen Browning, the American billionaire, or, rather, the Kurtline Group, of which he is the main shareholder. They're a powerful American investment fund whose shares—'

'Have just lost all their value?' guessed Loiseaux.

By way of confirmation Martin brought up on the screen a graph showing the collapse of the group's shares on the stock market, as well as an email announcing the forthcoming auction of the Paradise Key. Obviously Kurtline had decided to rid themselves of the gem.

'There's one thing I still don't understand though: if all the jewel does is cause misery and misfortune, why is everyone so desperate to get their hands on it?'

'The Paradise Key is a symbol of purity. According to the myth, it only brings bad luck if the owner is dishonest or greedy. If the opposite is true the stone brings long life and good luck.'

'What does all this have to do with Archibald McLean?'

'Think about it, most experts thought the stone had disappeared for good, or that if it hadn't it certainly wouldn't ever be reappearing on the open market. Its value is inestimable, and the price will soar. From what I've found out, certain collectors from Russia and China are prepared to spend an absolute fortune to get it. Everyone has heard about this auction and I'm willing to bet that it will sell for more than 50 million dollars.'

Loiseaux shook his head in disbelief, but Martin didn't give him time to argue.

'This jewel isn't just any diamond. It's a legend, something truly magical. And it's the only thing that could tempt Archibald at the moment.'

'What proof do you have that that's true?'

Martin decided to bluff.

'I don't need proof. I know McLean better than anyone else does; I feel what he feels; I can get into his head. I know that he wants this diamond, I know how he's going to get it and I know how to stop him. Put me in contact with the FBI and let me go and investigate in San Francisco.'

'Without any concrete evidence you know that's out of the question.'

'But the guys on the Art Crime Team over there know us. Last year we helped them when the Hopper was stolen. They know they can trust us.'

Loiseaux shook his head.

'This is nothing like that time, when we had evidence – phone tapping, tailing of suspects, photos. This time we have sod all.'

The two men fell silent. Looking like a sullen teenager, Martin sat on his boss's glass desk and defiantly lit a cigarette.

The colonel looked at Martin indulgently. This morning, the behaviour of his second-in-command didn't aggravate him. He just felt pity for him, and a little anger.

'For God's sake, what is it that you're after?' he burst out.

The question hung in the air, along with the cigarette smoke.

Loiseaux carried on. 'Even if you do manage to catch McLean one day, do you really believe that'll change

119

anything? Don't start thinking it's going to solve all your problems, Beaumont!'

Martin tried to defend himself. 'Well, what do you want, Colonel?'

'I don't want anything. I'm not looking for anything, because I've already found it. After a certain point in life, it becomes about trying to hold on to what you've already got.'

'So what have you got?'

'What everyone in the world is looking for: my missing piece.'

Martin suddenly didn't want to know any more. He had heard the rumours. Loiseaux had recently left his wife to move in with a young lieutenant who had just finished her training. Was it a midlife crisis? An infatuation? Or true love?

He thought of Karine, of the messages she had left on his answering machine, messages that he hadn't returned. Was she his 'missing piece'? He felt certain she wasn't. But the expression got under his skin like the venom from a snake bite, putting ice crystals in his veins and fracturing the wall of stone around his heart. As though suffering from vertigo, he felt himself falling. He shut his eyes and suddenly it was thirteen years ago, on a rainy summer morning, and he was standing in San Francisco airport. Wet hair became entangled with his own, green eyes shone in the rain and a voice implored him, 'Stay a bit longer!'

Stay a bit longer!

New York, Staten Island Hospital cafeteria

Dr Garrett Goodrich sat down opposite Archibald McLean.

He spread the contents of the file on the table, laying out the results of the tests he had just carried out.

Despite the doctor's warning, Archibald raised the flask of whisky and swallowed a gulp of the precious nectar, not because he really wanted to but more as a gesture of defiance. No one had ever told him what to do and they weren't going to start now. He sealed the silver flask and looked the doctor in the eye.

The two men were actually quite alike. They were about the same age and of a similar build. Neither was particularly tall, but both were powerfully built and both had a certain charisma and presence.

'So basically I'm going to die, aren't I?'

As always, Archibald preferred to get straight to the point.

Goodrich didn't break eye contact. He felt a strange kind of empathy towards this patient, who in another world might have been his brother, his best friend, his alter ego. What would he have wanted to hear if he'd been in his shoes? The cold hard truth or the sugar-coated version? He chose the former.

'You have a tumour in your pancreas that has already spread to your lymph nodes and your liver.'

Archibald took the news without flinching.

Goodrich carried on. 'Its size means it is now inoperable. I've rarely seen a case this severe. We could try surgery or chemotherapy to ease the abdominal pain but I doubt they'll work any better than the painkillers you're taking.

121

So if you want to know how long you've got, I'd say your chances of making it past the next three months are slim to none.'

Archibald closed his eyes and felt his heart racing. At least now he knew the situation. He was backed up against the wall, ready to fight one last battle, the outcome of which he already knew.

The two men faced each other for a short while without saying anything. Then Garrett Goodrich got up to ask at the counter for an empty glass, before returning to the table. He poured himself a measure of whisky and drank with his patient.

Archibald felt his heart slow down. Strangely enough, the fatal diagnosis had made him feel less afraid than he had before. Fearing the worst was far more frightening than knowing the worst.

Fear was the real enemy.

Always.

9

MADEMOISELLE HO

He wept tears of crystal,
And when to the earth they fell,
Together they made a music,
Ghostly and angelic.
Michel Polnareff

Gare Saint-Lazare
8.10 p.m.
The train from Rouen arrived half an hour late. Whether it was because of industrial action, technical problems or something on the tracks, Martin was too tired and depressed to care.

He was one of the first to get off the train. With his hands stuffed into the pockets of his jacket and his iPod turned up loud, he pushed his way through the crowd, anxious to escape the cold, urban setting of the station.

On the escalator, he felt someone standing a little too close to him; he turned round to find an enormous Asian man who was built like a sumo wrestler. Dressed in an Italian suit and sporting a pair of dark glasses, he looked as if he had just stepped out of a John Woo film.

Then a feline figure emerged from behind the giant.

123

The young woman, who was wearing a trench coat belted at the waist and held herself like a queen, came down a step to join him. His ears full of the music that was still playing, Martin could only lip-read when she spoke to him.

'Good evening, Mr Beaumont.'

He took off his headphones and squinted at her. She vaguely reminded him of someone.

'Moon Jin-Ho.' She held out her hand as she introduced herself. At first, the name meant nothing then it came to him.

Mademoiselle Ho, the 'Seoul Panther'.

'I think there are a few things we need to talk about, Mr Beaumont. But, firstly, may I call you Martin?'

Things we need to talk about?

Martin frowned. For a short while he looked down at the hand she was holding out to him, before finally deciding to shake it.

'I hope you haven't lost your tongue,' she said, moving a little closer to him.

Martin remained expressionless. He knew that this woman was anything but harmless and that behind the charming and friendly exterior lay an iron ambition that knew no limits. Mademoiselle Ho was famous in his world. She had attracted the media's attention for the first time five years previously, when she had been working for the State Prosecutor in Seoul. Leading a squad of fifty investigating officers, she had managed to put the heads of Jopok, the Korean mafia, behind bars for good. It had been a 'clean' operation that had succeeded in ridding Seoul of many of the criminal networks that had

124

once controlled prostitution and illegal gambling in the city through blackmail and extortion. This coup had made a heroine of the young Korean, but meant that she now required constant protection, as the criminals she had brought down wanted her dead. Martin knew she was now working for the American branch of Boid's Brothers, one of the biggest insurance companies in the world.

'Have dinner with me,' she said. 'Let me try and persuade you.'

'Persuade me to do what?'

'You have a very nice voice.'

'Persuade me to do what?' he asked, starting to get annoyed.

'Persuade you to work for me.'

'I don't work for anyone,' he said, shaking his head.

'You work for a state that doesn't acknowledge your achievements.'

He looked at her. The station was crowded, but her bodyguard seemed to create a barrier between them and the rest of the world.

'You would be working with me, not for me.' The Korean changed her tactics. 'Together we might actually stand a chance.'

'A chance of what?'

'Of catching Archibald McLean.'

*

The Bentley with the tinted windows cut across Rue Saint-Lazare, then Boulevard Haussmann before heading for Place de la Concorde. The inside of the car smelt of new leather. At the wheel the colossus in dark glasses drove with surprising care to the sound of Bach playing on the car stereo. In the back seat, Martin, lost in thought, watched without seeing the thousands of bluish lights that sparkled like a waterfall from the trees bordering the Avenue des Champs-Élysées. Sitting next to him was Mademoiselle Ho, who was looking furtively at him. Her gaze lingered on his overlong hair, his unkempt beard and the shabby leather jacket he hadn't bothered to take off. She also noticed the neckline of his sweater, above which she could see a painful-looking tattoo and the plaster near his lip. She thought he looked a bit like a down-at-heel rock star. There was something both sad and troubled about him. He was improbably good-looking, romantic, but with an edge. She managed to catch his eye, but only for a moment. His eyes were a pale washed-out blue and had the power to attract in the way that some men do when they have long given up on love. There was a glint in them that suggested a sharp intelligence.

The car crossed the Seine and turned right onto Quai d'Orsay before carrying on to Quai Branly and Avenue de Suffren.

Mademoiselle Ho suddenly shivered. She had confronted the most hardened criminals, and had had some of the world's most feared gang leaders sentenced to death, and taunted all the killers that the mafia had set on her trail. And not once had she felt afraid. But in this car, with this man, she was afraid. Afraid of herself and the sudden emotion she felt, which was both unexpected and disturbing. She was paid vast sums for her ability to see through people, to find their frailties and guess their weak spots. In theory, she already knew everything there was to know about Martin. The insurance company she worked for had been watching him for several months now. Mademoiselle Ho knew his file inside out, had read his emails and listened to both his private and business phone calls. She had thought she knew what she was doing with this man, but she hadn't anticipated the magnetic effect he would have on her.

She closed her eyes for a few moments, trying to suppress her growing desire. She knew that emotions could be more dangerous and destructive than a bullet from a 9mm or the sharp blade of a sword.

The Bentley pulled up near the Champ-de-Mars. The sumo wrestler opened the door for them, slamming it behind them.

It was cold outside. The temperature was close to zero and a mixture of rain and snow swirled in the wind.

'I hope you're not afraid of heights,' she said, pointing up at the metal structure of the Eiffel Tower, floodlit in blue.

In an effort to warm up a little, Martin lit a Dunhill and exhaled a cloud of pearly smoke.

'Not at all, I like standing over the abyss,' he replied, almost as though he were challenging her.

*

Martin followed the Korean woman up to the first floor of the Eiffel Tower and under the awning that led to the private entrance of the Jules Verne restaurant. The lift

127

took them up to the second floor where the 'Iron Lady's' famous restaurant was tucked away. The maître d' led them through the room, which followed the contours of the tower's four pillars so that its shape resembled a sort of Maltese Cross.

There were deep-brown carpets, a discreet piano, modern Italian chairs and a breathtaking panorama. It was truly a magical place. Their table looked out onto the Trocadéro with its spectacular illuminations.

They ordered quickly, then Mademoiselle Ho took a brown envelope out of her bag, which she handed to her dining companion.

The young *flic* opened it. Inside was a cheque made out to him from Boid's Brothers for the sum of 250,000 euros.

Ten times Martin's current salary.

*

Martin *(pushing the cheque away)*: What is it that you want exactly?

Mademoiselle Ho: Consider it an advance if you like. A kind of incentive for you to leave the police force.

Martin didn't reply to this. Speechless, he looked absent-mindedly at his citrus-caviar-vodka marinated salmon, whilst she savoured every mouthful of her coquilles Saint-Jacques. Then after a moment:

Martin: What do you want me to do for you?

Mademoiselle Ho: I've already told you. I want you to help me arrest Archibald.

Martin: But why me?

Mademoiselle Ho: Because you're the only policeman in the world who's actually seen his face and had him in your sights. Because you spend your evenings trying to get inside his head and because you seem to be convinced that your life is somehow inextricably linked to his.

Martin: What makes you say that?

Mademoiselle Ho (*bringing a flute of pink champagne to her lips*): Let's be honest with each other, Martin. I know everything about you, from your grandmother's bra size, to the name of your primary school teacher. I know your entire service record, how empty your private life really is, the type of cigarette paper you use to roll your joints, all your favourite porn sites …

Martin couldn't help but smile. He had known for a few weeks now that someone had been following him, and that his computer had been bugged. Thinking it was an investigation carried out by the police complaints authority, he had made sure to protect the most important things: Nico, little Camille and his secret file on Archibald. The Korean thought she knew him, but she had no idea of the things that truly mattered to him.

She could sense his disdain. Realising that she needed to approach this from a different angle and that she wouldn't get anywhere by intimidating him, she played her last card.

Mademoiselle Ho: You think you know everything there is to know about Archibald, but you're wrong.

Martin *(unmoved)*: Go on.

Mademoiselle Ho: For you, McLean is a skilled thief. For us, he's a kidnapper.

Martin frowned.

Mademoiselle Ho: Officially, there is no such thing as kidnapping works of art, because if it were recognised as a crime, people would start doing it left, right and centre. In my industry it's something of a taboo. No one would ever discuss it openly and no insurance company or museum curator would ever admit to having paid a ransom to retrieve a stolen painting.

Martin *(shrugging his shoulders)*: Yeah, but in reality it's a different story.

Mademoiselle Ho: Exactly. And McLean knows how to play this game better than anyone else. Apart from a few works that he won't part with for anything, he is willing to negotiate returning most paintings with the insurance companies, normally for vast sums. But the most surprising thing about all this is what he does with the ransom money.

She deliberately stopped there, leaving her revelation hanging. Martin forced himself not to react, pretending to concentrate on the grilled langoustines with truffles that the waiter had just put in front of him. Then he looked up at her, as if examining a work of art in a museum. Her skin was beautifully clear, with a rosy glow. Tall and model-thin, she wore a flared black skirt and a white shirt, which made her look more like Audrey Hepburn than Gong Li.

130

Mademoiselle Ho: According to the IRS, Archibald has created a complicated network of dummy companies to launder the profits from his thefts and donate much of the money to humanitarian organisations.

She showed him the screen of her BlackBerry, which displayed a list of the NGOs concerned. Martin recognised some of the names: Doctors without Borders, Flying Doctors, Wings of Hope.

Snowflakes swirled in the wind just inches from their table, before being dashed against the glass windows. She was still talking, but Martin had already stopped listening. In his head he now saw Archibald as a kind of modern-day Robin Hood, using his passion for art for altruistic charitable ends. He had already constructed hundreds of theories in his head, which all led to the same question. What was it the thief was trying to atone for?

Mademoiselle Ho: I assume you are familiar with Boyd's Brothers, the insurance company I work for?

Martin nodded. Boyd's Brothers was a major player in the art world, made up of a conglomerate of smaller companies, which had managed to absorb most of their rivals, creating a kind of monopoly that snapped up all the most important contracts on the market.

Mademoiselle Ho: For the last five years Boid's Brothers has had to pay out millions in compensation because of Archibald McLean.

Martin *(shrugging)*: That's your problem, not mine.

131

Mademoiselle Ho: Because of Archibald's increase in activity over the past year, the company is now in an extremely precarious financial situation. We've had to dip into company savings to the tune of tens of millions of euros.

Martin: Well, what do you expect? It's tough for everyone at the moment.

Mademoiselle Ho *(trying to control her anger)*: We can't take much more of this, and neither can the FBI. We work side by side with the Feds and we've both decided that we need to solve our McLean problem. Once and for all.

Martin: I'd love to know just how you're going to manage that.

Mademoiselle Ho: Our company has agreed to insure the Paradise Key, which is going to be put up for auction in San Francisco very soon. Like you, we think that Archibald will try and get hold of it, but this time he won't succeed, because you'll be there to stop him.

Before he could ask any questions, she put a plane ticket on the table.

Mademoiselle Ho: I'm working with the Feds and I want you to be my partner on this assignment. Whatever you decide, you have fifteen minutes before I retract my offer.

Martin looked at the plane ticket. It was a one-way ticket to San Francisco, for the day after next. His Korean friend didn't waste any time. She was probably used to winning this kind of bet. But the young *flic* had one more ace up his sleeve.

Martin: I want permission from the FBI to carry a gun on American soil, and authorisation to arrest Archibald McLean myself if the opportunity arises.

Mademoiselle Ho: I can't possibly grant you that.

Martin: You can negotiate anything in that country; it's both its strength and its weakness. You know that as well as I do.

Mademoiselle Ho: It's still impossible.

Martin: Look, even if you mobilise the FBI, the IRS, and the American army, you'll never be able to catch him, unless you know who he really is. But you don't know the first thing about his past, or what drives him now. You have no solid facts to rely on, no biographical knowledge to help you. I, on the other hand …

He took a small clear plastic bag out of his pocket, the kind that was normally used to hold pieces of evidence. Inside was the label from a bottle of champagne.

Martin: I have one of his fingerprints.

She looked at him incredulously.

Martin: Six months ago he sent me a bottle of champagne. I think he was trying to provoke me. Anyway, he left a clear fingerprint on the label. A fingerprint that you won't find in any file. I'm the only one who knows

133

it exists. I've already looked on the national fingerprint database but you'd also have to check it against the prints on Eurodac, and the IAFIS, the FBI database.

She held out her hand, hoping for a moment that Martin would give her the bag. Their eyes met for a few seconds before Martin proposed a final deal.

Martin: The fingerprint in exchange for permission from the Feds to arrest Archibald McLean myself in the United States.

He got up from the table without having touched his dark chocolate soufflé and warned her, 'I'm not giving you fifteen minutes to think about it though. You have five.'

10

LIFE'S WHIRLWIND

So together we took off
Into the whirlwind of life
And we kept on turning
Entwined together
Entwined together
Music by Georges Delerue
Lyrics by Cyrus Bassiak (Serge Rezvani)

Eiffel Tower, Jules Verne Restaurant
10.03 p.m.

Escorted by the maître d', Martin headed for the restaurant exit, passing the huge glass doors that led to the kitchens. In this temple of luxury, no one even thought of monitoring the comings and goings of diners, and so, flouting all the rules, Martin slipped unnoticed through the doors and grabbed a can of Coke Zero from a fridge before leaving the room.

He went down in the lift, doing up his jacket and putting his headphones back on. He still listened to the same brand of edgy and aggressive hip-hop as he had in the nineties when he was at school and then university. The same songs that had acquired cult status over the years:

'*J'appuie sur la gâchette / Paris sous les bombes / Pose ton gun*'. This was his music: the music of a kid from an estate in Essonne, the angry freestyling, which was in turn explosive and soothing. The music of someone who had no place in a restaurant full of tourists on their honeymoon.

*

On the Champ-de-Mars the air was clear and icy cold. Martin rubbed his hands together to warm up and headed onto Quai Branly. As though drawn by a magnet to the river, he turned onto Pont d'Iéna, which linked the Eiffel Tower to the Trocadéro. On the banks of the river, he lost himself in the dancing lights of the houseboats and streetlamps that glittered like fireflies. Snowflakes were still fluttering in the air, but instead of cotton wool they now looked more like fine grains of cocaine.

He took out of his pocket the plane ticket that he had made sure not to leave lying on the table.

San Francisco.

Even the thought of the place sent a shiver down his spine. It was neither a pleasant nor an unpleasant sensation. First came the deceptive caress of nostalgia, then a wave of pain, which he had to struggle to master.

Once more, the memory of that magical summer resurfaced, the security of Gabrielle's arms, and the only time he had truly felt a connection with another human being.

Why was love such an addictive drug?

Why did loving someone cause such suffering?

The sound of a barrel organ brought him back to the present. He recognised the lively melody from a Truffaut film. He remembered the name of the song: 'The Whirlwind of Life'.

It was true. Sometimes life was like that, a wonderful whirlwind that fills us with joy, like a ride on a merry-go-round when we are children. A whirlwind of love and drunkenness when you sleep in someone's arms, in a tiny bed, getting up for breakfast at midday because you've spent the morning making love.

But sometimes a whirlwind destroys things, like a violent typhoon that tries to drag us down, when we have been caught by the storm, when we realise that we have to face the tempest alone.

And we are afraid.

*

'Martin!'

He heard his name pronounced in an English accent.

A few feet behind him Mademoiselle Ho, still accompanied by her bodyguard, was calling him over.

He was sure that she had given in and that he had won.

He had won the right to follow Archibald to America.

The right to continue his duel with the greatest thief of all. It was the only thing that kept him from going under, that gave meaning to his life.

The only thing that made him still believe that in life everyone had a purpose. His was to stop Archibald

McLean. It was an irrational belief that he held on to fiercely and had carried within him for years.

And with the fingerprint on the label of the champagne bottle, Martin felt sure he was within touching distance of success.

Even though he knew that the print was too clear, too obvious to be anything but a trap. Archibald would never have made such a simple mistake.

Martin hadn't found the fingerprint – Archibald had given it to him.

Because from now on the rules of the game had changed: it was no longer Martin pursuing Archibald, but Archibald drawing Martin closer.

But why?

11

THE DAY YOU LEAVE ME

But here's the worst part: the trick to life lies in hiding from those we hold most dear how much they mean to us; if not, we'd lose them.
Cesare Pavese

The following day, 21 December, headquarters of the Police Judiciaire in Paris
10.40 a.m.
As he handed in his letter of resignation, Martin had goosebumps. He saw himself as a young man again, stepping for the first time into this mythical building on Quai des Orfèvres, a stone's throw from Notre Dame.

He remembered how he had walked down the building's narrow corridors, and down the staircases that belonged to another era, surrounded by the ghosts of legendary policemen who had all worked in this charmingly antiquated place, which was too small and hadn't been adapted to the demands of the modern police force, but had a strong emotional charge for all those who had worked there.

Between the drugs squad and the OCBC, the police had been his life for the last eight years. A life in which he

139

had never felt comfortable and had never really found a family, but a life he found difficult to leave.

Half an hour later, he left the building. The pavements alongside the banks of the Seine were bathed in golden sunlight. He had handed in his badge, his ID card, his gun and his handcuffs. He felt naked without them. He was filled with a combination of regret and relief. Well, that was the end of his police career.

It was going to take some getting used to.

Institute for adolescents, boulevard de Port-Royal 3.30 p.m.

From the outside, the Solenn Institute resembled a giant glass steamship, with two arms stretched out invitingly towards the centre of town. Martin walked across a green esplanade and followed the paths of a small garden which led to the hospital building. For three years now he had been coming here once a week, every week.

The hallway was spacious and light, covering an area of over six thousand square feet, with a pale wood floor and an immensely high ceiling, from which hung posters depicting various adolescent afflictions.

Strangely, Martin always felt very calm in this place, which seemed to be anything but a hospital: the vast spaces, the glass walls and the landscaped surroundings dispelled any sense of being enclosed.

He went straight up to the third floor where the arts therapy centre was located. The various rooms led into each other and included a multimedia library, a kitchen, a music and dance studio, and a radio studio. Martin didn't believe in much, but he did believe in the healing powers of art, in culture as a means of restoring one's self-image, and in the resilient power of creativity.

He noticed someone standing in the doorway of the art room.

'Hi, Sonia.'

'Hi, Martin, you're early today!' answered the young woman in white scrubs.

She gave him a friendly kiss on the cheek and showed him into the studio, which was filled with artworks done by the residents. Each time he came, Martin was amazed by how moving the pieces were. There were tormented paintings, filled with death, guardian angels and exterminating demons. There were casts of the emaciated bodies of anorexic patients, depicting them at the time of their hospitalisation, then casts of the same bodies six months later, rounded and healthy. In this room, angels and demons seemed to be waging a bitter war, the outcome of which was uncertain.

Just like in life.

'Could you help me move the trestles?'

The young policeman happily obliged, then asked, 'Has she come out of her session yet?'

'Yes, I said to her you'd meet her up there.'

'Will you come up with me?'

'Come on, Martin, you're a big boy.'

'I've got something to tell you, Sonia …'

She followed him into the corridor and as they waited for the lift she suddenly challenged him.

'Come on, lazybones, let's take the stairs! Last one up buys lunch!'

Before she had even finished her sentence she ran off, taking the stairs four at a time.

Martin had difficulty catching her but when he did he pinned her up against the wall.

'I have to tell you something.'

'What, that you love me? But that can't be – you know I have a boyfriend.'

'Can you be serious just for one minute, please?' he replied, letting her go.

'What do you want to tell me? That you're going away? Then it's not me you should be telling. It's Camille.'

*

Martin had met Dr Sonia Hajeb, child psychiatrist and head of the clinic, three years previously when she had appeared in his office at the OCBC.

She was a slim woman, with a youthful face, and thick dark hair that was always pulled back into a ponytail. Barely older than he was, she often wore jeans and a leather jacket and lived in Saint-Denis. She could have been the sister he'd never had.

Every day in her work she fought against anorexia, bulimia, depression and the destructive kinds of behaviour that drove teenagers to suicide. From the moment she had opened her mouth, Martin had been able to tell that she was a good person.

'I am forbidden by law and by my profession from saying what I'm about to say to you.'

He had immediately been impressed by these opening lines, which indicated a strong personality and fearless determination.

'In telling you, I'm putting my job on the line.'

'Then why are you telling me?'

'Because I believe it will help a young girl get better.'

Martin had frowned at this. He didn't understand what this could possibly have to do with him.

'Do you remember Camille?'

He had shrugged his shoulders vaguely.

'I know a lot of Camilles.'

'Women maybe, Casanova, but I'm talking about a little girl.'

Martin had closed his eyes for half a second and in that moment adrenalin had started pulsing through his veins and the memory had come rushing violently back to him.

*

Winter 2000, Le Luth, north of Gennevilliers

Blocks of flats stand twenty storeys high and 650 feet long. It is drizzling, the rain is grey and dirty. It is only five o'clock, but already night is falling. The dark-blue Peugeot 309 pulls up at the bottom of building C. He is one of the three policemen who are going to arrest the girlfriend of a drug dealer that they've had under surveillance. He knocks at the door and reels off the standard lines. There's no answer. One of his colleagues breaks down the door. Martin steps inside, gun poised.

They find the woman lying on a mattress. She seems feverish, with dilated pupils and slashed wrists. Her nightdress is stained with blood and urine. Beside her there is a homemade crack pipe – an empty bottle of Coke with a biro wedged in it. Martin remains at her side while an ambulance is called. He knows it is already too late for her. She is going. By the time the ambulance arrives, she's gone.

The search doesn't come up with much. A few joints, some crack cocaine, a little heroin.

A shit day.

He goes back to Nanterre, forces himself to get through all the paperwork and closes the case. He wants to vomit, to sob. He wishes he were somewhere else. In the evening he goes home. Another sleepless night. The feeling that something is missing from his life. The look in the dying woman's eyes comes back to haunt him …

A shit night.

Martin wakes up, gets in the car and drives out to the suburbs, onto the ring road, through Saint-Ouen, then Gennevilliers, finally arriving in Le Luth. He wanders around the estate on foot for a bit, questioning the dealers who are hanging about, and goes back to the apartment. He is looking for something, though he doesn't know what. He goes through the bedroom, the kitchen, the stuff on the floor. He is still looking. He goes downstairs and lingers in the stairwell. He looks through the letterbox, examines the lift ceiling. He is still looking. Outside, in the night, the cold, that damned rain, he is still looking, in the car park, in the cars, the scooters, the cardboard boxes that are everywhere. He is still looking for something, or someone. Is that a shout he hears? Or is it his intuition?

He opens the bin nearest to him and searches through it. He shivers suddenly. There it is! He knows it's there, before he even knows what 'it' is. Inside a plastic carrier bag he finds a baby, no more than a few hours old, naked, frozen, wrapped in a jumper and a towel. There are still bits of the placenta on its head. It's not breathing. Wait, yes, it is. Well, perhaps. Martin doesn't bother to call an ambulance. He wraps the newborn in his coat, bundles it into the passenger seat, puts on his siren and speeds off, heading east to Ambroise-Paré. The blood they saw on the woman's dress a few hours ago wasn't just from her wrists, it was from a haemorrhage during childbirth. And the idiot paramedics hadn't even noticed! He calls the hospital to tell them he's coming. He keeps looking at the baby beside him. It's a little girl. Well, at least he thinks it is. He is at once horrified and fascinated by her tiny size. Obviously the birth was premature, but how long could she have been in her mother's womb? Seven months? Eight?

He reaches the hospital. She is taken from him. There are dozens of forms to fill in. The baby's name? Surname? At first, he is not sure what he should put down. He struggles to remember what the mother was called. For the baby's first name, Camille is the only one that comes to mind. Then he waits for hours, with no news of the child. He comes back the following day. Like most drug addicts the baby is experiencing violent withdrawal symptoms. All they can do is wait. But why is the baby so small? Crack cocaine restricts the blood flow from the placenta to the foetus, resulting in poor foetal growth. He comes back the

145

next day as well. The little thing is fighting for her life. He wants to fight with her. On the third day, he is told that the worst stages of withdrawal have passed, but the baby has HIV and there could be serious side effects, even deformities. On the fourth day, he does not go back to the hospital; instead he chooses to spend the evening in a seedy bar, with a bottle of vodka. Because Camille was Gabrielle's favourite girl's name. The name she would have liked to give her little girl. On the fifth day, he does not go to work. On the sixth, he buries the incident in his memory and decides to forget Camille completely. Years go by. Until one day Sonia Hajeb steps into his office.

*

On the roof of the hospital, the terrace had been turned into a garden with trees and a few wicker chairs and tables.

A little girl of around eight, with short hair and a turned-up nose, innocent as anything, seemed engrossed in *A Distant Neighborhood,* the cult manga by Taniguchi.

'Hi, Camille.'

'Martin!'

She looked up from her book and ran to hug him. He picked her up in his arms and spun her round at top speed, following the ritual that they stuck to religiously.

Three years earlier, when Camille had been going through a difficult time with her adoptive family, Sonia Hajeb, the psychiatrist who had looked after her from the beginning, had taken it upon herself to tell her what had really happened when she was born. Camille had then insisted on meeting this odd sort of big brother who had saved her life. These secret meetings had had an extremely positive effect on the young girl, proving that Sonia had been right to take such a risk.

Whatever happened, they met once a week, always in the same place, always on a Wednesday.

Camille was a pretty girl, full of energy and vitality. When Martin looked at her, he saw life blossoming in front of him, a reminder that fate did not always bring misfortune but also sometimes bestowed unexpected gifts. The risks of deformity had disappeared entirely, the HIV virus had been contained and the likelihood of her leading the life of a victim had been averted.

'It's freezing out here,' said Martin, rubbing his hands together. 'Don't you want to go back inside?'

'No, I want to enjoy the sun! And, anyway, I like the cold – it wakes me up!'

He sat down next to her, and gazed into the distance, at the ocean of rooftops below them.

'So which comic are you reading now, then?'

'Oh, it's brilliant! Thank you so much for recommending it,' Camille enthused.

'You're welcome.'

He opened his rucksack and fished out the apple-green iPod that he had given her a few months ago.

'Here, I've made you a great playlist. There's some Marvin Gaye, The Cure, U2, Jacques Brel …'

'But I wanted Beyoncé and Britney Spears!'

'And why not the Spice Girls, too, while you're at it?'

147

Suddenly serious, he moved his chair closer to her. 'There's something we have to talk about.'

She looked him in the eye, sensing that the delicate balance that held her life together was being threatened.

'Have you ever heard the expression "out of sight, out of mind"?'

She shook her head.

As he explained to her why this expression would never ever apply to them, an angel passed by above and lightly brushed the last rays of the winter sun with its wings.

12

LET ME SHED A TEAR

It is important that we do not lose our fragility, for it is this that brings us closer to those around us, while our strength divides us.
Jean-Claude Carrière

Avenue Kléber: The motorbike sped through the night
Place de l'Étoile: Martin wiped the rain from the visor of his helmet.
He had one last thing to do before he left France.
Avenue de Wagram: One person left to see. A woman.

*

The first time Martin had met Nico was on a weekday evening, in the queue at the supermarket in Les Ulis. Martin had only been in the area by chance, visiting his grandparents who were living at the time in a retirement home in Bures-sur-Yvette. He had never got on with them very well, but nevertheless felt it his duty to go and see them once a month, generally to listen to a litany of criticism. On the way back, he had stopped at the local

149

shopping centre to pick up a few supplies, some spaghetti with pesto sauce, a tube of condensed milk, some Coke Zero, the new Michael Connelly paperback and the final season of *Six Feet Under*.

The woman standing in front of him in the queue immediately caught his eye. She was tall and blonde, with a pretty face, but a fragile expression. He had picked up on her Slavonic accent when she exchanged a few words with the cashier. It was her eyes that especially caught his attention, with their faded, yet fascinating sparkle. They reminded him of another pair of gold-flecked eyes.

She had paid for her shopping and then moved away, walking quickly. In order not to lose sight of her, Martin had left his items at the till and followed her into the main shopping arcade, driven by an impulse that was as sudden as it was unexpected.

'Mademoiselle!'

When she turned to face him, he was reminded of a startled gazelle encountering a hunter. He would have liked to say to her 'Don't be scared', but instead he pulled out his badge and said: 'Police, ID check, your papers please.'

*

Half an hour later, she was sitting in his car. He had given her a lift home – she lived in a tower block on the Daunières estate where she shared a flat with a friend. Her name was Svetlana but everyone called her Nico because of her striking resemblance to the Velvet Underground singer.

She had an MA in History of Art which hadn't really been of any use to her, so she had left her home town of Kiev to live in Moscow where she struggled to make ends meet as a model with a minor agency until her agent offered her the prospect of a shiny new life in the West.

It had turned out to be a false Eden that had forced her into selling her body on the streets, demeaning herself a little more each day.

He had gone as far as to ask her hourly rate. She had looked him straight in the eye and answered that it ranged from fifty to two hundred euros, depending on what you wanted. He had handed over two hundred euros.

'Close your eyes and do what I say,' he had instructed.

'Here, in the car?'

'Yes.'

*

She had closed her eyes, and he had switched on the stereo and put on one of his all-time favourite CDS: Ella Fitzgerald singing with Louis Armstrong. He had headed down the N118 into Paris.

She had not been expecting any of this, but she let herself be led, keeping her eyes closed for the whole journey, comforted by the voices of Ella and Louis.

Half an hour after that, they were looking down on the city from the top of the Ferris wheel at Place de la Concorde. She had relaxed a little by this point, and although she was still not completely sure she was safe, life had taught her to live in the moment and take the pleasures that were available to her.

Nico had gazed with childlike wonder at the sea of lights that illuminated the Champs-Elysées. When their cabin reached the highest point on the wheel she had put her head back, as if offering herself to the heavens. Martin had watched her, seeing hundreds of stars reflected in her eyes.

Afterwards, he had taken her to eat ravioli with porcini mushrooms and polenta biscotti in a little restaurant on Rue de Bassano.

Then he had taken her back to Les Ulis, to her block of flats.

She had started to run her hand over his leg, his knee, his thigh, his—

'No,' he had said, putting his hand on hers.

Svetlana had got out of the car, and he had watched her walk away.

She was both happy and unhappy.

*

They had met up again the following week, and over the next year it became a regular occurrence. He always paid the same price, two hundred euros. It was his insurance against falling in love, and her insurance against romantic delusions.

He imagined he was giving her a chance to escape the sordid reality of her daily life: blowjobs in the back seats of cars, quickies in Novotels, seeking destructive solace in coke and heroin, the feeling of being a prisoner in her own life.

He remembered each of their meetings clearly: the time they had visited the open-air ice rink at the Hôtel de Ville, the Bouglione Circus, the Police gig in the Stade de France, Picasso and Courbet exhibitions at the Grand Palais, *La Vie devant soi* at the Marigny theatre.

He had saved all her emails on his mobile, the ones she always left him the day after one of their evenings together, messages that, like an idiot, he had never replied to.

From: svetlana.shaparova@hotmail.fr
To: martin.beaumont1974@gmail.com
Sent: 12 February 2008; 08:03
Subject: Life's not worth living

Dear Martin,

It's cold. I'm taking the metro to 'work'. I'm pulling along my little suitcase on wheels. With all the odds against me, I'm clutching the book you gave me. I'm listening to the Serge Gainsbourg song you played me for the first time, 'La Javanaise', the one that says that without love life's not worth living.

Thank you so much for the delicious dinner yesterday evening on Avenue Montaigne. I loved the restaurant above the theatre. I was so happy to look down on Paris for once, to be above the world, to share an instant of life with you, smiling, taking care of me. Even tiredness couldn't ruin it. I was so happy.

Thank you, thank you, thank you! I don't even regret that trip to McDonald's!

I'm yours,
Your Cinderella

Boulevard Malesherbes: The motorbike sped over the wet ground, passed Boulevard Berthier and the ring road.

Avenue de la Porte-d'Asnières: Martin slowed down and lifted up his helmet's visor.

Rue Victor-Hugo: He did a U-turn in the central reservation.

Three provocatively dressed eastern European women were waiting in the rain for customers, next to a large billboard. He approached the trio, slowing down. They mistook him at first for one of their customers, then Svetlana recognised him. He held out her helmet and told her to get on the bike. She shivered, looking thin and hollow-eyed. He could tell she wasn't sleeping properly, that she now spent most of her income on drugs.

'Come on!'

She shook her head, walking away. She had guessed what he had in mind and she was scared. She was scared of the violent retaliation of the gangsters who had put her on the streets, scared of the threats these guys made to her family back home.

But you couldn't spend your life being scared.

Martin caught up with her on the pavement. She was so weak that she couldn't even put up a fight. He took her by the shoulders, almost carrying her to his motorbike, all the while telling her: 'You're going to be OK, it's all going to be OK.'

*

One hour later they were in Montparnasse, in a discreet hotel on Rue de l'Abbé-Grégoire. She took a shower and he rubbed her with a towel to warm her up. Her pupils shrank because of the withdrawal and she started to shake violently. He saw her marked arms, bloodied from the scratching, and heard her stomach growl with hunger.

Before she went to the bathroom, he made her take three spoonfuls of methadone to reduce the withdrawal symptoms. Sonia had told him that the first analgesic effects would take between thirty minutes and an hour to kick in. While he waited, he helped her wrap herself in the duvet and held her hand tightly, until finally she stopped shaking.

*

'Why, Martin?' she asked him in her Slavonic accent.

Lying on the bed, she seemed relaxed, almost serene. Of course, this calmness was artificial and chemically induced, but it was still the first step.

'You'll never get out on your own.'

'But wherever I go they'll find me.'

'No, they won't.'

He got up and fetched his rucksack and pulled out a battered passport.

'It's more realistic than a real one,' he explained, opening it at the first page. 'From now on, you're no longer Svetlana, you're Tatiana, and you weren't born in Kiev, you were born in St Petersburg.'

That was how he had spent his last day as a *flic*. He had found her a new identity.

'And the second thing,' he said, putting a plane ticket on the bed. 'Tomorrow morning, you're leaving for Geneva, to stay in the Joan of Arc Clinic. They'll help you get better, I promise.'

'But how …?'

'Everything's already been paid for,' he answered, anticipating the question.

What he didn't tell her was that it had been paid for using money from his savings account, which he had emptied that afternoon.

Then he gave her Sonia Hajeb's business card.

'If you have any problems, call this number. She's a psychiatrist and a friend of mine. She knows who you are and she's willing to help you.'

By this point, Svetlana was tearful, but they were tears of gratitude that brought an animation to her eyes that Martin had thought was extinguished for good.

'Why are you doing this, Martin?'

He put a finger to her lips, telling her implicitly that there were some questions that didn't have an answer, and said that it was late and she should get some sleep.

He lay down next to her and held her hand until she drifted off.

*

It was the middle of the night, on a housing estate in Essonne. In the small apartment, all the lights were turned out. There was an eastern European-sounding name on the doorbell.

Inside everything was grey and sad. In the bedroom, on a bookshelf there were a few books that he had recommended to her and a Walkman with a CD of songs he had told her to listen to.

On the wall hung posters of the films that they had seen together that year: *Two Lovers*, *We Own the Night*, *Into the Wild.* A beautiful music box lay on the bed, which when opened played a traditional, nostalgic melody. Inside, there were also a few photos of a Ukrainian childhood. Hundreds of little memories.

In the bottom of the box there was an envelope, which contained some banknotes. It was all the money he had given her after their encounters. She had never touched any of it, even in her most desperate moments. Even when she would have done anything for a hit of heroin.

Hundreds of little memories, proof that something real had happened between them, that year when, for a few months, he had been a part of her life. And she had, in some way, been a part of his.

13

SOMETHING MISSING

Day after day,
The dead affairs
Go on dying.
Serge Gainsbourg

Her, San Francisco
7 a.m.

The first light of day. A salty taste in her mouth. An aching head, weary body and a heavy heart.

Gabrielle got up silently so as not to wake the man asleep at her side, the dickhead, whom she had already completely forgotten, even his first name, and whom she wouldn't be seeing again. The dickhead with his eco-friendly 4 x 4, his hi-tech job and his sea-view apartment.

She gathered her things and dressed hurriedly in the bathroom: pale jeans, black roll-neck, belted leather jacket and high-heel ankle boots.

She grabbed a small bottle of mineral water from the fridge in the kitchen. She yearned to smoke, to pop a Lexomil under her tongue to stifle the emptiness that devoured her insides and the loneliness that had been stalking her since childhood.

Rays of sunlight played on the open picture window that looked over the marina, onto the Pacific and the island of Alcatraz. Guided by the light, she left the house and crossed the long strip of lawn. The wind had picked up and carried with it the sound of foghorns from the ferries.

She headed out across the beach, took off her boots and stepped into the water. The sand was lukewarm. Fiery particles of light glinted in her hair. From a distance, it looked like she was dancing at the ocean's edge and that she was happy.

And yet her torn heart was an icy wasteland.

In two days it would be her thirty-third birthday and, just like every other year on that date, she would be alone confronting her inner self.

So alone.

She closed her eyes, stretched out her arms and lifted her face to the gusts of wind and the sea air. She knew she was barely getting by.

Why did I let go of your hand?

She felt she was being sucked into the abyss and she quivered like a flame.

She fought back. She would not be snuffed out. She would not fall. Because if she did no one would catch her, no one would stop her being crushed.

Him, Paris
1 a.m.
The hotel bedroom was in semi-darkness.

Martin lay on the bed, arms folded, eyes wide open. Beside him, Svetlana had fallen asleep. He knew that he wouldn't sleep a wink. Sleep wasn't really his thing. He got up without a sound, leant over her and pulled the covers up over her delicate shoulder. He slipped on his jacket, turned out the light and left the room.

In the lift, he had a feeling of violent turmoil; a chasm had suddenly gaped open. It was an absence that he struggled to pin down, an unending sadness that formed a knot in his stomach.

He crossed the ornate foyer, greeted the receptionist and went out into the street.

Raining, as always.

He got on his motorbike, fired it up and hurtled off into the night.

As a *flic*, he'd played with fire a fair bit and got his fingers burnt. Tonight, he felt both invincible and yet deeply vulnerable, caught between contrary desires to be embraced, but also to play Russian roulette, like some tightrope walker treading the wire between two rocky peaks.

In his guts, the knot continued to tighten. He thought it was anger boiling inside.

He didn't yet know that it was love.

Her, San Francisco
7.30 a.m.
The sound of barking jolted Gabrielle from her introspection She opened her eyes and pulled herself together. On the

160

beach, a golden Labrador yapped around her, nuzzled at her. She stroked him and played with him for a few minutes.

Then she headed back to the sidewalk around the marina, lined with picturesque houses looking out to sea. Her car stood out a mile: a 1968 Mustang coupé convertible, in red, that had once belonged to her mother. An unenvironmentally friendly car, from way before the oil crisis and global warming. An aberration perhaps in these politically correct times. That didn't put her off. She still loved it and drove it with pleasure.

She turned the ignition and drove down Marina Boulevard and Redwood Highway before crossing the Golden Gate Bridge.

She adored the suspension bridge, which she went over every day. She loved its reddish-orange colour, its two enormous towers, which seemed to shoot up ready to take on the sky, and like all the city's other residents, she was proud of it.

Her spirits somewhat brighter, she selected a CD of Lou Reed and turned up the volume on 'Walk on the Wild Side'.

With the wind in her hair, she felt as if she were hovering over the sea, soaring up into the sky and touching the light. Then, abruptly, the pain returned and the feeling of emptiness overtook her again.

Instead of slowing down, she accelerated.

So what if I have an accident? No one's going to miss me.

Him, Paris
1.30 a.m.

Plugged into his iPod, his face battered by the wind, Martin sped through the curtain of rain bucketing down on the Paris ring road, now as slippery as an ice rink. He flashed past Porte de Vincennes, Porte de Bagnolet and Porte de Pantin.

Hundreds of lights danced before his eyes, whirling about him, blurring his vision. From his headphones, Brel sang of a quest for an unreachable star, the crazy romance of old lovers, the whores of Amsterdam, Hamburg and elsewhere.

He accelerated, weaving through the cars, sensing obstacles rather than actually seeing them. Feverish, drenched in tepid rain, he gave himself up to the road, as if intoxicated.

He accelerated again, putting himself in danger, abandoning himself to fate, almost as if it were no longer him in control, almost as if he were asking for an invisible hand to steer him towards something or someone.

Them

Two fireballs hurtling towards each other despite the ocean that separated them.

Two free-wheeling stars heading for collision.

A reunion postponed for far too long.

A dangerous reunion.

Would love or death triumph?

PART TWO

THE STREETS OF SAN FRANCISCO

14

VALENTINE

If two people love each other, there can be no happy end to it.
Ernest Hemingway

The next day, 22 December, over the Atlantic
'Some champagne, sir?'

Flying at more than 20,000 feet, Flight 714 continued on its course to San Francisco, soaring like a silver bird above a sea of clouds.

Martin politely refused the air hostess's offer. Around him, the first-class passengers savoured their foie gras and figs served on toasted *pain d'épice*. To his left, Mademoiselle Ho, escorted as ever by her sumo wrestler bodyguard, was delicately sipping her Martini Bianco.

'You were right,' she conceded, drawing a cardboard file from her briefcase.

Martin looked at the folder. It was marked with the initials FBI, followed by *Highly Confidential*.

'Have you had the lab results of Archibald's fingerprint?'
She nodded and offered him the file.

'Let me introduce you to Joseph A. Blackwell, inmate of San Quentin prison until 1981, number IB070779.'

As he looked at the sheaf of papers before him, Martin felt a shiver of excitement run down his spine. He reached for the folder and his eyes lit up as he opened it.

*

The photo had been taken at San Francisco police headquarters, at the time of the arrest of a certain Joseph Archibald Blackwell, on the night of 23 to 24 December 1975, on the charge of grievous bodily harm. The mug shot showed a man of about thirty, with dark circles under his eyes, his face ravaged by grief.

A short biography provided brief details of the suspect's background.

He had been born in Fountainbridge, Edinburgh, of a seamstress mother and an artist father, who would never sell a single painting. Gifted in childhood, but undisciplined, he had left school at fourteen to take up various odd jobs: builder, mechanic, coffin varnisher, and general handyman at the Edinburgh School of Art.

At twenty, he had signed up with the Royal Air Force as a low-ranking mechanic, but went on to pass his flying exams. Five years later, he was working as a pilot for an organisation of flying doctors, airlifting multiple-trauma victims in central Australia. Several photos from this time showed him looking tanned beside an old Cessna in the arid Australian bush.

Then another set of prints showed his involvement in various humanitarian missions for another association, Wings of Hope: accompanying children in need of emergency care in Biafra; airlifting refugees; transporting pharmaceutical supplies in Nicaragua; transporting rescue teams after an earthquake in Sicily, and so on. So many airlifts of hope. A few drops of water on an inferno. A few drops of water which changed nothing. A few drops of water which changed everything.

Martin was mesmerised by each of the prints. So, in his youth, the future thief had been a pioneer of humanitarianism, a lone warrior with a hollowed-out face whose steely gaze spoke of melancholy, rebellion and a lack of love.

The final two images stood out from the others. The first showed Archibald embracing a young woman on a sandy beach. Behind them were the deep-blue sea, the snow-capped mountains and the battlements of a fortified town that Martin knew well.

Intrigued, the former *flic* turned the photo over. On the back, written in faded fountain pen, was the inscription *Antibes, January 1974*, then a message in French:

Garde-moi auprès de toi.
Pour toujours.
Je t'aime.
Valentine

(Keep me close to you.
For ever.
I love you.
Valentine)

So, Archibald was holidaying on the Côte d'Azur the very year that he himself was born. This discovery reinforced his feeling that their fates were linked somehow.

Martin generally shied away from delving into someone's private life without being asked. So it was with some unease that he studied Archibald's female companion: he could tell she was beautiful, even though her face was partly hidden by long tresses of chestnut hair, blown across her eyes by the wind. Clearly, the thief's good taste was not just confined to works of art …

The last snap was a close-up of Archibald sitting outside a Provençal restaurant. The sunlight on his face softened his appearance somewhat. He looked completely relaxed. Martin was looking at the face of a man who had happily let his guard down. The face of a man in love who was not looking at the camera but at the attentive smile of a woman.

There was no inscription on the back, but Martin was prepared to bet that it was Valentine who had taken the photo.

Who was she? And what could Archibald have done to wind up in prison?

More and more intrigued, he read on through the file, which included a police cross-examination and an indictment, as well as the official account of a trial.

The case went back to a night in December 1975.

A night which should have been one of untold joy.

And which was instead one of high drama.

23 December 1975, San Francisco
5 a.m.

'Honey, it hurts!'

Archibald opened his eyes at once.

Beside him, Valentine was writhing in pain. She was six months pregnant and for some time had been suffering from terrible heartburn. She had lost her appetite and vomited regularly. The doctor she'd seen had diagnosed gastroenteritis, but her condition seemed to be worsening.

'We're going to the hospital!' he decided, coming over to her side of the bed.

He stroked her forehead then helped her to her feet. He had just come back, in the middle of the night, from an assignment in Africa. His plane had been three days late, because for the last week the US had been experiencing an extreme cold snap: snowstorms, ice and blizzards were sweeping the country from coast to coast, causing major power failures, and disrupting air and road travel, slap bang in the middle of the Christmas holidays. Even in California, the cold had disrupted everything: numerous stretches of highway had been shut and San Francisco had been hit by frost for an unprecedented six days running.

Luckily, their bed was surrounded by three little electric heaters which emitted reassuring warmth and made their houseboat, barely bigger than an igloo, at least habitable.

Supported by Archibald, Valentine stood up with difficulty. Her feet were swollen. A growing sense of fear and a splitting headache were making her nauseous.

They went out, limping along. Outside, the little port of Sausalito was still shrouded in darkness. In front of their houseboat sat the bright-red Mustang coupé which they'd just treated themselves to, its windscreen totally covered in ice.

Archibald helped Valentine in, then began scraping off the ice with his fingernails.

'There's a scraper in the back, honey,' she told him kindly.

No sooner said than done. Key in the ignition, the engine purred and they were off to the hospital.

'This time, we're taking no risks – we're going to Lenox!'

'No, Archie, we're going to Mission; it's where I'm due to give birth.'

Archibald didn't like to contradict her, but he had no confidence in Dr Alister, the gynaecologist looking after her. He was arrogant, too sure of himself, the type you couldn't ever reason with.

He tried to persuade her: 'There's Elliott Cooper at Lenox.'

'Elliott's a cardiac surgeon, baby ...'

He looked at her. Despite her pain, she smiled tenderly at him, almost enjoying their little quarrel.

Then, because she was always right, Archie turned onto Richardson Avenue after exiting the Golden Gate Bridge.

'You don't want to put on any music, honey?'

'But, Valentine, you're—'

'Stop arguing and turn the radio on! It'll take my mind off the pain!'

On the radio that morning, it was the voice of Leonard Cohen that accompanied them as they snaked through the dips of Divisadero Street up to Pacific Heights and Haight Ashbury.

170

Valentine looked beautiful. In spite of the throbbing pain, the migraine and the nausea, she looked beautiful.

She smiled at him.

They didn't yet know it, but that was the last song they would hear together.

*

They arrived in the Castro District – a place that was just becoming known as the 'gay quarter' now that the city had proposed the Gay Rights Bill, outlawing sexual discrimination. They then took a left, passed Dolores Park and arrived at Mission District, the Hispanic neighbourhood. The area, snubbed by tourists and not written up in any guidebook, was nonetheless the oldest part of the city. It was here in 1776 that the Spanish had built their first chapel, the region's centre of Franciscan evangelism.

Archibald hated the area. He found it seedy, violent and dilapidated. Valentine adored it, thinking it colourful, flamboyant and electrifying.

Due to the enormous building site of the BART, the suburban train network, which had been pulling the guts out of the city for months, the entrance to the hospital had been moved to the back, which forced them to go round the building. The neon signs of Mexican tacos bars flashed in the night. Even with the windows shut, they could smell cooking odours: chilli, burritos, corn on the cob with melted butter.

When they finally got to the emergency room, they were struck by the chaos of the place. Judging by the overflowing waiting room, the hospital was understaffed. What's more, the hallway was full of junkies and tramps, waiting for a consultation at the free clinic which shared the same premises.

This was the dark side of the city: the number of homeless people seemed to increase every day amid an almost unanimous indifference, and the boys returning traumatised from Vietnam haunted the corridors of the psychiatric hospitals before bedding down in cardboard boxes or on subway benches. But it was mainly the democratisation of drug use which had caused the most horrifying damage: San Francisco was paying a heavy price for the hippie movement. No, LSD and heroin hadn't raised spirits and freed minds. They'd only transformed those who didn't know how to kick the habit into emaciated zombies dying on the sidewalk, a needle in their arm and vomit around their mouth.

'We're going!' declared Archibald, turning to Valentine.

The young woman opened her mouth to object, but suddenly she was gasping for breath and she crumpled to the floor.

*

'Well?'

In a pretentious-looking office, Archibald sat opposite Dr Alister, who had just got the first of Valentine's test results back.

The two men were about the same age. They could have got on quite well, but, from their very first encounter, they'd felt a blind hostility towards each other.

One was born on the streets, the other in Beacon Hill.

One wore a bomber jacket, the other a tie.

One had a past, the other had qualifications.

One was instinctive, the other rational.

One loved, the other wanted to be loved.

One was not so tall, not so good-looking but he was a real man. The other had the handsome face of a seducer and all the patter to go with it.

To one, life had given nothing, so he had taken it for himself. To the other, life had given a lot, so he hadn't developed the habit of saying thank you.

One had struggled for years before waking up beside the only woman who mattered to him. The other had married his first girlfriend from college but made out with nurse interns beneath the dim light of the radiography room.

One detested everything about the other.

And it was mutual.

'Well?' repeated Archibald, losing patience.

'The blood tests show a drop in platelet levels: 40,000 when the minimum should be 150,000. Liver function is not looking good, but—'

'What are you going to do about it?'

'We've given her something to bring down her blood pressure and we're going to give her a transfusion to increase her platelet count.'

'And after that?'

'We'll wait and see.'

'We'll wait and see what?' retorted Archibald, annoyed. 'High blood pressure, albumen in her urine: this is pre-eclampsia.'

'Not necessarily.'

'You've got to do something about the pregnancy.'

Alister shook his head. 'No, the pregnancy can continue if we manage to stabilise your wife's general condition. For now, there's nothing too much to worry about and no reason to think anything's going to go wrong.'

'Nothing to worry about? Are you joking or what?'

'Look, you're not a doctor.'

'That's true,' Archibald said, 'but I've certainly seen more women dying of pre-eclampsia in Africa than you have.'

'This isn't Africa. And your wife is only in her twenty-fifth week. To do a Caesarean now would put the child's life at risk.'

Archibald's face took on a hard, bitter air.

'I don't give a damn,' he replied. 'It's my wife I want to save.'

'It's not quite as clear-cut as that,' Dr Alister explained. 'We're looking for a delivery time which both ensures the child will survive and safeguards the mother's life.'

'The only thing you'll wind up doing is screwing up her brain, her liver, her kidneys …'

'I've already talked this over with your wife. She is aware of the risks, but she does not want a Caesarean at present.'

'It's not up to her to decide.'

'No, it's up to me. And I can see no valid medical reason why this pregnancy shouldn't go to full term.'

*

174

Archibald went back to Valentine's room. He sat by her side and gently stroked her face. He thought back over the long journey they had both taken in order to live a love which should never have been. He thought of all the obstacles they had overcome, all the fears they had conquered.

'I don't want a Caesarean!' she begged. Her skin was waxy. She had dark circles under her eyes and they were full of tears. 'I'm only twenty-five weeks gone, honey! Let me keep it a little longer!'

She needed him but he was powerless. He had promised her that he would be there, through good and bad, in sickness and in health. He had promised to protect her and watch over her, but we always promise more than we can deliver.

She looked at him, wide-eyed. 'Let me give it a little more strength.'

'But you might die, my darling.'

Hooked up to tubes and drips, she managed to cling on to his arm and, in spite of the pain which took her breath away, she said, 'This child, I want this child for you. I can feel it's so alive inside me! It's a little girl, you know. I'm sure of it! You will love her, Archie, you'll love her!'

He was about to say that it was her he loved. Then he saw her eyes rolling back. Then her facial muscles and her hands tensed violently, and …

*

'You're going to do that goddamn Caesarean!' Archibald yelled at Alister across the corridor.

175

Taken aback, the doctor watched him surge towards him, boiling with anger and ready to do battle.

*

In bed, Valentine bit off the end of her tongue as she clenched her teeth. Her arms and legs stiffened and her breathing tightened and faltered.

*

Without actually seeming to do so, the security guard had already moved over to Archibald and advanced, revolver in hand, just behind him. He was used to overcoming violent junkies who had been refused a dose of Subutex. But Archibald wasn't a drug addict. Sensing the guard's presence, he ducked quickly and, in a move as sudden as it was violent, he kicked back at the guard with his foot. Thrown to the floor, the guard dropped his gun, which Archibald then snatched up.

*

Valentine was shaken by violent spasms. Foamy, bloody saliva spilt from her lips and started to choke her.

*

'She's having convulsions, you bastard!'
    Later, at the trial, Archibald would explain that he had only wanted to threaten the doctor with the gun, just to

intimidate him, that the shot had gone off on its own and that he'd never intended to pull the trigger. The guard would also testify that the revolver was badly maintained and that a similar situation had happened to him twice already. In any case, the accidental nature of the action did not alter the outcome: Dr Alister took a 9mm bullet in his right lung.

Archibald dropped the weapon at the very moment his wife lost consciousness and plunged into a coma. He was surrounded and wrestled to the floor, before being cuffed amid an almighty commotion.

When the police took him away, he turned back towards Valentine's room and it seemed to him that he heard the intern on call shout, 'We're losing her!'

Then the voice of the nurse: 'It's a little girl.'

*

That Thursday, a little girl born three months prematurely was taken to the intensive care unit of the public hospital in Mission District. She weighed one pound two ounces and measured barely twelve inches. Like many premature babies, she was a well-proportioned child, with a delicate face and thin, jelly-like skin through which her veins were visible.

The doctor called in a panic to carry out the delivery had hesitated a moment before attempting to revive her, and, even having done so, he wouldn't have bet a dollar on her surviving.

But she was placed in an incubator, on a ventilator.

The midwife who took care of her was called Rosalita Vigalosa. She'd lived in the neighbourhood for twenty years and everyone called her Mamma. It was she who cleaned the baby's premature little lungs every three hours to help them become fully functioning.

Every day, on her way to work, she had taken to lighting a candle in the chapel of Mission Dolores and saying a prayer for this infant's survival. After a few days, she started calling the baby a 'miracle child'.

When it came to writing a name on the child's wristband, Rosalita said to herself that she would surely need some guardian angels to help her get by in life.

So, by way of a talisman, she decided upon the name of the pre-eminent angel: Gabrielle.

15

ALTER EGO

*There are things in our souls which we know not
how much they mean to us. Or rather, if we live without
them, it is because, either through fear of failing or
suffering, we daily postpone the moment of coming under
their thrall.*
Marcel Proust

'*Ladies and gentlemen, our plane will shortly begin its
descent towards San Francisco. Please fasten your
seatbelts and return your seat to the upright position.*'

Still staggered by what he had just read, Martin didn't
hear the cabin crew's announcement.

That name ... that date of birth ...

Engrossed in the papers, his hands clammy and his
heart beating, he hurried feverishly to finish reading
through the account of the trial. It was a trial in which
Archibald had been sentenced to ten years' imprisonment
for grievous bodily harm against Dr Alister.

The photocopied record of his time in San Quentin
State Prison noted a few fights he'd been involved in,
which meant he had not been eligible for early release,
and also his assiduous attendance at the library and at

history of art classes given on a voluntary basis by a professor from Stanford.

But the most surprising thing was that while in prison Archibald had never had a visitor. No friend to tell him to hang in there, no relative to bring him news of his family, no one to introduce him to his daughter.

Following his escape in November 1981, Joseph A. Blackwell had vanished into thin air, leaving no address, and turned into Archibald McLean, the king of thieves.

Martin studied the last page, a recent photocopy dated the day before. It was most likely some additional, cursory investigation, made in a hurry by the Feds, and livened up with a photo that he had hoped for and yet feared at the same time: that of a young woman, with an elusive face, sunglasses perched on her nose, at the wheel of a bright-red Ford Mustang. It was a young woman with long silky hair, whose green eyes, shining in the rain, he had never forgotten. A young woman who, at the end of one summer, urged him to: 'Stay a bit longer!'

To disguise his emotion, he turned towards the window. Beyond the arid mountains, he could make out the Californian coastline, the rolling waves of the Pacific and San Francisco Bay.

He realised that he and Archibald shared that same heartbreak of a love that had been snatched away.

Above all, he realised that his obsessive hunting of Archibald represented more than just the arrest of a criminal. It was an investigation of himself. A kind of therapy. Not the kind where you sat on your backside on some shrink's couch, but a confrontation with his past, with the fears he'd fled from, and with the least admirable features of his personality.

*

It took barely a second for Archibald to pick the lock of the house on stilts where Gabrielle lived.

He had the impression of entering a sanctuary and the emotion of it gripped him suddenly, as if an animal had leapt at his throat. It was in this houseboat that he had woken up thirty-three years earlier, at Valentine's side, on that fateful morning in December that had catapulted them both into a nightmare.

He carefully made his way inside. The scent of incense hung in the air. The house was empty, but full of memories. He immediately recognised the white wooden furniture that they had repainted together, the little wardrobe bought for a song at the flea market in Carmel, the free-standing mirror found in a second-hand store in Monterey …

A gentle breeze wafted in through the still-open door, rustling the flimsy curtains through which the light filtered. When he went into the kitchen memories of the past rose painfully to the surface: romantic dinners for the two of them, him making his special pasta with pesto, Valentine's favourite dish, wine glasses clinking together, laughter, mouths forever seeking one another.

To blot out the scenes from the past, he turned on the tap and splashed his face with cold water. Two days earlier, the cancer gnawing at his pancreas had left him so weakened that he couldn't make the slightest effort.

Today, he felt surprisingly better. Taken at high dose, the painkillers were having their desired effect, helping him contain his illness and offering him relief, which might allow him to talk to Gabrielle for the last time.

The last time that would also be the first.

*

In prison, sorrow had almost driven him mad and he had always refused to acknowledge his paternity. Gabrielle was left in the care of her somewhat unpredictable French grandmother, who was married to a wine-grower in the Sonoma Valley. Once he had escaped from San Quentin in the early 1980s, he had made discreet enquiries about his daughter, only to learn that she had been told that her father had died while rock climbing well before her birth, that his family lived in Scotland and that Scotland was far away.

Perhaps things were better that way, after all.

Yet he could not stop himself from going to see her coming out of school at least once. He had watched her from afar and what he'd felt had filled him with fear. He was angry with the child! He was really angry with her for having torn him away from the woman he loved. It was unfair and irrational but he could not help his resentment.

So he decided to disappear and he knew just how he was going to do it.

October 1977, San Quentin Prison
'And you managed to get past them?'

'Just like I said, son. But back then I didn't have these screwed-up lungs.'

Sitting on their respective bunks, Archibald and his cellmate, Ewan Campbell, were chewing over their pasts. Or, rather, it was Campbell doing the talking. Archibald was happy to listen most of the time.

The two men had shared the same cell for several months. After a few teething problems, a real bond had developed between them, reinforced by their common Scottish origins.

Campbell was in for several years for stealing paintings. With his cheeky humour, he managed to tease Archibald, who since being put away had sunk into a deep depression.

'With all the security they have now, you wouldn't have made it,' Archibald replied dismissively.

'Don't you believe it. People think that no sooner has a fly landed on a painting than twenty cops will turn up with flashing lights. That's what happens in the movies. It's a bit different in reality. Believe me, every museum in the world can be burgled. You just have to know their weak points.'

'And you know them, these weak points?'

'I know a fair few. Yeah, I'd say I know a fair few ...' the old man said with an air of satisfaction, then added pointedly to Archibald, 'You want to learn a few tricks?'

Archibald shook his head slowly and replied jokingly, 'I don't intend to end up like you.'

Then, as if to show that the conversation was over, he stretched out on his bunk and picked up *The Count of Monte Cristo.*

But his companion refused to give up so easily.

'You haven't heard the last of this, son. We'll talk about it later.'

*

That was how over the course of several months Ewan Campbell had taught him everything he knew about burglary before dying in prison from lung cancer.

At the point of changing his life, Archibald decided to put to good use all he had learnt and to take on, in some way, the personality of his 'teacher'. Exit Joseph Archibald Blackwell, enter Archibald McLean!

Once he had adopted the 'prince of thieves' persona he was forced to be constantly on his guard, to lead the life of a fugitive, to have a number of identities and hideouts, and to perform daring feats. It was both physically and intellectually demanding, and kept him from dwelling too much on his remorse and his regrets.

It worked for a while. Then he began to realise that his obstinacy in denying the existence of his daughter did not correspond with what Valentine would have wanted. In the nights, which grew shorter and shorter, he was increasingly woken by the same nightmare, which ended with the cry: *'It's a little girl, you know. I'm sure of it! You will love her, Archie, you'll love her!'*

It was like an appeal from beyond urging him to a course of action.

So, on Gabrielle's fifteenth birthday, he decided to make contact with her to explain the truth and to explain himself.

But, while he had the will, he lacked the courage.

He was as ashamed of his behaviour – which he did not know how to justify – as he was afraid of his daughter's reaction. If the kid resembled her mother, she would have a pretty strong character and something told him that she would not welcome him with open arms.

In order not to give up without having exchanged a few words with her, he found a way: disguise.

23 December 1990: the taxi driver who took her to the airport. That was him.

23 December 1991: the eccentric old man with whom she was stuck in the shopping mall lift. That was him.

23 December 1992: the cheeky homeless guy who played the saxophone on Market Street and to whom she gave a dollar. Him.

23 December 1993: the florist who delivered one thousand and one roses from a secret admirer. Him again.

Him, him, him … present but incognito at each of her birthdays, which were full of fateful memories for him.

During each encounter, he told himself that this was the right time, that the time for lies and disguises was gone. But each time he changed his mind.

Yet these secret meetings with Gabrielle had stirred paternal feelings in him that he didn't know he possessed. Worried, he made up his mind to hire a private detective so he could keep track of his daughter's daily life. It was a choice that was neither ethical nor entirely fair, but it was the only effective way for him to play the behind-the-scenes role of her guardian angel.

An overdraft at the bank, a boyfriend who was a little violent, a shortfall in her finances, unexpected medical bills: he anticipated and resolved all the problems. It was better than nothing, but still so inadequate.

He knew that his illness didn't leave him any choice now, and in a way that simplified things.

*

Archibald went to the fridge and opened a Corona.

Holding his beer, he strolled around the sitting room, inspecting each trinket, discovering with interest which books she liked reading, which films she liked watching.

She had forgotten her BlackBerry, which was recharging on the fruit dish. He picked up the little machine and shamelessly scrolled through her emails and text messages: some not very subtle messages from guys she'd met at parties, invitations to go out for a drink, one-night stands who didn't give their name. Why did Gabrielle give out her number to all these wasters?

On the bookshelf, there were only two photo frames. The first photo he knew because he'd taken it. It was Valentine smiling, and splashed by the waves, on the rocks above Antibes, during a holiday in France. The second image was that of a young man in his twenties. Martin Beaumont, in the summer of 1995.

Martin Beaumont, who had been hunting him down for years. Martin Beaumont, with whom, to his amusement, he'd played cat and mouse, and whom he'd had followed for months.

Archibald put on his glasses to study the photo more closely. He'd already seen dozens of photos of Martin, but this one was different. The face reminded him of another

186

face. It was the face of a man who had happily let his guard down. The face of a man who was looking at the attentive smile of a woman. The face of a man who was in love for the first time.

Out of instinct, he prised open the frame. Behind the photo, a folded-up slip of paper fell onto the parquet floor. Archibald scooped it up and unfolded it. It was a letter dated 26 August 1995 which began with the words:

Dear Gabrielle,

I just wanted to tell you that I am going back to France tomorrow.

I wanted you to know how much the time we spent together meant to me. Those moments in the campus cafeteria discussing books, movies, music and generally putting the world to rights meant more to me than anything else I experienced in my time in California …

Perplexed, he remained standing for a long time, reading and rereading this declaration.

When he placed the frame back on the shelf, he stared hard at the portrait of Martin and, as if throwing down the gauntlet, said, 'Let's see what you're made of, son.'

16

CALIFORNIA HERE I COME

*The map of our lives is folded in such a way that we do
not see one great road stretching ahead of us, but, as it
unfolds a little more each day, hundreds of smaller ones.*
Jean Cocteau

San Francisco

The light.

The softness.

The soothing breeze, under a perfect spring-like sky.

A Beach Boys song blaring on the car radio.

All the dull greyness of Paris nothing but a bad memory.

In his rented convertible, Martin hurtled over the
undulating streets lined with Victorian town houses. It was
as if he were driving over a mountain range. Although it
was just a few days before Christmas, the city was flooded
with sunlight, and the sea's proximity created an almost
Mediterranean atmosphere.

This unusual city gave the impression of having been
repainted in every pastel tone, and still had the relaxed
atmosphere and magical air that he had discovered in his
youth. It all came rushing back to him: the sounds that

came up from the port, the fresh ocean air, the cable cars that looked straight out of the 1950s, with their wooden panels and brass bells.

He overtook an electric bus flying an Obama flag and saw the turquoise bay surrounded by hills as he descended towards the marina.

For the first time in his life, he drove across the Golden Gate Bridge, admiring the view of the sunny bay in his rear-view mirror. He followed the sharp turns of the winding road that led to Sausalito. The sumptuous houses that stood on the side of the hill had long ago replaced the houses of the first hippies in the city, but even in this opulent setting Martin could think of only one thing: he was going to see Gabrielle again.

Their story had started here, in the summer sun of 1995. It had almost ended one Christmas Eve, in a cold and lonely bar in Manhattan. Thirteen years later, fate had dealt them a card that neither of them had been expecting.

*

'Fuck!' Gabrielle swore as she slammed her toolbox shut. 'The bloody carburettor's still not working!'

She had been crouching on the engine of her seaplane, but now she sprang to the ground with feline agility.

'It's fine, we'll get it fixed somehow,' Sonny tried to console her.

'You always think it's fine. How am I supposed to pay my bills if I can't take people up any more?'

'There's always the Cessna.'

189

'Three seats instead of six? That's half our income gone up in smoke!'

Hands on hips, she stood still for a moment, looking at the cause of her torment: *La Croix du Sud,* a vintage Latécoère 28 – an elegant, glossy cedar-wood seaplane. The deep burgundy of the wood was set off by yellow piping that shone fiery gold in the sun, attracting the attention of passers-by.

At first glance, the plane might have seemed more at home in a museum than on the water, but Gabrielle had managed to restore it to perfect condition. Much of her spare time and savings had gone into it. Along with her houseboat and the Mustang, it was the only thing she had inherited from her mother, and it was her most treasured possession.

The young woman checked the knots that were keeping the plane tied to the pontoon and went back to the log cabin, where Sonny took care of reservations and sold ice creams and drinks to the tourists.

The edge of the golf course resembled a lake surrounded by pine trees. The late-afternoon light was soft, the air was pure and the pale blue of the sky cast a shimmering reflection on the water.

Gabrielle had been working in the nature park for ten years now. After a long struggle, she had finally obtained a licence to use the two seaplanes to take tourists on an unforgettable ride over the bay. Sonny, a former hippie, was her business partner. He had long since passed retirement age, but his tie-dye shirts, his ponytail and his tattoos were straight out of the 1960s and reminded tourists of the Summer of Love, and of San Francisco when it had been at its most exciting and vibrant.

In the summer, the 'lake' was overrun with swimmers, kayaks, windsurfing boards and jet-skis. But on this winter afternoon, a bucolic calm reigned over the man-made stretch of water, where herons, cormorants and pink flamingos came and went as they pleased.

Gabrielle approached the counter looking anxious. Sonny handed her a small bottle of mineral water, which she gulped down gratefully.

'Problem with your ride?'

She turned round to see who was talking to her. A man was standing at the counter, sipping an ice-cold Corona, with a motorcycle helmet at his side. He seemed to be in his sixties, with dishevelled black hair, a hint of stubble and a kind of laid-back elegance. He was wearing jeans and a red polo-neck with a tweed jacket. He wasn't the grandfatherly type, nor was he the handsome older man. Not the sort to have hair implants and probably not even old enough for Viagra.

'Is it the engine that's playing up?'

'Yep.' She sat down on a stool next to him.

He raised his bottle in her direction, as though toasting her health. She decided to play along.

'I'll have a beer, Sonny. This guy's paying.' This was her number one rule. Always move faster than them, catch them on the hop to see how they react. See if they take the bait and lose all credibility, or earn the right to stay in the game.

He gave an almost imperceptible smile.

'I'm Archibald.'

'Gabrielle.'

She too raised her bottle of Corona to him, and before taking a swig, bit into the slice of lime. She felt his gaze on her and looked up.

His eyes were not fixed on her breasts, or her behind, or her mouth. They were looking into hers. He was looking at her with real affection. Not a grandfather's affection, nor that of a husband who still loved his wife but didn't touch her any more. This was different. This was genuine warmth. Something she had not felt in a long time.

She was sometimes reminded of the courses she had taken in linguistics. 'We think in words,' Hegel had said, 'the spoken word gives thought its most pure form of existence.' However, the words of the men who approached her sounded increasingly hollow. Most of them came out with the same spiel, the same chat-up lines, the same half-hearted dates, the same unimaginative texts that said nothing in particular. So she tended to rely on the essentials, things that couldn't lie, like gestures, looks, facial expressions and body language. And Archibald had a confidence that could not be faked. Something she had rarely seen before, distant, yet strangely comforting.

*

The GPS instructions led Martin to the nature park where Gabrielle worked. He parked by the pine trees and lingered in his car for a moment, unsure what to do next. He had scoured the FBI report, which had not mentioned any contact between Archibald and his daughter, but how much could he rely on the report? He himself had asked her and she had said that she had never known either of her parents. Why should he doubt that now? Because Gabrielle had always been slightly secretive. Because she was living in San Francisco, and because he knew Archibald would waste no time in getting there and trying to seize the diamond for himself. Assuming he wasn't in the city already ...

Martin pressed a button and in a few seconds the two sections of the aluminium roof slid over the top of the car, turning the convertible into a coupé. When he got out to lock the doors, he almost didn't recognise his reflection in the car window. Boid's Brothers certainly didn't do things by halves; when he had arrived at his hotel, he had found three Smalto suits, made to measure and beautifully cut. The next surprise was a hairdresser waiting for him in his room who had transformed him from a scruffy *flic* into someone who could have been mistaken for the hero in a Jerry Bruckheimer movie. This new look made him feel as though he were walking in someone else's shoes. Someone slicker and more presentable but who was no more him than the depressive *flic* dragging his Converse trainers through the streets of Paris. Since when had he felt so uncomfortable with himself anyway?

Since *her.*

He sighed with dissatisfaction and walked towards the water. The surrounding area was peaceful and filled with light. It reminded him of Provence when he was a child. All that was missing was a few cicadas to complete the picture. He headed for the little log cabin by the water's edge that served as a café. It was then that he saw them.

*

'I could have a look at the engine if you like?' Archibald asked invitingly.

'Are you a mechanic?'

'Not really. I'm in the art business.'

'Well, I don't think that's going to help much here.' Gabrielle couldn't help smiling a little. 'It's a very delicate engine, and a very old plane.'

'Yes, I know. It's a Laté 28.3.'

Gabrielle raised an eyebrow, at once impressed and suspicious.

Archibald decided to get technical. 'That's not the original Hispano engine though, is it? What did you replace it with?'

'A Chevrolet.'

'Six hundred and forty horsepower?'

'Yes ... yes, that's right.' There was no doubt about it; the guy clearly knew his stuff. In a last attempt, she held up her hands, which were smeared with grease and oil. 'You'll be covered in it!'

But Archibald had already taken off his jacket and started rolling up his sleeves.

'Well, you asked for it then,' she said with a smile, handing him her toolbox.

Amused and curious, she followed him onto the pontoon where he hauled himself up onto the fuselage as if he'd been doing it all his life.

'So what do I get if I manage to fix it?' he asked, opening the cover of the engine. 'Dinner?'

She blinked, heart racing.

Calm down!

She knew that there was something about her that men liked, that made them believe they could get her, and that encouraged them to try their luck with her. They all did, some with more subtlety than others. This guy was no different from all the rest. She didn't let her disappointment show. She only pretended to enjoy the attention.

'Here we go again. You act like the perfect gentleman at the beginning. But it all comes to the same thing in the end. A little dinner, a little glass of wine, a little screwing.'

Archibald carried on as though he hadn't heard anything. She persisted.

'You're just like all the others.'

'Maybe,' he said, looking up from the engine. 'But maybe not.'

'OK then,' she said defiantly. 'Dinner, if you can fix the engine.'

*

His heart beating fast, Martin retreated to his car. Feverishly, he opened the glove compartment and took out the Glock 19 Parabellum that Mademoiselle Ho had provided him with. She had kept her word; he now had a weapon and authorisation from the Feds to use it. In another compartment he found a torch, a flare gun, a hunting knife and a pair of binoculars. He picked up the binoculars and pointed them towards the water.

195

Gabrielle was talking to her father!

She was wearing a long cable-knit sweater over a pair of worn-out jeans. Martin noticed that his hands were shaking slightly. He had not seen Gabrielle for thirteen years, but it felt like yesterday. Just as in the past, her light-brown, almost blond hair hung over her face, often covering her eyes, without her bothering to brush it away. The fading light accentuated the harmonious lines of her face and animated it briefly with something that was quickly dispelled.

Martin understood then that neither time nor distance had lessened his love for her.

But was a love that made him ache with suffering truly worth fighting for?

*

The plane's engine spluttered as though something were caught in its throat, backfired loudly, then started to purr again. Without a word, Archibald jumped modestly down onto the pontoon and wiped his hands on a cloth.

'The problem wasn't with the carburettor, but with one of the cylinder heads. Even if it holds for a while, you'll have to think about buying a new part.'

He put his jacket back on and smiled at Gabrielle. 'Obviously I was joking about dinner. Unless, that is, you really want to have dinner with me?'

Momentarily caught off guard, she hesitated. She wanted to prolong the moment, she wanted to get to know this man better, but she didn't want to look too interested.

196

'No, I don't really want to.'

Archibald accepted the verdict, picking up his helmet.

'Goodbye, Gabrielle.'

'Goodbye.'

He started walking away from the log cabin towards where he had parked his motorbike.

She didn't want him to leave. Something about him made her feel happy. She wanted to find out what it was about him that made him different from all the rest. She wanted to, but she didn't dare.

He had already got on the bike when he called back to her: 'So it's just the ones you don't like that you have dinner with then?'

'Yes,' she answered breathlessly.

'Why?'

'Because I'm afraid of losing the others,' she admitted.

She had given up struggling. She saw that he could read her like a book, and that he had discovered her flaw, her shame, her hidden wound that still bled, that ate away at her.

He put on his helmet, raised the visor and looked back at her one last time.

Her eyes were glistening as though she had been crying.

Standing in the middle of the pontoon, she felt vulnerable and gave the impression that the wind could have carried her off like a feather.

Something was happening between them. It wasn't seduction, it wasn't desire but it felt like it.

Archibald switched on the ignition and the four cylinders kicked into life. He was just putting it into first gear when

Gabrielle ran to catch up with him and jumped onto the seat behind him. He felt her hold on to him and rest her head against his shoulder.

Archibald accelerated and the motorbike sped away under the setting sun.

17

THIRST FOR THE OTHER

Each one of us has in our heart a royal chamber;
I've bricked it up, but it is not destroyed.
Gustave Flaubert

'The bastard!'

Boiling with anger, Martin struggled to follow Archibald's motorbike. Back in Paris, he would have had his flashing light and radio to call for back-up, but here he felt alone and powerless.

The dragster – a riot of aluminium, chrome and steel – wove between the cars. On the other side of the highway the traffic was bumper to bumper but the road back into the city was clear, with cars still moving and Archibald obeying the speed limit. He was anxious not to attract the attention of the California Highway Patrol officers and police motorcyclists, nor to risk the life of his daughter, who was riding without a helmet.

Martin didn't know how to interpret the scene he'd just witnessed. Was this the first time Gabrielle and Archibald had seen each other? Did the young woman know the truth about her father?

When it came off the bridge, the motorbike cut across the wooded zones of the Presidio before skirting along the marina. The setting sun turned the sky aglow, thrilling tourists with the perfect picture-postcard image for their photos. But for Martin, the advancing twilight made tracking the bike more difficult.

In Russian Hill, he lost sight of the bulky, muscular form of the Yamaha, only to spot it again more clearly a few moments later, heading into the Italian district.

Right now, the four-cylinder machine was back on the Embarcadero, the main arterial route running parallel to the seafront. This one-time industrial zone had been spectacularly transformed after the 1989 earthquake. The docks had made way for a wide six-mile-long palm-lined boulevard, which snaked along the coast to the delight of cyclists and rollerbladers.

Archibald sped past the ferry terminal, whose 230-foot tower, boxed in by four clocks, had survived all the earthquakes. Its brick arches and marble floor gave the building an Iberian air, transporting the visitor to Miami, Lisbon, or Seville.

Then the bike turned onto an elegant-looking pier that jutted out to the very edge of the Pacific, offering a privileged few access to a luxury restaurant right on the seafront.

Caught unawares, Martin slammed on the brakes and parked up suddenly in a space reserved for buses, while a valet took care of Archibald's mount and the maitre d' found him a table outside.

200

It was nightfall.

The skyscrapers of the business district glinted in the dusk. In the distance, on the slopes of Telegraph Hill, the Coit Tower blazed in the darkness like some kind of protective sword.

The flame of a Zippo lighter fleetingly lit up the interior of the car and Martin took a long drag on his cigarette.

Waiting again.

Wondering again, with binoculars trained on Archibald, whether it was the right time to step in.

But things were different now. This man was no longer the jaunty thief who intrigued him; he was now Gabrielle's father and Valentine's lover.

He was a man in love, and one who resembled him so much.

*

What the hell am I doing here?

Gabrielle looked at herself in the mirror. Upon arriving at the restaurant, she'd headed for the ladies' room. She needed a few moments to gather her composure and take stock. What strange force had driven her to follow this man? Why this sudden impulse?

Distractedly, she washed her hands and hurriedly tidied her hair, somewhat annoyed at finding herself so badly dressed in such a high-class establishment.

She wasn't doing too well at the moment and she didn't try to persuade herself otherwise. She was working hard,

201

partying hard and getting little sleep. She'd also kept up her voluntary work for the humanitarian organisation founded by her mother, Wings of Hope. And she was still involved with the firefighters: each time a fire broke out in the bay, she would fly a Canadair water bomber, scooping up water from the nearby lakes and ponds.

It was a very full life, geared towards helping others; a life with which she tried to do something positive; a life she wanted to be proud of. And yet this hyperactivity was not much more than a kind of headlong rush, a desire to lose herself in action, like a moth battering itself obstinately against a light bulb. Never settling, never stilling its beating wings, even to the point of exhaustion, to the point of getting burnt. Never stopping to admit to herself what she knew really: that she needed a compass to guide her, arms to embrace her and fists to protect her.

She took out the mascara that she always carried with her. With the brush fully coated, she delicately combed her eyelashes, lengthening them and accentuating their curl.

Always properly made up. Not for the sake of looking beautiful, but for hiding behind.

A tear trickled down her cheek. She brushed it away mechanically, before going out to join Archibald at the table.

*

Martin adjusted his binoculars to get a better view.

Positioned between the sea and the sky, the restaurant's covered terrace offered its clientele a panoramic view and gave the impression that they were dining on the water.

Chic and low-key, the interior design of the place spoke of refinement. Elegant arrangements of orchids harmonised with the white and beige tones of the decor, while subdued lighting and armchairs draped with throws created an intimate ambiance.

Martin was stubbing out his cigarette just as Gabrielle came back and sat down beside Archibald.

Martin's heart suddenly lurched and his mind grew confused, torn between competing desires.

The desire to prove that he could actually arrest Archibald wrestled with the desire to learn yet more about him; the desire to love Gabrielle because she was destined for him, but also the desire to pay her back for the hurt she'd caused him.

Because your soulmate can also be your downfall.

*

Noticing that Gabrielle was shivering, Archibald signalled to the waiter to bring the patio heater a little closer.

She thanked him with a forced smile. Despite the convivial atmosphere of the place, she felt so disconcerted that she couldn't relax. To dispel her awkwardness, it was she who started the conversation.

'You seem to know quite a bit about planes.'

'I've flown a few,' Archibald agreed.

'Even seaplanes?'

He acquiesced with a nod of the head while at the same time pouring her a glass of the white wine he had ordered.

'I didn't really understand what it was that you did,' she continued. 'You said that you worked ... in the art world, is that right?'

203

'Actually, I steal paintings.'

She smiled uncertainly, thinking he was teasing her, but he remained deadpan.

'What, that was your real job? Stealing paintings?'

'Yes,' he confessed without a hint of mischief.

'But where did you steal them from?'

'Oh, all over. From museums, billionaires, kings, queens ...'

On the sideboard next to their table, a waiter had left a silver platter laden with an assortment of appetisers presented in small glasses: oysters on a bed of caviar, a salad of snails and cherries, shrimps grilled in peanut butter, a fusion of lobster and frogs' legs with pistachios ...

With a mixture of curiosity and apprehension, they set about exploring the distinct flavours of the dishes in front of them. Gradually, the atmosphere began to lighten. Archibald made a joke or two, Gabrielle relaxed, he poured some more wine. She even laughed a little. While she let herself be lulled by his enveloping voice, he did not take his eyes from her face. In the candlelight, he'd noticed tiny lines of tiredness round her eyes, but, as if by magic, these softened and her gaze regained its sparkle. She looked so much like Valentine. She had the same way of tilting her head to one side when she smiled, the same habit of rolling a lock of hair around her finger, the same gentle expression when her face relaxed. The same light in her eyes – eyes which could make 'the sky jealous after the rain', as the poem went.

Tell her! Tell her now that you're her father! For once in your life, be brave with her. If you shrink from this tonight, you'll shrink from it for ever ...

'And apart from paintings, do you steal anything else?' she laughed.

'Yep,' he said. 'Jewels.'

'Jewels?'

'Diamonds … and phones as well.'

'Phones?'

'Like this one,' he said, sliding across the tablecloth the BlackBerry that he'd stolen from her place hours earlier.

Once she recognised it as hers, she placed her glass back on the table and immediately stopped laughing.

What on earth …?

She knew that she'd left it at home that morning. This guy, whom she hardly knew, had gone through her apartment and violated her privacy. What kind of weirdo had she ended up with now?

Archibald put his hand on his daughter's forearm, but she was not reassured and brusquely pushed back her chair before getting up from the table.

'*Attends, Gabrielle, laisse-moi t'expliquer!*' he shouted, urging her to stay and listen.

For a second, she was thrown by the man's sudden desperation. Why was he speaking to her in French?

But, furious at having been deceived, she fled, not wanting to hear any more, and began running along the pier as if someone were hot on her heels.

*

Martin dropped his binoculars when he saw Gabrielle pacing up and down the Embarcadero, on the lookout

205

for a taxi. He got out of his convertible without being seen and stayed crouched down behind it, his eyes fixed on Archibald, who, on the other side of the street, was apparently resigned to letting his daughter go.

For the moment, Martin decided against crossing the highway. At this time of day, the traffic was always heavy and he wasn't keen on finding himself face to face with Gabrielle.

A car finally drew up alongside the young woman. She was about to dive into the taxi when her mobile vibrated in her hand. She hesitated a few seconds, then …

*

'Don't hang up, Gabrielle, please. Let me speak. I've been trying to do this for eighteen years.'

Gabrielle turned round. The jetty was still heaving with people. A motley crowd were flocking to catch the last ferries, or grab a drink in the bars and clubs lining the avenue.

At the other end of the line, Archibald went on speaking hoarsely.

'I need to explain something to you.'

She tried to search him out. She didn't understand. She didn't want to understand.

'I'm not dead, Gabrielle.'

Finally, she could see him, 150 feet below, where the sea wall met the pier.

He made some conciliatory gesture with his hand and carried on with his confession.

'It's true that I abandoned you …'

206

She gave up on the taxi and stayed stock still for an instant, frozen in the middle of the sidewalk.

'... but I've got the right to tell you why.'

Archibald could hear his heart beating too hard and too fast within his clapped-out old body. The words, stuck in his throat for years, now poured from him and flowed like lava down the sides of a volcano.

My father ...

After a moment's hesitation, Gabrielle decided to go and meet him. She signalled to him with her hand and ...

'Watch out!'

*

It was she who had called out to her father. On the other side of the sidewalk, a man was walking towards him, holding a gun. And that man was ...

*

'Freeze! Put your hands above your head!' Martin yelled out to the thief.

Taken by surprise, Archibald slowly raised his arms. In his right hand, above his head, a worried voice came from his mobile: 'Dad? Dad?'

Arms outstretched, both hands clasped over the butt of the semi-automatic pistol, Martin had Archibald in his sights. They were only separated by the flow of cars heading from west to east.

This time, he'd decided to be done with it all: the past, the fascination he'd developed for this criminal in spite of himself, the absurd and insane love he'd felt for Gabrielle. He would get Archibald banged up, go back to France and grow up. Become a man at last.

'Hands up!!' he bellowed over the din of the traffic.

He pulled out the plastic badge emblazoned with those three magic letters – FBI – as much to do things by the book as to reassure suspicious and alarmed passers-by. Above all, he had to take him in according to the rules. Above all, he mustn't make a blunder or a procedural error.

As he tried to cross the two lanes, a blaring horn rooted him to the spot and a long bendy bus travelling at full speed narrowly missed him. Archibald took advantage of this diversion to flee towards the pier.

By the time the ex-policeman had managed to reach the other side, the thief had stolen a march on him. Martin called out his command again, then fired a shot into the air. He'd have to do more than that to scare Archibald …

Martin changed tack and darted back to the car in order to block his enemy's escape.

Breaking all the rules, the convertible drove through the open-work fencing which led to the back of the small parking lot, next to the restaurant. But Archibald had already got on his motorbike and donned his helmet. Martin chased him all along the pier, and this time he didn't fire into the air but took aim at the bike. Two shots cracked in the night. The first bullet put a hole in one of the aluminium stanchions of the fork and the second ricocheted off the exhaust pipe. Despite the bullets, Archibald managed to avoid being trapped at the water's edge and instead found his way back to the road. They lurched onto the avenue almost simultaneously, but while Martin was expecting the bike to slip into the traffic, Archibald seemed to want to go back up the Embarcadero against the flow.

He wouldn't dare.

It was a mad gamble, suicidal almost, and yet …

… yet Archibald clung on to his handlebars and let rip the enormous machine's two hundred horsepower, producing a blistering acceleration. In the wake of such power, the tyre left a long skidmark on the tarmac and, like a rocket, the bike was propelled into the thick of the traffic.

Martin hesitated, then he, too, took the plunge. Amid a cacophony of blaring horns and flashing headlights, the vehicles rained down on him like a shower of asteroids. He only managed to stay the course for a hundred yards or so before being forced off at Fountain Plaza to avoid an accident. Aware of having flirted with disaster, he could feel his heart beating fit to burst and his hands shaking on the wheel.

He did a quick U-turn.

Yet again, he had played the game and lost.

*

He looked for her everywhere: at the restaurant, on the sidewalk, on the pier …

He looked for her for ages.

But Gabrielle hadn't waited for him.

18

MEMORIES AND REGRETS TOO ...

If you ever want something badly, let it go.
If it comes back to you, then it's yours for ever.
If it doesn't, then it was never yours to begin with.
Extract from the film *Indecent Proposal*

1 a.m.
Martin was stretched out on the beach, his hair in the sand, his face to the wind, his eyes raised to the stars.

He'd called Gabrielle on her mobile, but she hadn't picked up. He'd looked all over for her – at the log cabin near the seaplanes and in all the places they used to go to in the past. But he hadn't found her anywhere.

The story of his life.

Just like when he was twenty-one and had a touch of the blues, he'd washed up on this small beach behind Marine Drive, between the marina and the Golden Gate Bridge.

Tonight, it was almost a full moon and the ocean sang an enigmatic song. Despite the lateness of the hour, the shore was far from deserted. Ignoring the warning notices, a group of young girls had lit a bonfire and were poking fun at an old fellow dressed like a spaceman as he tried out his sand yacht. Paddling in the water, an androgynous-looking Asian – with wraparound shades, a revealing purple kimono, but a body-builder's torso – was handling a huge dragon-shaped kite. With his headphones on, he was in his own world. Each to his own: that was the philosophy of this city, and what gave it its charm, its euphoria and its vileness.

Far from the shore, hidden by the rocks, a young couple were kissing each other timidly, apparently just discovering the delights that love can bring.

'Don't you think they're a little like us?' a voice behind him asked.

Martin shivered as he recognised it. Gabrielle came and sat down a few feet away from him and drew her knees up under her chin.

He tried to remain impassive. He forced himself to turn his head to glance at the young couple, before conceding: 'Sure, that was us, back then.'

'A better-behaved version perhaps. I don't know if you remember all that we got up to on this beach?'

'That was a long time ago.'

'Not so long,' she suggested. 'Do you remember that line from Faulkner that you wrote in one of the letters you sent me: "The past is never dead. It's not even past"?'

He didn't try to hide his bitterness. 'I'm pleased to see that, having failed to reply to my letters, you did at least read them.'

'And I remember them, even thirteen years later.'

For the first time, he turned to look at her properly. In spite of himself, he felt himself blinking more rapidly almost as if it were written somewhere that every moment with Gabrielle could only be fleeting, and that he should hurry to etch this image in his mind.

When he had left her, she had been more of an adolescent than a woman. It was the opposite today, but she had retained that tomboyish air which made her so different.

'Did you come to San Francisco to see me?'

'No, I came to arrest your father.'

'So, this Archibald, he really is …'

'Yes, he's your father, Gabrielle.'

'How long have you known that?'

'Since this morning.'

'He's my father and you tried to kill him.'

'That's my job!'

'It's your job to go around killing people?'

'I'm a *flic*, Gabrielle. That is, I was a *flic* …'

'I know what you do.'

'How?'

'Have you ever heard of Google?'

He shrugged his shoulders and then attempted to explain. 'I wasn't trying to kill him. I just aimed at his bike; it's different.'

'Oh yeah, sure! You "just" aimed at his bike! What kind of a man have you become, Martin Beaumont?'

That riled him.

'Your father is a criminal and he has to pay for what he's done.'

'He only steals paintings.'

'Only! Every police force in the world has been tracking him for years.'

212

The wind whipped up and the surf became rougher. There was a long pause and each withdrew a little, gazing out over the horizon, their minds tormented by memories which were reopening old wounds.

'Is this the first time you've seen your father?'

'Yes!' she insisted.

'What did he tell you?'

'He wanted to explain why he'd abandoned me.'

Gabrielle's face was bathed in moonlight. Her shining eyes betrayed the pain and emotion she was feeling.

'You've denied me that explanation,' she said in rebuke.

'No, it's all here,' he said, opening the rucksack lying next to him on the sand.

He handed her the FBI file.

'That's also why I wanted to see you, so you could know the truth.'

'I'm not sure I want to know the truth, Martin.'

'You don't have a choice. And you need to know as well that, whatever his crimes, your father is a good man.'

'A good man?'

'Yeah, well, it's kind of complicated. But, anyway, he did really love your mother, with a rare, deep and passionate love.'

'If he's such a good man as all that, why are you so determined to arrest him?'

'To hurt you maybe.'

She shook her head, dumbfounded and saddened by what Martin had just said. She could feel the rawness of those wounds still, the pain that still raged.

'No! The Martin I know is incapable of hurting me. That's why I loved him: for his kindness, his—'

'Oh please, give me a break from the phoney affection and back-handed compliments! In any case, the Martin you knew doesn't exist any more. And that's thanks to you!'

'Because I didn't turn up to meet you in New York? Isn't that a bit of a cop-out?'

'I'd worked for months in order to arrange it! I waited for you all day and all night at the Café DeLalo. Not only did you not turn up, but you never even gave me the slightest explanation. You knew my number, my address, you had—'

'And what about you? You never bothered to look me up again after that. You dropped me pretty quickly for someone who said I was the love of his life! And you never even tried to find out why I didn't come.'

'Because you were with someone else, isn't that it?'

'What does it matter? The slightest hurdle and you—'

Staggered by such hypocrisy, he didn't let her finish her sentence.

'I hate you for even daring to say that!'

'And yet it's the truth!' she said, rapping out the words. 'You were annoyed. Your masculine pride was hurt and you couldn't stand that. So you shut yourself and your anger away and decided to sulk for thirteen years! And I thought that you were different from the rest, that you were above all that!'

'Above what? You broke my heart, Gabrielle!'

'No, Martin, it was you and you alone who did that. And in the process you broke my heart too.'

'Spare me the role reversal and the melodramatic tirades!'

214

A gust of wind took them by surprise, forcing them to shield their eyes from the clouds of sand. She huddled in her coat and, as she did, he recognised it as the three-quarter-length moleskin coat he'd given her thirteen years ago. He pushed up the sleeves of his shirt, got out his lighter and lit a cigarette. The sound of ambulance sirens and police cars could be heard intermittently, then the beach resumed its usual noises: the rolling of the waves, the shrieking of the gulls, the howling of the wind.

'Why didn't you come that day?' he asked, less angrily.

'We were only twenty, Martin, only twenty! We knew nothing about life or love. You wanted certainty, some kind of vow.'

'No, all I wanted was a sign.'

She tried to smile at him and, her voice full of hope, said, 'Come on, Martin, let's bury the past. Here we are, in the same place, together, thirteen years on – it's like magic, don't you think?'

In a flash of tenderness, she stretched out her hand to stroke his cheek, but coldly he pushed her away. She had tears in her eyes. There was hardly a twinkle in those eyes now, he noted. There was nothing that he wanted to see in those eyes any more. Maybe he had no more feelings for her after all. And maybe this was the best thing that could have happened to him.

He got up, buttoned his jacket and went back to his car without turning round.

*

Gabrielle did not sleep that night.

It was 2 a.m. by the time she got home. She made herself a flask of tea and went online to learn more about this Archibald McLean, whose 'exploits' she'd only vaguely heard about through the media.

Then she plunged into the thick file Martin had given her. Over the course of her reading not only did she discover a father whom no one had ever mentioned, but she also saw her mother in a new light: as a woman very much in love and determined, at all costs, to bring her child into the world, even at the risk of her own life.

And then she wept until she was empty of tears, convinced that her birth had wrecked four lives. Her mother's to start with, then Archibald's, as he had been sent to prison unfairly. Then her own – she had always been a lonely, sullen orphan who had never found her place in the world. And finally Martin's. She had made him suffer in spite of herself.

At 4 a.m. she swapped the tea for raspberry vodka and went rummaging through the cupboard in the cellar, on the hunt for old photo albums. She looked at the photos of her mother with fresh eyes, discovering that some of them – those in which Valentine looked at her happiest – had been cut up with scissors. Methodical censoring by her grandmother had eliminated the presence of someone she guessed to be Archibald. She knew these photos by heart – she didn't have many of her mother – so how come she'd never asked herself why there'd been such graphic, almost Stalinist censorship?

But maybe she had subconsciously asked the question. Already, her mind was buzzing with memories of her grandparents – the ambiguous words and knowing looks – which had intrigued her at the time, but which she understood better now. Like all family secrets, the drama surrounding her birth had probably hung like an invisible lead cloak, stifling her childhood and adolescence, and causing damage that she was still struggling to deal with.

By 5 a.m. she'd swapped the vodka for coffee, while rereading Martin's old, impassioned love letters. The image of the young man in love merged with that of the hardened man she'd encountered that night. From one line to another, from one second to another, she went from joy to sadness. One moment a smile played on her lips, the next she had crumpled, her head in her hands, giving full vent to her misery.

She had loved him so, she had loved him so much. She had never stopped loving him. Ever since the first kiss, no, since the first letter. The one that began *I just wanted to tell you …*

At 6 a.m. she had a long shower. She felt lighter, as if freed from some burden.

Contrary to her feelings of a few hours earlier, the tragic circumstances surrounding her birth now seemed to endow her existence with more value. Should she not show herself to be worthy of it?

Having spent much of her life thinking that she was one of those people destined for unhappiness, she now

217

sensed a new determination stirring within her. For the first time in her life, she was resolved to take the risk of being happy.

At 7 a.m. Gabrielle opened the blinds and saw the rosy-pink rays of early dawn bathing the bay in glory. A new day, full of promise, was breaking over San Francisco.

The night before, by some curious combination of circumstances, the two most important men in her life had reappeared, both at the same time.

Now she was determined not to let them go.

She only hoped that she'd never be forced to choose between them.

19

YOU SEE, I HAVEN'T FORGOTTEN A THING ...

Love is the right we give to another to persecute us.
Fyodor Dostoevsky

23 December
8 a.m.
The gold and silver needles glinted in the light.

As fine as a strand of hair, four inches in length, they twirled in the air, guided by the brisk, precise movements of Miss Euphenia Wallace.

Effie had joined Archibald in this beautiful rented house, perched on the hillside. Part bodyguard, part governess, this Englishwoman, a medical graduate from Manchester University, was giving her boss a session of acupuncture to ease his pain.

Working swiftly, she inserted thirty-odd needles along the length of Archibald's entire body, altering the angle and depth of each one to maximise the flows of energy.

Lying flat on his stomach, the thief had closed his eyes.

He was in pain.

The night before, he'd managed to contain it, but this morning it had come back with a vengeance.

Her blond hair neatly swept back in a chignon, her toned, long-limbed body clad in a red tracksuit, Effie went on with her work. Once the needles had been inserted, she would adjust them to reinforce their therapeutic effect, pulling on some, twisting others by rolling them between her thumb and index finger. It was a subtle, complex art, and, just like love, it demanded gentleness and skill.

Archibald let the different sensations wash over him: numbness, shivers, heat, muscle twinges, tiny electric shocks …

Was this type of treatment any good? He had absolutely no idea. For weeks, he'd been swallowing painkillers all day long. Yesterday, they'd worked, but today something else was needed. And Effie had a gift for combining modern Western medicine with ancient Chinese medicine, practised since the dawn of time.

Once the needles had been positioned, she left the room to allow her patient to relax entirely. Archibald tried to breathe deeply. He became intoxicated with the scent from the sticks of incense burning in the four corners of the room, their fragrance blending with the headier odour of mugwort. The softly playing piano music of Erik Satie calmed him somewhat, taking him back to the images and emotions of the night before: his confession to Gabrielle and his duel with Martin.

He forced himself to smile. The lad had not lost his cool: he had followed him right to California and, last night, he'd come really close to arresting him. But coming close was not the same as actually doing it. Coming close was not enough. At the last minute, Martin had chickened out again, and had lost his nerve when it came to driving against the traffic in pursuit.

His feelings towards the young Frenchman were becoming more and more ambivalent. Goodwill fought with jealousy, as he had an urge both to provoke him and to protect him, to help him and to flee from him.

He grimaced with pain. He had little time left to find out what Martin Beaumont was made of. He had no intention of playing for extra time: he wanted to go out with a bang, not as an invalid stuck in some hospital bed.

Up until now, the kid had risen to the challenge, but the test was not over yet.

*

Perched on a stool upstairs at Lori's Diner, Martin nibbled his way through an organic breakfast: wholemeal bread, muesli, a shrivelled-up apple and yellowish coffee. Yawning, he gazed through the diner's picture window at the crowds filling Powell Street.

'Hey, what's this then? You're not usually that abstemious!'

The voice shook him as if waking him from a sleep.

Fresh and spruce, Gabrielle smiled as she looked at him. She'd changed into a pair of pale jeans, a white shirt and the belted brown leather jacket that he thought he recognised from thirteen years ago.

'So,' she said, sitting down in front of him. 'Pass me the menu, and we'll order something a bit more substantial.'

'Did you follow me?'

'You're not very difficult to find. You seem to be on some kind of pilgrimage to all the landmarks of our youth! Do you remember how many banana splits we shared here? I'd always let you have the cherry on the whipped cream, because I knew you liked it. Do you remember how adorable you thought I was?'

He shook his head, sighing. 'What are you doing here?'

She became serious again. 'First of all, I wanted to thank you for this,' she said, handing him back the file he'd given her the night before.

'Fine, and then what?'

'Then I wanted to have breakfast with you!'

She beckoned the waitress and ordered an espresso, some vanilla French toast with red berries, and eggs Benedict with salmon.

Martin turned his head and pretended to study the decor. The place was trying to recreate a 1960s vibe: jukebox, pinball machines, a Harley Davidson display, film posters with James Dean and Marilyn Monroe.

'I read a lot of stuff about my father last night,' Gabrielle confided. 'Have you been trying to catch him for a long time?'

'Several years.'

'And it didn't seem a bit strange to you?'

'What?'

'That the man you've been tracking for all these years just happens to be my father.'

Martin frowned. That question had kept him awake all night. It was true that it was hard to put it down to chance, but could there be another explanation?

Gabrielle's order arrived. Just as in the good old days, she cut her French toast into two equal portions. Even

222

though Martin spurned her offer, she feigned indifference and continued the conversation.

'What was it that interested you about Archibald?'

He shrugged his shoulders.

'I'm a *flic* specialising in art and he's stolen more paintings than anyone else in the world. That should be motivation enough, don't you think?'

He took a sip of his watery coffee, grimacing as he did so.

'But, to begin with, what was it that fascinated you about him?' she carried on, holding out her espresso for him.

'Nothing! I was angry, that's all.'

'What, about something specific?'

He pondered for a few seconds.

'In February 2005, he stole *The Kiss* by Gustav Klimt from a museum in Vienna. It was my favourite painting and—'

'Our favourite painting,' she cut in.

'Yeah, well, where are you going with this?'

'Well, doesn't it seem bizarre to you that he happened to steal that very painting just after you joined the OCBC?'

He dodged the question. 'I see you've been researching my career.'

'Archibald did everything to spark your interest in him,' Gabrielle said softly. 'He's been the one pulling the strings for years. I think it's time you realised that.'

Annoyed, Martin got up to leave. Perhaps Gabrielle was right, but in order to be certain he had to arrest Archibald – whatever the cost.

He left three 10-dollar bills on the table and crossed the diner without a backward glance at the daughter of his enemy.

'Shall we have lunch later?' she called out.

He didn't look back.

One hour later

The Palace Hotel was located on Montgomery Street, between the business district and Union Square.

Martin and Mademoiselle Ho scanned the room on the ground floor – the prestigious Garden Court – which was hosting the exhibition and sale of the Paradise Key.

Protected by bulletproof glass, the famous blue diamond dazzled with its mesmerising brilliance. In spite of the early hour, a dense crowd of people was already clamouring to admire the jewel. In the middle of the room, a string quartet played music from the film *Breakfast at Tiffany's*.

The luxury and elegance of the place provided a sumptuous backdrop for the event. The hotel was the preferred choice of the city's oldest families, who would come for Sunday brunch or book it for their lavish wedding receptions and christenings. Most of all, it was a place steeped in history: Oscar Wilde used to stay there, as did the tenor Caruso and President Roosevelt. Sarah Bernhardt, for her part, had provoked a riot when she arrived with her pet tiger.

The old courtyard, where in bygone days the carriages would draw up, had been transformed into a magnificent winter garden with majestic vaults supporting an enormous glass roof. Martin marvelled at the dome's stained glass, the Austrian crystal chandeliers, the Italian marble

224

columns and the amber-hued candelabras covered with gold leaf. You only had to close your eyes to feel yourself transported back to a Victorian-era ballroom, and yet, at the same time, the dozens of lush palms in giant glass pots, bathed in natural light, gave the room the feel of a modern atrium.

'So?' Martin's Korean colleague asked.

'It's magnificent,' agreed Martin. 'But as for security—'

'Yes?'

'As leaky as a sieve!'

*

They had gone back to their headquarters in one of the hotel suites on the top floor. On a long, lacquered table, a bank of screens beamed images from the surveillance cameras installed in the Garden Court.

Martin studied the monitors sombrely, looking worried.

'There are gaps everywhere!'

Mademoiselle Ho leant over his shoulder. Her perfume smelt subtly of cut flowers.

'No, there aren't. All the exits are guarded, security men are patrolling every floor and the diamond is in a glass container sealed to the floor. What more do you want?'

Martin got up, freeing himself from the invisible hold the woman exerted over him.

'The place is stuffed full of people! Archibald could cause chaos in an instant: start a fire, set off an alarm for no apparent reason, a gunshot … There would be pandemonium, a total scrum.'

Mademoiselle Ho disagreed.

225

'Everyone is briefed on how to handle an evacuation.'

Martin remained standing and tapped the keys on his laptop to call up the security guards' rotas.

'Sure, there are plenty of security guards during the day, but they're few and far between at night! And, frankly, exhibiting a diamond behind a glass case … It's as if we're asking for it! How many times has Archibald come at something from the air? It's his speciality!'

Mademoiselle Ho was silent, as if she were suddenly aware of the gaps in her strategy.

Martin went back to his desk and downloaded onto his computer the plans of the hotel that the management had just sent him. He was printing them out when his mobile emitted a sharp, metallic beep, alerting him to a text message.

— *Am I disturbing you?*

He glanced at the number: it was Gabrielle's. He decided not to reply, but, less than two minutes later, she sent it again.

— *Am I disturbing you?*
— *Yes!* he replied, in irritation.

Using her texts like instant messaging, she pursued him with questions:

— *Shall we have lunch together?*
— *No.*
— *What are you doing?*

226

— My job.
— You're killing people?
— Stop it, Gabrielle.
— Do you remember when we used to make love?

Almost as if caught *in flagrante*, Martin glanced over towards Mademoiselle Ho. At the other end of the office, half hidden behind the screen of her MacBook, his colleague was watching him with curiosity.

I hope they haven't got me under electronic surveillance, he thought to himself as he turned back to his mobile to tap on its tiny keys.

— Stop it!
— Making love was always good, so gentle, but so intense. It was you ...

He would have to tell her to stop again, but he no longer had the slightest desire to. Instead, he waited for a good minute, eyes fixed on the little screen, hoping for a new message, which wasn't long in coming:

— It's never been that good, that intense, that sensual for me since.

He couldn't let that pass.

— If it was so good, why didn't you come and meet me?

227

Without replying to the question, Gabrielle went on reliving her memories with a flurry of steamy texts.

— *Do you remember our kisses and caresses?*
— *Do you remember your hands on my breasts?*
— *Do you remember my breasts in your mouth?*
— *Do you remember your body in mine?*
— *Do you remember your head in my hands, your tongue in my—*

Suddenly, it was too much. He stopped reading and, with all his strength, hurled his mobile at the wall of the office, smashing it to pieces.

*

He headed back up Market Street, hurtled down Geary Street and came out on Grant Avenue, in front of the Café des Anges. He was sure to find her there!

Just on the edge of Chinatown and a few streets from the French consulate, the brasserie looked like a little corner of France right in the heart of San Francisco. Even though it didn't sell cigarettes, the café still bore a 'Bar-Tabac' sign, an exact replica of the façades of old-fashioned 1950s Parisian bistros.

Martin pushed open the door and went inside.

It was where they had gone on their first date as young lovers.

The charm of the place worked every time: with its checked tablecloths, zinc bar and wooden chairs, you were transported back into some old French film. Looking at its customers, you half expected Lino Ventura or Bernard Blier to appear suddenly, while you caught yourself listening out for sophisticated dialogue.

On the blackboard, the menu gave a real taste of France from another era: egg mayonnaise, herring fillets with steamed potatoes in oil and vinegar, leek vinaigrette, blanquette de veau, beef bourguignon, coq au vin, Caen-style tripe, and so on.

Behind the counter hung a French Post Office calendar and ancient postcards from the Tour de France, commemorating the adventures of the cyclists Anquetil and Poulidor. Next to this stood an old Garlando table football, its players long past their prime. Even the music was from another era: remixed Edith Piaf, Renaud and his Saturday night bops, Zaza Fournier and 'her man' …

Having quizzed the waiter, Martin found Gabrielle sitting at the most romantic table in the restaurant, set apart a little by a small arbour covered by a vine.

'So, that's the way you want to play it!' he said, seating himself opposite her.

'Will you have *rillettes* for starters?'

'Hang on, first tell me how you managed to get this table.'

'Just like you did that first night: I greased the waiter's palm!'

'What do you want exactly?'

'I want to find him again,' she said, shutting the menu. 'Who?'

'The Martin I used to know. The one I loved.'

'You can't bring back the past.'

229

'And you don't have the right to destroy it!'

'I don't want to destroy it, I want to understand it: understand why you didn't come to meet me.'

Their voices were rising. She softened her tone with a suggestion.

'Wouldn't you rather look to the future instead?'

He looked away. She warmed to her theme.

'They say you only get one bite of the cherry, but look, we're entitled to have another go at it, Martin! Let's not spoil it! We're still young, but only just. We've got as much time before us as behind us, but only just. We could have children, but we'd have to start trying right now ...'

She blushed to the roots of her hair, shocked at the audacity of her declaration, which seemed to have left him stony-faced.

Still she ploughed on.

'I wasn't ready thirteen years ago. I wasn't up to it; I wasn't strong enough. I doubted everything. And you, too, you weren't ready, whatever you want to make yourself believe.'

He looked quizzical. She went on.

'Now, I am ready. You see, love's like oxygen. If you go without it for too long, you end up dying because of it. You loved me so much for those months that I had enough love to last me for years. Thanks to that love, I managed to confront many things, but I've reached the end of my reserves, Martin.'

Her hand went up to the back of her neck, caressing the hairs at the nape, almost as if it were her way of urging herself on, since there'd never been anyone else to do it for her.

230

'I know I hurt you. Forgive me,' she concluded.

Finally, Martin opened his mouth to pour out his heart.

'The problem isn't the pain. Pain hurts but it doesn't destroy you. The problem is the solitude the pain generates. That's what kills you little by little, what cuts you off from others and the world around you. And what brings out the worst in you.'

She didn't try to duck the issue.

'Loving is always dangerous, Martin! To love is to hope you'll win it all while running the risk that you could lose it all. And sometimes it's also about accepting that there's a risk that you'll love more than you are loved.'

'Yes, well, you see,' he said, rising from the table, 'I don't think I'm ready to run that risk any more.'

*

Martin returned to the security HQ at the hotel and spent a good part of the afternoon working on the plans of the Garden Court. He then had to go to a meeting with the head of the team of security guards hired by Boid's Brothers and with the few FBI agents who were also on site.

The sun was beginning to dip as he wrote a lengthy memo to Mademoiselle Ho: a list of measures aimed at bolstering security around the diamond. He tried to contact his colleague, but there was no answer from any of her numbers. He sent her an email that he also copied into a text, then he headed down towards the exhibition room.

In the Garden Court, it was a crush. For several days, the sale of the diamond had been front-page news and the media had taken it upon themselves to turn the exhibition into a must-see trip for the Christmas holidays. Such a big crowd worried Martin because it made his job so much more complicated.

In amongst the throng, he briefly closed his eyes, as if to concentrate better. He had to get inside the thief's head. *How would I steal the diamond, if I were Archibald?*

During the afternoon, his brain had processed an enormous quantity of data, practically non-stop, like a computer. Now in the early evening, everything seemed to order itself in his mind, falling into place like pieces of a puzzle.

How would I steal the diamond, if I were Archibald?

Images scrolled through his head: the glass roof, the number of exits, the excessive crowds, the choreographed movements of the security guards...

How would I steal the diamond, if I were Archibald?

And suddenly, the answer came to him with absolute clarity: if he were Archibald, he would never try to steal the Paradise Key!

Because that would be too easy.

It was a set-up! Some kind of bait!

Martin was suddenly aware that he was just a pawn on a chessboard, playing a role in a game over which he had no control.

Neither Boid's Brothers nor Mademoiselle Ho had ever wanted to protect the diamond.

What they wanted, on the contrary, was to lure Archibald into a trap.

This surprise last-minute sale and the media hype surrounding it were nothing more than a decoy to force Archibald to stick his head in the lion's mouth.

The diamond on show couldn't be the real diamond …

20

TWO LOVERS

My father gave me a heart, but you set it beating.
Honoré de Balzac

When Martin arrived in Sausalito, the last rays of the sun were fanning out across the Pacific, fleetingly turning the sky and ocean purple.

He found a space in the parking lot in the floating village where Gabrielle lived. This slightly absurd, vibrant mix of houses on stilts and houseboats was one of the most unusual sights in California. In the 1960s the houseboat town had become a key symbol of the counterculture when a group of hippies and drop-outs had seized on this scrap of land to create an environment in their own image, a place to patch up old boats, fit out barges and erect what looked like shacks on stilts.

Now, though, the town was becoming gentrified – thanks to the make-overs by fashionable architects, homes were snapped up for astronomical prices. The old battered Jeeps and flower-power camper vans had long since been replaced by 'boho' eco-friendly 4 x 4s and Porsche convertibles.

Martin glanced at the quaysides, edged with flowerbeds, shrubs and painted wooden benches. Many of the houseboats had large picture windows that gave the impression that you could delve right into people's private lives. An elderly couple were enjoying drinks outside while discussing the ways of the world; a school kid was poring over his books as he finished his homework; a teenager alone in her bedroom was giving it her all in a Britney dance routine; and an elegant young couple were hurling insults at each other: *'You've been with your slut again, haven't you?'* *'Hang on, Rita's not a slut!'* *'So, you were with her then?'*

People, time, life …

Martin recognised the house from the Cessna seaplane moored next to the little wooden landing stage, shared by two neighbouring properties. He followed the landing quay up to the veranda.

'Come in, it's open!' Gabrielle called out to him through the window.

He pushed the door and immediately found himself in the sitting room. It was charming and had a very convivial atmosphere. A large bouquet of multicoloured orchids brightened up the wood-panelled room, while a bow window let in the fading evening light.

'Have you come to make peace?' she asked, welcoming him in.

'Sort of.'

'In that case, you're very welcome.'

He held out a bottle of wine. 'I was looking for something original …'

235

She looked down then exclaimed, 'Château-Margaux 1961! Are you crazy or what?'

'I found it in the "secret" cellar at the Palace Hotel.'

'How do you mean, "found it"?'

'Stole it,' he clarified.

'You're clearly not much better than he is!'

Martin chose to ignore that remark, adding instead, 'Apparently, it was an exceptional year.'

But Gabrielle was not going to fall for that.

'I'll put it in the cellar and take it back to the hotel when I can.'

She slipped out for a few seconds. He pretended to be offended.

'If that's how it is, then I won't bother giving you anything again!'

'How did you get into their cellar?' she asked, coming back into the room.

'I had the plans.'

'I hope you didn't leave any incriminating marks.'

'No, that is one advantage of being taught by a master.'

She gestured for him to sit down, but he preferred to remain standing.

'Can you help me choose?' she asked, guiding him to a shelf full of music.

She spurned the flashy pink iPod on its speaker and instead urged him to look through her mother's collection of old LPs.

Martin joined in the game and for a few minutes they rediscovered their former bond, glancing through the varied record collection and commenting on the albums of legendary artists that Valentine had bought way back then: Janis Joplin, the Beatles, Pink Floyd, David Bowie, Joni Mitchell, and so on.

They settled on an LP by Bob Dylan that included the track 'Lay Lady Lay'.

As Martin was putting the disc on the record player, Gabrielle remarked, 'You're lucky I'm here. Normally I'm still at work at this time.'

'Why did you come back early?'

'There was something I needed to do.'

'What?' he asked, getting up.

'This,' she replied, as she started to kiss him.

*

Their breathing becomes one, their lips touch, their tongues search and tease.

She touches his face; he caresses her neck.

She pulls off his jacket; he unbuttons her jeans.

She removes his shirt, which falls to the wooden floor; he pulls off her sweater, licks her shoulders, savours her skin.

She notices a tattoo he never had before; he recognises her scent and contrasts it with his memories.

So time is derailed. The past contaminates the present.

And fear resurfaces.

Fear.

Buried deep in the body, lurking in the shadows of the mind.

It's a fear that grows.

A fear that knows no limits.

And that only love can conquer.

At first, fear infects everything.

At first, fear begets fear and there is an urge to flee.

And yet, their hands join and their bodies cling to each other.

She holds on to him as if to a raft.

He finds the strength to anchor himself in her.

She manages to tie herself to him.

His gaze seeks hers. He beckons her on, halts an instant to contemplate her in the glow of the port lights: her body gleams in the night and illuminates her face. She smiles at him, wants to be radiant for him. She runs her fingers through his hair; he lets his tongue explore her breasts.

Of course, their kisses could be considered nothing more than an exchange of saliva, a clashing of teeth.

And yet ...

Yet, in the blink of an eye, their bodies tremble and their fear ebbs.

*

Wrapped in sheets and blankets, Martin was the first to go out onto the veranda. Night had fallen, but it was still warm in this unique city, protected as it was from the Pacific winds and enjoying an incredible microclimate, which transformed this winter night into an evening in springtime.

Martin gazed all around him. The veranda provided a panoramic view over the ocean. On one of the other

238

quays, an 'old hand' from the area was just setting himself up with his fishing rod and portable radio. As he listened to the opening arias of *La Traviata*, he teased the cackling seagulls whose staccato cries ended up becoming part of the opera.

The clinking of glasses roused him from his reverie.

Enveloped in a check rug, Gabrielle came to join him, skipping as she did so, two empty glasses in her hand. She kissed him and leant her head on his shoulder. Then with a mischievous smile she said, 'What about opening that bottle you brought?'

He took her at her word.

'I'll go and fetch it!'

Alone on the veranda, she shivered as goosebumps crept over her body, while a solitary tear trickled down her cheek.

That tear was pure concentrated gratitude.

Gratitude that she felt towards life, chance, karma, luck, providence, the great architect who controls all our destinies, God Himself if He existed – what did it matter? Martin was back in her life. And this time, she knew it would be for ever. By some strange alchemy, the harmony of their bodies had led to the harmonising of their souls. They were now both ready, not to begin from scratch, but to continue with a love that had survived for thirteen years in hibernation. Martin was right when he said that one couldn't look to the future with equanimity unless one had understood and accepted the past.

They were no longer travellers without baggage. They were no longer twenty. They'd both been around the block a bit and had suffered without the other. They'd both lost their way without the other.

Each had tried to find love with other people.

But all that was now finished.

From now on, she would tell him everything, explain everything, beginning with the real reason why she hadn't come to meet him in New York.

She would tell him about her lovers too, about that feeling that she'd always had, since adolescence, of being a kind of bait or prey in some game she wanted no part of and that she would never win. For a long time, in her relationships with men, she had said 'no' a lot and then had said 'yes' a lot too. The reason being, when you've no self-esteem, finally saying 'yes' to someone can be more negative than saying no. She knew Martin would understand this.

As they had embraced, her defences had fallen away at the same time as his.

From now on, they had no need of them, because they had love.

From now on, nothing could disturb their happiness.

Except perhaps …

'Good evening, Gabrielle.'

*

She jumped, taken by surprise.

Archibald's face stood out in the light cast by a candlestick lamp.

'What are you doing here?'

'I came to continue our conversation.'

'Not tonight.'

'It'll have to be tonight or never, I think.'

'Why?'

'I'll tell you.'

'No, get lost!' she ordered, pushing him away. 'Martin is here!'

'So I see,' he said, sitting down on the sofa.

Gripped by panic, she begged him, 'Please don't spoil this night for me.'

'You're the one holding all the cards, Gabrielle. If he wants to arrest me this time, I'm not going to resist. You choose: talk things over with your father for one last time, or send him to end his days in prison.'

'But where do you want to talk?'

'I've got an idea,' he said, nodding towards the little seaplane.

'Why are you asking that of me? Why are you making me choose between you and Martin?'

'Because life is all about making choices, Gabrielle. But I think you know that already.'

For a couple of seconds, she remained rigid, terrified by what Archibald was asking of her. Then she dashed back into the house and ran down to the cellar.

'I've found the bottle!' shouted Martin, hearing her arrive.

He was shutting the drinks fridge when Gabrielle put her head round the half-open door.

'I'm sorry, my darling …'

'What?'

Before he could understand what was going on, she'd turned the key in the lock to trap him in the cellar.

'I'm sorry,' she said again in a broken voice as she went to join Archibald.

21

WE LOVED EACH OTHER
SO MUCH

*Loving someone means robbing them of their soul,
and in doing so, teaching that person how great,
inexhaustible and clear is that soul. We all suffer from
this: from not being sufficiently robbed. We suffer from
the forces within us that no one knows how to plunder,
so that we too can discover them for ourselves.*
Christian Bobin

With its rounded undercarriage and its great floats, the seaplane resembled a pelican.

Archibald put on his flying goggles and settled at the controls of the Cessna aircraft while Gabrielle silently went through the final safety checks. He started up the engine, letting it run at low throttle to protect the propeller from the erratic gusts of wind sweeping the water and so he could familiarise himself with the plane.

The night sky was clear, but a sharp breeze and the waves were making the plane turn like a weathervane. Archibald carefully moved away from the pontoon until he detected a space for take-off where the water was less choppy. He screwed up his eyes, conscious of needing to avoid the splinters of wood and flotsam bobbing around on the surface in order to prevent damage to the floats.

As the seaplane gained momentum, Archibald drew up the flaps and the rudder before gradually pulling up the front of the floats, which were clipping against the waves.

When he increased the throttle, the plane transformed itself into a hovercraft, skimming the surface of the ocean, before pulling away from the water, gracefully moving from one element to the other.

Then he began to climb, flying over the centre of the city with its skyscrapers, Bay Bridge and Angel Island, before heading south.

*

Barefoot and in boxer shorts, Martin was livid with rage. There was no window in the cellar and the only access was the metal door that Gabrielle had just closed on him. Three times he rammed it with his shoulder, but he only succeeded in hurting himself.

Once again, Gabrielle had humiliated him. She'd disarmed him, stripped him bare, got him to drop his guard, all the better to betray him, only a few moments after giving herself to him.

He didn't understand, he would never understand.

Along with the suffering and the pain, he felt a ferocious hatred.

Sick with frustration, he seized the bottle of Bordeaux and hurled it against the sheet of steel.

*

243

The Cessna reached its cruising speed. It had passed Carmel and was flying over the southern end of Monterey Bay, tracking the panoramic coastal road pinched between Los Patres forest and the Big Sur cliffs, which plunged sheer into the ocean.

Throughout the flight, Gabrielle did not say a word to her father, content just to help him with the piloting. The thief followed the road that, many feet below him, was snaking through tight bends all along the rocky, wild and jagged coastline. Now and again, his gaze drifted out to sea and, without actually seeing them, he imagined the grey whales on their silent migration from Alaska to Mexico in search of more clement climates for breeding. As for Gabrielle, all she could think of was Martin …

A little before San Simeon, Archibald reduced the plane's speed and began the descent. With the winds constantly changing direction, Gabrielle knew it was a tricky manoeuvre.

Archibald nosed the plane up lightly to try to land it in the mouth of a little cove. It was such a starry night, the moon so bright, that the seaplane was reflected in the water as if in a looking glass, making its altitude difficult to gauge. Despite this, he managed to guide it down gently.

Archibald was one hell of a thief, but he was also a great pilot.

*

The little inlet was lapped by calm waters that gleamed and shone enchantingly. The beach could only be reached from the sea, which enabled the place to retain its slightly wild air.

'This cove was one of your mother's favourite places,' Archibald explained, as they drew alongside the shore.

Torn between curiosity and anger, Gabrielle asked him, 'How did you meet my mother?'

'I was a pilot at the time and one summer I worked for her, I mean, for the humanitarian organisation she set up, Wings of Hope. I met her then, during a job in Africa.'

A slight swell ruffled the ocean's surface and a mild breeze caressed their faces.

'Was it love at first sight for you both?'

'For me, yes, I loved her at first sight,' he said. 'For her, it took more than five years.'

'Five years!'

'Before me, your mother had been in love with the singer of quite a well-known rock group. He was a nasty piece of work and made her suffer for years.'

For a few moments, Archibald's gaze clouded as he thought back to the 1970s, through the twists and turns of a still-painful past.

'He was the sort of guy who took a lot without giving her anything back,' he went on. 'And worst of all …'

'Worst of all what?' asked Gabrielle, pushing him to finish his sentence.

'He forced her to have an abortion twice.'

There was silence again, this time heavier than before. Then, in unspoken unison, they jumped feet first into the water and headed for the beach.

While they were tying up the seaplane to stop it drifting, Gabrielle resumed the conversation.

'So did she stay with the singer a long time?'

'Six years, I think, on and off.'

'Six years!'

Under her searching gaze, he went on: 'The more he hurt her, the more desperately she loved him. Life's strange, eh? Sometimes things happen almost as if we're punishing ourselves for some fault that we can't really identify.'

They walked along the shore a little. The place was breathtakingly beautiful, with its natural crescent-shaped beach, sheltered from the winds by a giant granite cliff.

'But what were you doing all that time?'

'Well, I was waiting for her. I put up with her rejections and I waited for her.'

'And were you always hopeful?'

'Initially, yes. By the end, I didn't hold out much hope.'

She liked the frank way he replied.

'So, you were hurting?'

'Yes,' he admitted. 'It was more than hurt: it was a kind of wrench, or punishment, or torture.'

'But how come you could love a woman, from that very first encounter, when you didn't know what she was like?'

'I know it's hard to comprehend,' Archibald conceded. 'It seemed as if I could see in her things that others couldn't see, qualities which not even she was aware of. It was as if I could already see in her the woman she would later become.'

'That's only in books and films.'

'It sometimes happens in life,' he assured her.

'And how do you explain that it took her five years to realise that you were the love of her life?'

246

He looked into her eyes.

'It's scary being loved, that's why. Because life is complicated and all too often it throws you off balance by sending you the right person at the wrong time.'

'Did you love anyone before her?'

'Before her, I'd been married for a few years to a nurse in the Red Cross.'

'Did you leave her for Maman?'

'No, I left her because I was spending too much time thinking about your mother, even though, at the time, she wasn't interested in me. I left her because being unfaithful to someone begins in the head.'

'And finally, five years later, Maman said yes.'

'She didn't say yes, she said simply that I had healed her.'

'That you'd healed her?'

'Yes, and, believe me, that's worth all the "I love you"s in the world.'

*

At the end of the inlet, he pointed out a waterfall which tumbled directly into the ocean. The beach was edged with redwoods, willows, eucalyptus and sycamore trees.

'It's in this cove that we kissed each other and made love for the first time – and more than likely where you were conceived!'

'OK, spare me the details!'

He pulled a cigar from his shirt pocket.

'Make the most of this landscape because you'll never see it so unspoilt again. They're building a footpath to link it to the Eagle's Nest car park.'

'That's sad,' Gabrielle mourned.

'That's life,' he sighed, rolling his Havana cigar with its supple, oily coating between his fingers.

'Nothing stays the same – is that what you're trying to tell me?'

'Yes, it all gets crushed. It all gets broken. It all passes with time. Only the moment you're in has any meaning.' Archibald cut off the end of his unlit cigar.

Gabrielle challenged that.

'No, there are things that stand the test of time, there are things that last.'

'Like what?'

'Like love,' she ventured.

'Love! There's nothing more fragile or ephemeral. Love is like a fire on a rainy day: you've got to spend all your time protecting it, feeding it, tending it, because if you don't, it goes out.'

'There are some loves that last.'

'No, what lasts is the pain that comes after love.'

'I don't like what you're saying.'

'If there are some answers you don't want to hear, it's best not to ask those questions.'

His face inscrutable, Archibald struck one match, then another, to fully light the end of his cigar.

'But what about Maman? You still love her!'

'Yes,' he agreed.

'Well, as long as you remember the person who loved you and whom you still love, then you're making love endure.'

'That's what people want to hear but I don't really believe it.'

Caught up in her thoughts, Gabrielle chose not to pursue the discussion. She comforted herself by watching the end of her father's cigar glowing in the night. The wind was still mild and the murmur of the waves on the sand very gentle.

'There's something I wanted to give you: a letter,' he said, rooting around in a leather satchel slung over his shoulder.

'A letter?'

'Yes, you know, the thing people used to write to each other before emails came along.'

'I know what a letter is! I've had a few myself, you know!'

'Oh yes, from your Martin.'

'Enough already, if you don't mind!'

'Anyway, this letter, I wanted you to have it, as a keepsake from that time,' he said, holding out a pale-blue envelope, faded over the years. 'Your mother sent it to me, just when we were starting out together. It was her way of telling me that she wanted us to have a child. I've carried it with me always, and I would prefer you to read it when you're alone.'

Gabrielle pretended not to hear. She sat down on the sand and opened the envelope.

*

Stretched out on the beach, propped up on his elbows, Archibald studied the horizon.

Sitting next to him, Gabrielle finished her reading. Relieved of a burden, she was crying. These were the same tears as the night before: tears of gratitude.

Gratitude for having had the chance to get to know her parents at last and to be able to love them.

Archibald took a few light, short puffs of his cigar, savouring the smooth aromas that lingered on his tongue. Always relishing the moment, trying to stretch out the little time he had left.

'I've got a tumour on my pancreas, Gabrielle.' Held back for so long, the words popped out on their own.

'What?'

Tenderly, he studied her tear-soaked face.

'I'm in the terminal stages of cancer. I'm going to die.'

She looked at him disbelievingly.

'You're going to die?'

'In a few weeks. Three months at most.'

'But are you sure? You've had all the tests?'

'Yes, there's nothing that can be done, sweetheart.'

Overwhelmed, she buried her head in her hands, then asked in choked tones, 'How long have you known?'

Just now, the words stuck in his throat.

'For sure? About two days.'

She wiped her eyes and, full of anger, cried out, 'But … why bother to come back then? A few hours ago, I finally found my father and already we've got to part. Why are you inflicting that on me?'

'Because you had to know that I hadn't abandoned you. All these past years, I've been there, in the background.'

'How do you mean, in the background?'

To calm her, he rested his hand on her arm. Then he explained how, for nearly twenty years, he had tried to renew the ties, so he could tell her the truth. He told her about his shame, his guilt, his sadness at his own

250

helplessness. He told her also of the various schemes he'd concocted to spend a few moments with her, in disguise, every 23 December.

Disconcerted, Gabrielle realised that still-fresh memories were coming back to her. Of encounters which had struck her then without her being fully aware of why and which now took on a different meaning.

The door-to-door salesman who had let her have the latest top-of-the-range laptop for a song, the very week when her own had given up the ghost.

That had been him!

The philosophical street clown, whose impassioned mini-show had moved her so much that she'd felt his words were directed at her.

That was him.

The gardener pruning the roses at the Japanese Tea Garden, who had had her in stitches of laughter, after sensing her sadness, on a day when things weren't going well.

Him again.

So many surreptitious encounters that now only left her with regrets. If only she'd known before …

But the regrets were shaded with anger when Archibald spoke of the detective he'd hired to trail her for years.

'How dare you interfere in my life without my permission!' she demanded, outraged.

'I just wanted to help you,' Archibald pleaded.

'Help me?'

'You're not happy, Gabrielle.'

'What do you know about it?'

He opened the leather satchel next to him and took out various 'pieces of incriminating evidence': the photocopied pages of his daughter's private diary, photos taken at the end of a night out, never with the same man. He'd made enquiries into some of them: no-good guys, self-centred, sometimes violent, sometimes cruel, to the extent that he'd had to 'take care' of one of them himself.

'Why do you do that, sweetheart?'

Her eyes were full of tears as she looked at him. She was ashamed to have to justify something to her father when she herself didn't know how to explain it.

'Well, you know, it's a bit like you were saying earlier: sometimes you're trying to punish yourself for something, without even knowing what it is.'

*

Gabrielle had retreated into silence and Archibald was absorbed in his memories.

He was thinking back to the first night in springtime that he'd spent here with Valentine, entirely alone, amid the irises and poppies.

Now in his twilight years, he could say for sure that he'd never known a feeling stronger than that of being at one with another person – that rare feeling of not being alone any more.

He turned to his daughter and got straight to the point. 'Do you truly love this guy, Martin?'

She hesitated before replying, then said, 'Yes, I've loved him for a long time. He's nothing like the others.'

'And does he love you?'

'I think so, but after what you've just made him go through, it's going to be difficult to win him back.'

'I haven't done anything to him,' Archibald replied with a thin smile. 'You're the one who locked him in the cellar! And yes, I'd agree that he's not going to like that and you're going to have a hard time winning him back!'

'You sound like you're pleased about it!'

He shrugged his shoulders and took another puff of his cigar.

'If he really loves you, he'll come back. It'll do him good actually, to see nothing can be taken for granted. For me, it took five years of fighting before your mother said yes!'

'But he's been waiting for me for thirteen years—'

'Waiting isn't the same as fighting!' Archibald cut in.

She shook her head; he tried to understand.

'So if you love him, why keep him waiting for thirteen years?'

She replied, as if it were obvious, 'Because I was afraid.'

'Of what?'

'Of everything.'

'Everything?'

'Afraid of not being worthy, afraid of not knowing how to love him, afraid of waking up one day and not loving him any more, afraid of not being able to give him the children he wants ...'

Imperceptibly, Archibald frowned. His daughter's words were too reminiscent of Valentine's. They were words he didn't like to hear because they were meaningless to him.

'What do you think of Martin?' Gabrielle dared to ask.

'You mean, setting aside the fact that he's tried to put two bullets in me?'

'Yes,' she smiled.

Archibald grimaced.

'I don't know if he's capable.'

'Capable of what?'

'Capable of protecting you.'

'But I'm not a child!' Gabrielle exclaimed, annoyed. 'I don't need a man to protect me.'

'That's a load of crap! A woman needs—'

'Oh, give me a break from your old-fashioned sermons!' she interrupted. 'In any case, Martin is stronger than you think.'

'You must be joking! He hasn't even managed to protect you from me. Even you were able to lock him in the cellar!'

'Do you think I'm proud of that?'

But Archibald hadn't finished his critique.

'And I find him too tender, too sensitive, too sentimental …'

'You were sentimental at his age as well,' she pointed out.

'Exactly. It was those sentiments that made me lose my cool, clouded my judgement. They stopped me from protecting your mother.'

'What do you mean?'

'I should never have driven her to that hospital, I should never have shot that doctor, I should never have screwed up my life and yours, I should never …'

His voice trembled before breaking into a sob.

All of a sudden, the wind became chill and swept through the trees with a low rustling.

For the first time in thirty-three years, father and daughter were finally able to fall into each other's arms.

22

VALENTINE'S LETTER

Life is not a rehearsal for love.
It's the only chance we get.
Pascal Quignard

13 April 1973, San Francisco

Archie, my love,

First, the night.
First, the worst.
All that hurts us.
All that kills us.
Our fears, the ghosts of our two pasts.
They're all there and we can look them in the face:
your first love, my first love, the dizzying emptiness, the
'devilishly handsome' singer who destroyed my heart and
my body and whom I would still have followed to the gates
of hell, your first wife, that blonde angel whose altruism so
impressed you.
It's important to look them in the face in all their
seductiveness, important also to know that they won't
give up that easily, that a day will come when the singer

will call me up to say that he's always thinking of me and that this time he is available, that he's written me a song to say 'I love you' and that, even if the last time he saw me he called me a whore as he slapped me, that wasn't the real him and it was only because he loved me ...

And perhaps for a few seconds I'll believe him ...

There'll also come a day when you'll bump into your blonde nurse and you'll remember that there were some perfect mornings and, for a few seconds, you'll want to protect her all over again, she who loved you so much because she thought you were 'different from the others'.

Important too to know that temptation will take other forms: that there'll be men who will try to win me over, and that there will be women whose fragility will touch a chord in you.

Look, they're all still there: dangers past and those still to come, but the ghosts, the mirages and the easy seduction will eventually fade. Even though they will resist, merging into one another to form a thick cloud. The earth will tremble, a livid bolt of lightning will shake the doors and windows and the wind will sweep into the room. Its powerful gust will caress us, but will violently expel the menacing fog.

And once the wind has passed through, we will find each other again, just the two of us, alone, in our little apartment perched on the water. Rays of sunlight will splash the parquet floor. I will hold your hand, you will hold mine. We will smile at each other. Fear will have passed over us without affecting us.

The mirror reflects back our image: that of a still young couple with a life before them.

The best is yet to come. The best is those years ahead, dozens of years opening up before us.

We are young, but we've already experienced enough to know the price of happiness.

We are young, but we already know that in life's great game those who are most unhappy are those who haven't taken the risk to be happy.

And I don't want to be one of those.

In years past, to keep their men close, women would wear a ring and bear children.

It doesn't work like that today.

Nowadays, how do we hold on to those we love?

I've no idea.

All that I can promise you is that I'll always be there for you, from now on, whatever happens.

In good times and bad, for richer and poorer, as long as you want me, I will be there.

I smile at you and you smile back. There is light everywhere. Such a beautiful light.

In our home there is a magic window: a window that sometimes lets you look into the future.

To begin with, we're a bit reticent. We're doing fine, the two of us, in the here and now. We're so warm, our hearts and bodies intertwined, your lips sealed on my lips.

Why take the risk of wanting to know what's in our future?

'Come on, Archie! We're going!'

Hand in hand, we move closer to the window and we see ourselves through it.

There we are, in a hospital room.

It is a hospital, but we're not unwell. The room is full of warmth, soft light and bouquets of flowers. In the room, there's a cradle and in the cradle, a new-born baby.

You look at me, I look at you. Our eyes shine. That's our baby.

It's a little girl. She opens her eyes. She looks at us too, and all at once, we are three, and we have become one.

All at once, we're a family.

Archie, my love, when you're with me, I'm afraid of nothing.

Archie, I love you.

Valentine

23

HALFWAY TO HELL

Destiny is usually just around the corner. Like a thief, a hooker or a lottery vendor: its three most common personifications. But what destiny does not do is home visits. You have to go for it …
Carlos Ruiz Zafon

24 December
5 a.m.
It was not yet daybreak when Gabrielle made it back to her house in the floating village of Sausalito. She hoped with all her heart that Martin had waited for her and that they could discuss things calmly. She didn't want to fight any more; what she longed for was mutual trust and understanding. And most importantly she wanted to explain her actions to him and to confide in him all that Archibald had revealed to her.

The cellar door was broken. Inside, shards of glass were strewn across the floor, splashes of wine covered the walls and the drinks fridge was overturned on the floor. Gabrielle guessed that Martin had used it to break open the lock.

He'd managed to escape and had left before she'd got back.

Holding out little hope, she rang his hotel and left messages on his mobile, then she got into her car and did the rounds of the favourite haunts of their youth.

But this time Martin was nowhere to be found.

We think that some ties are so strong that they can withstand anything, but it's not true. When trust is broken, weariness sets in. Then poor choices, the deceptive lure of seduction and sorry twists of fate, all conspire to kill off love. In this type of unequal contest, the chances of winning are slim, more the exception than the rule.

Reaching the little beach near the marina, Gabrielle sat down on the sand and stared at the horizon. She was tired. Her eyes stung. Always the same pain, always the same loneliness, always the same heavy weight on her shoulders.

Some say that you know real love when you realise that the only person in the world who can console you is the one who has hurt you. Martin was her real love.

And she'd lost him.

6 a.m.

The sun was just rising over Alamo Square, the little public garden in the residential area of Western Addition. It overlooked the city, providing a panoramic view of the Bay Bridge and the dome of City Hall.

A row of elegant Victorian-style houses bordered the garden; these were the famous Painted Ladies, so-called

261

because of their pastel shades: lavender blue, aqua green and straw yellow.

Like everyone else, Archibald knew these archetypal San Francisco dwellings well, but would never have thought that one day he would sneak inside one of them.

The house in question belonged to Stephen Browning, the largest shareholder in the Kurtline Group, which was putting the diamond up for sale. Once inside, the thief easily deactivated the alarm and surveillance cameras before heading to a back stairway. He'd thought about stealing the Paradise Key for many years, but he'd always resisted the temptation. To do so now, in a low-key operation while dozens of halfwits stood around waiting for him to fall into some crude trap, did have something delicious about it. He came to a wide corridor that curved round and led him to the entrance of a fortified room. A panic room! It was the latest craze among the well-heeled: to have a giant vault installed where they could take refuge in the event of an attack from outside.

With its reinforced hinges and armoured door, the steel bunker resembled a nuclear shelter. Riding the security-conscious wave of the Bush years, firms of architects had lured rich homeowners with promises of building them impregnable citadels. Archibald knew, however, that its combination lock would hold out for only a few seconds against his electronic box, but today, as he went about his work in the old way, he felt an urge to take his time, to draw out the pleasure of what would probably be his last heist. He placed his toolbox on the floor, digging out a whole arsenal of tools along with an old-fashioned radiocassette player, and, to the sounds of Bach's *Sonatas for Cello*, he set to work, just as in the good old days.

*

The door opened with a metallic click.

Several fluorescent bulbs came on at once, flooding the small space with a garish light.

Archibald frowned. In the middle of the room, a man and a woman were sitting back to back, bound and gagged. Wrapped in a dressing gown that gaped open over a paunchy stomach, the elderly Stephen Browning had his back to his mistress, the beautiful Mademoiselle Ho, who had the sexy allure of a manga heroine in her satin baby-doll nightdress with turquoise lace.

'Is this what you're looking for?'

Archibald flinched before turning round abruptly.

Leaning against the wall of the corridor, Martin was rolling the diamond between his fingers. The Paradise Key shone with the opalescent brilliance of a moonstone.

Archibald's face showed denial and then anger before gradually giving way to acceptance.

In his thirty years of burglary, it was the first time that someone had beaten him to it. Yet, he wasn't really surprised. Hadn't he started this duel himself? Hadn't he himself selected a worthy opponent, with all the risks that it entailed?

'It's beautiful, isn't it?' Martin said, watching Archibald's reactions through the prism of the diamond.

Archibald gave a little laugh. 'It's said that it brings bad luck to whoever wins it by foul means. That doesn't worry you?'

263

'No,' Martin assured him. 'In any case, I've nothing left to lose.'

Archibald shook his head. He didn't care for that type of categorical statement.

Martin pulled his jacket open to show that he was unarmed and had no intention of arresting Archibald. His eyes were bloodshot, red from lack of sleep, humiliated rage and the desire for revenge.

In the panic room, Mademoiselle Ho and her elderly lover let out muffled cries beneath the gaffer-tape gags, but neither of the 'duellists' took any notice.

'So what do we do now?' Archibald asked.

As if tossing for it, Martin lobbed the diamond into the air with one hand then snatched it back with the other, taunting the thief before throwing down the gauntlet.

'If you want it, come and get it.'

And he turned on his heel, briskly climbing the short narrow staircase to the ground floor.

Archibald sighed. He didn't really understand what Martin was hoping to achieve by behaving like this. He wondered vaguely whether he was drunk or high. A moment before, it had seemed to him that Martin's clothes stank of alcohol. What on earth had he cooked up while he'd been shut in that cellar? One thing was certain: the lad had lost it. He himself was exhausted – his back was aching, he felt sick, his joints were as fragile as glass – yet there was nothing for it but to pick up the gauntlet and go off in pursuit. He had to do it for Gabrielle, all the time trying, as far as possible, to limit the damage for which he was largely responsible. In any case, he couldn't stay here in the house.

264

*

Since early morning, San Francisco had been wreathed in fog: a thick, menacing mass that hung over the city, like something out of a film noir.

Martin had 'borrowed' the cherry-red Lexus convertible belonging to Mademoiselle Ho and was heading down Divisadero Street towards the ocean. Hot on his heels, Archibald's motorbike sliced through the opaque curls of fog, making him look like he was sinking into the clouds.

For the first time, Archibald understood that he had gone too far. His confrontation with Martin had reached such a pitch that not even he knew who was the hunter and who was the prey. He'd wanted to remain in the background, pulling the strings, protecting Gabrielle and ensuring her happiness. Then he'd got it into his head to test Martin, her first and only true love. But it couldn't be done, playing with other people's feelings and forcing them to be happy in spite of themselves. Because of him, Martin had quit the police and had overstepped the mark several times. Right now, he had to tell him the truth and salvage whatever could be salvaged, for Gabrielle's sake.

On Lombard Street, he tried to regain the initiative, and with a burst of speed he caught up with Martin. For a short while, the two vehicles travelled side by side, brushing up against each other, and refusing to give one inch of space.

There was probably some biological explanation for their shared brinkmanship: that damned testosterone that turned men into predators, giving them an urge to dominate. But Martin and Archibald were also both engaged in a more unusual combat. For each man, it was a personal confrontation with their inner demons, their fear of failure, and their death wish.

One was seeking out a father to kill, the only way to erase the insult of a love that had never been.

The other had sickness and death hot on his heels, and didn't know how to lessen the guilt that had been eating away at him for more than thirty years.

Both were at an impasse.

The sports car drove at full speed onto Route 101, which went through the wooded areas of the Presidio park.

Perhaps this morning as never before San Francisco lived up to its nickname of Fog City. Dancing in the beam of his headlights, Archibald saw a pallid mist that engulfed the traffic and blotted out the sidewalks and road signs.

He slowed down to manoeuvre into the car's slipstream. He had no idea what Martin was playing at, nor where he was trying to lead him.

Visibility was barely ten feet. When the Lexus left the park, heading onto the Golden Gate Bridge, the fog was so dense it seemed to have swallowed the bridge whole. The symbol and pride of San Francisco had lost its glorious rich red colour. The mist lingered, unfurling its pale ribbons that twined like creepers around the metal structure and its thousands of cables.

Martin slowed down in the middle of the bridge and came to a stop in the right-hand lane.

Archibald hesitated for a moment, then he too pulled over behind the car, well aware of the huge risk he was

266

running. Already, a chorus of horns hooted in reproach. It was explicitly forbidden to park here, and in a few minutes more, the traffic cops would show up to check their ID and book them.

In spite of the early hour, the Golden Gate Bridge was very busy on this Christmas Eve. Over the six lanes of traffic, cars passed each other, just missed each other and overtook in a frenzy of blaring horns, insults and screeching tyres.

Martin slammed the door and straddled the blocks separating off the cycle lane. Just like Archibald had done six months earlier with the Van Gogh self-portrait, Martin brandished the diamond threateningly in one hand, as if he were going to hurl it into the ocean.

'Are you ready to go looking for this in hell?' he yelled wildly.

But the Golden Gate Bridge wasn't Pont Neuf.

With its colossal size, it dwarfed you. Its towers soared more than 650 feet above a wild and dangerous sea.

Archibald too stepped into the cycle lane.

'Listen, son, come back, don't be a fool!' he yelled over the noise of the wind.

The security barrier was high, but it wasn't high enough to stop the dozens of people who every year jumped from it to their deaths.

'So are you coming or not?' the young man demanded impatiently.

Despite the grey light, the Paradise Key now shone between his fingers like an intense flame, producing an almost unreal, mesmerising halo.

Martin then shoved the diamond deep into his pocket and began climbing the safety rail.

'I couldn't give a damn about the diamond!' Archibald shouted to him.

Instinctively, he craned over to look down. It was terrifyingly beautiful and dizzying. Without seeing them, you could imagine the waves smashing against the gigantic pillars anchored deep in the Pacific.

Archibald knew that time was running out. The bridge was studded with cameras and, in a few seconds, they would hear the sirens of a police car or a Transportation District patrol car.

'Listen, son, don't throw it all away! Come down from there! We've got to talk!'

He moved closer and tried to pull Martin down by tugging his jacket, but the Frenchman managed to shake him off. Just as Archibald was ready to try again, Martin threw him a fierce punch. As he sought to dodge the blow, Archibald grasped his opponent and the two men grappled until Martin suddenly toppled backwards. The thief tried to hold on to the younger man, but Martin struggled and, without really wanting to, he pulled Archibald down with him towards the icy Pacific currents.

*

A leap of 230 feet into the abyss.

A fall lasting more than four seconds.

Four seconds is a long time, especially when you know they are the last moments of your life.

At the end of those four seconds, your body smashes into the water at a speed of over sixty miles an hour. The impact is as violent as if you'd dropped onto concrete.

During those four seconds, you don't see your life pass before your eyes like a film on fast forward.

During those four seconds, you're scared.

During those four seconds, all you have is regrets.

Even if you chose to fall, there is always a moment, mid-descent, when you would give anything to turn the clock back.

That's how it is.

Every time.

As he was falling, Archibald told himself that he'd tried to do his best, but that he'd failed. That all he'd managed to do was destroy the lives around him and that in wanting to make amends he'd gone on to make even worse mistakes. Then, in a last bid not to die in bitterness and resentment, he squeezed the lad tightly in his arms.

Martin, for his part, thought of Gabrielle. She was his enigma, his love and his wound. For always and for ever. Because there are pains in this life which you never get over.

On the point of parting, he thought of the letter that he'd written to her, with the naiveté and idealism of a twenty-one-year-old.

… When I close my eyes and imagine us in ten years' time, I see in my head pictures of happiness: sunshine, children's laughter, the intimate glances of a couple who are still in love …

269

What a joke! There'd never been any sunshine, at the most a few sunny spells, intense but always fleeting.

There had only been suffering, blackness, fear and …

PART THREE

IN THE COMPANY OF ANGELS

24

THE GREAT ESCAPE

To fly with ease,
Eyes shining, hair blowing in the wind,
Before the flood, before the sled
Leaves the road and then ...
... nothing, the end.
Clarika, 'Escape Lane'

24 December, Nob Hill
8 a.m.
Sirens wailing, the ambulance screeched to a halt in front of the ER at Lenox Hospital.

The medical team on hand to attend to the injured people split into two groups.

—'What have we got here?'   —'What have we got here?'
—'A 34-year-old male,   —'60-year-old male,
coma with multiple trauma.'   coma with multiple trauma.'

The trolleys carrying the two stretchers seemed to be taking part in a race through the hospital corridors to see which would reach the operating theatre first, which would receive the first scan, which would be operated on by the

273

best surgeon … Almost as if the contest between Martin and Archibald was continuing even at death's door.

— *'He threw himself off the Golden Gate Bridge half an hour ago ...'*   — *'a 230-foot fall from the bridge.'*
— *'Fished out by the river police ... '*   — *'less than three minutes after the impact.'*
— *'Multiple fractures ...*   — *numerous internal injuries.'*

The two men had been intubated at the scene of the accident. Each was sedated and on a ventilator, and both wore a cervical collar and had a catheter connected to five drips. As many tubes as were needed to keep them alive, but for how long?

*

As luck would have it, that morning, Elliott Cooper, one of the hospital's most senior surgeons, happened to be walking past the ER parking lot after finishing his long night shift just as the ambulance brought in the two men fished out of the ocean after their fall from the Golden Gate Bridge.

Thirty years before, Ilena, the woman he loved, had ended her life by throwing herself off the same damned bridge. Ever since then, this symbol of San Francisco had held a painful fascination for him, which had prompted him to fight actively for the installation of a suicide barrier above the guardrail – a measure that had yet to be adopted.

274

Automatically, Elliott's ears pricked up and he watched the two medical teams bustling around the two injured people: a young Frenchman, Martin Beaumont, and a man his age of unknown identity.

A sort of sixth sense made him stop in his tracks and go to the aid of his colleagues. As a hospital administrator he knew that on Christmas Eve there wouldn't be many staff around. But there was also something he wanted to check. That figure he had glimpsed lying on the stretcher … those aquiline features, that greying hair, that mystery man … could it be …

Leaning over the second stretcher, the surgeon recognised his old friend Archie Blackwell. Without hesitating, Elliott went to put his name down on the list of doctors on call. He put on his scrubs and just before switching off his phone he dialled Gabrielle's number.

*

I always get the smashed-up ones …

Claire Giuliani, one of the on-call interns, observed with horror the injuries of her young patient, a Frenchman not much older than her: a fractured spine and ribs, broken legs and foot, a broken collarbone, a smashed rib cage, and a dislocated right shoulder and hip. Not to mention the internal injuries, which needed urgent treatment: a burst spleen, a ruptured intestine …

*

Elliott was astounded: the violence of the impact ought to have killed Archibald. He'd fallen flat on his back, as though in an attempt to shield Martin and to take the brunt of the impact.

His pelvis and spine were fractured, his kidneys badly damaged, his spleen and bladder had burst, he had a cerebral oedema and multiple internal injuries. There was no need to be a doctor to see that in this state his chances of survival were almost zero and that even in the event of a miracle, the probable injuries to his backbone and spinal cord meant that his friend would never walk again.

Midday

In the corridor leading to the operating theatres where she'd been told she could wait, Gabrielle tried desperately to glimpse what the surgeons were doing behind the frosted glass doors as they attempted to save the lives of the two men she loved.

Although she didn't know exactly what had led up to Martin and Archibald making that 'death-defying leap' from the bridge, for her this tragic dénouement was consistent with their ruthless battle.

She had refused to choose between the two, wanting to keep them both, bring them together, love them at the same time, but no doubt some duels can only end in death.

8 p.m.

It had been dark for several hours when Claire Giuliani left the operating theatre, face drawn, dark circles under her eyes. Glumly, she tossed her gloves and apron into the waste bin, before taking off her surgical cap and letting down her hair, damp with sweat. An auburn lock fell over her face. She left it. She got herself a coffee from the machine and walked out into the parking lot. The air was crisper that night; she liked it. She'd only been in San Francisco a few weeks and already found herself missing Manhattan. She was sick of the so-called laid-back lifestyle, the cool, friendly people, the positive attitude that contaminated everything. She was neither cool, friendly nor positive. She felt constantly restless and preferred the harsh New York winter to the mild Californian one. She stifled a yawn. Her eyes were stinging from the exhaustion of having operated all day, and the frustration at having made little difference. The handsome Frenchman was a big mess and barely alive: facial trauma, pulmonary bruising, a pneumothorax … And, judging from the results of the scan, he would almost certainly suffer a brain haemorrhage during the night. In that case, he'd need another operation and, given the state he was in, he was unlikely to survive it. And, even if he did come out of the coma, it was unthinkable that a fall like that wouldn't have left him with cerebrospinal injuries that would render him permanently paraplegic.

Angrily, she ripped a nicotine patch off her arm and went to rummage through the glove compartment of her car for a packet of stale cigarettes.

277

Leaning against the bonnet of the piece of junk that was her car – a VW Beetle spray-painted an intentionally hideous mauve colour – she lit her first cigarette in two months with a mixture of remorse and defiance.

Come on, nicotine, kill me softly.

Cigarette in her right hand and telephone in her left: the grand total of her addictions. All day, Claire had been checking her BlackBerry, frantic to see the little flashing red light showing she had an email or a text message. She was waiting for a call or a sign from a man. A man she'd left New York to get away from. A man who loved her, but to whom she'd never said 'I love you'. A man whom she'd treated badly. A man she'd cheated on, disappointed and hurt. For the sole reason of seeing whether he would still love her. Of seeing whether he was capable of putting up with the worst. Because it was the only way she knew how to love. One day, maybe, if the man stuck around, if he was patient and obstinate enough to wait for her, she would open her heart to him, say things to him that would change everything.

She fiddled nervously with her phone. The man hadn't rung her for a whole week. Maybe, like the others, he'd given up. She tried not to think about him and absent-mindedly connected to the hospital server. Clicking on the various links, she came across a paper by Elliott Cooper about the accidents on the Golden Gate Bridge. She discovered that since it had been opened in 1937, 1,219 people had killed themselves by jumping into the ocean: approximately 20 a year. Only 27 had lived!

About 2 per cent, she thought sadly.

She knew from experience that that kind of statistic did not lie.

8.15 p.m.

The repetitive beep of a submarine sonar.

A cold bluish room: the intensive care unit at Lenox Hospital.

Two steel trolleys, separated by only a few yards.

Between the two trolleys, a woman sitting on a chair, bent over, face in hands, exhausted from crying.

A guard, a sentinel.

On the trolleys, two men, eyes closed, in a coma.

Two men who'd preferred to fight rather than try to understand one another.

Two men who'd loved the same woman each in their own way.

Or, rather, who hadn't known how to love her.

8.30 p.m.

Claire Giuliani stubbed out her last cigarette and buttoned up her army coat, its collar studded with large safety pins. In theory, her shift was over. It was Christmas Eve. She was going to turn thirty. If she'd been like other women, she'd have been celebrating now with her family or with a boyfriend or in the staff room, which the interns had decorated for the occasion. But Claire was incapable

279

of pretending. She only liked the troubled exclusivity of intimate relationships and, failing that, had learnt to make do with the solitude which her profession forced on her anyway. A profession whose proximity to death destroyed her a little more each day while at the same time allowing her to form invisible links with some of her patients. Links that kept her going, and which on nights like this felt like her only connection with the rest of humanity.

Outwardly, she'd succeeded in life. She was a surgeon, and with a little more time and effort she could have been pretty, could have played at being one of life's daily heroines à la *Grey's Anatomy* – one with a hot body and a sexy intellect. But that wasn't her style.

She looked at her phone screen again. Still no flashing red light.

And what if she called him?

What if she dared to reveal her vulnerability to this man? She'd done it once, a long time ago, and had emerged bruised and bleeding, feeling as though she'd been through a firestorm. She'd vowed never to expose herself to that again, but as she grew older she realised that it was easier to live with remorse than with regret.

She scrolled down her address book on the tiny screen, stopping at the enigmatic entry: *Him.*

She placed a shaking finger on the call button, paused to reflect for a few seconds and then, feeling a sudden surge of affection, was about to press it when …

Another ambulance came hurtling in, pulling up in front of the automatic doors, where a young girl was taken out on a stretcher, unconscious, her face streaked with mascara.

280

Claire walked over. Why wasn't anybody there to take charge of the injured girl?

She automatically leant over the stretcher. The girl was wearing a pair of jeans that were too low cut and a pink T-shirt that was too tight and had the ambiguous words *Not a saint* printed on it.

'What have we got?' she asked one of the ambulance drivers.

'Fourteen-year-old female attempted suicide from swallowing toxic products: sodium chlorate, glyphosate and pentachlorophenol.'

'Claire, is everything OK?' a muffled voice asked. She glanced down at her phone. It was his voice. She hesitated for a second then decided to switch her phone off and attend to her patient. A real suicide attempt at fourteen …

The past really was coming back to haunt her in a strange way that night.

25

THE DEPARTURE
LOUNGE

Don't dream of what you do not have as if it were already yours; count the treasures you do have, and think how much you would dream of them, if they were not already yours.

Marcus Aurelius

Blackness.
Blackness.
Blackness.
A whisper:
... my love ...
Blackness.
A buzzing sound.
The repetitive beep of a submarine sonar.
A loud rhythmical sound like mechanical breathing.
The awareness of a faint light and then ...
Martin opened his eyes with difficulty. He was drenched in sweat; he felt groggy and short of breath. His eyelids were sticky, full of a thick gluey liquid. His face was burning up; he wiped his eyes with his sleeve and looked around.

He was in an airport, slumped over the metal seats in a departure lounge. He sat up straight and leapt to his feet.

He looked at his watch: it was 8.10 a.m., 25 December.

In a chair next to him, a young girl with dirty-blond hair had experienced the same painful awakening. He noticed the look of terror on her face, the streaked mascara, the T-shirt with the words: *Not a saint*.

Where was he?

He walked over to the picture window. The airport terminal was one big space flooded with light: a futuristic cathedral made of steel and glass, a transparent elliptical dome, the far end of which stretched out to the sea like an enormous ship. On the runways, a row of silvery planes were waiting to take off. Bathed in a warm golden light, the building resembled a transparent bubble sitting next to the water, cut off from any outside noise.

Was this heaven? Hell? Purgatory? No, even when he went to Sunday School as a child, Martin had never believed in church dogma or in its representations.

What then? A dream?

No, everything was too precise, too vivid to be anything but real.

He massaged his temples and his neck with his thumbs. He remembered everything he'd done in the past few hours: Gabrielle's betrayal, the theft of the diamond, his confrontation with Archibald on the bridge and their 230-foot plunge. That he hadn't dreamt, therefore he could only be … dead.

He tried to swallow some saliva, but his throat was parched. He wiped the sweat off his face.

At the end of the row of departure doors, he noticed a bar with tables looking out over the runways: the Golden Gate Café.

An appropriate name, he thought as he approached the counter where a beautiful mixed-race girl wearing shorts and a low-necked tank top was serving.

'What can I get you, sir?'

'Er ... could I have some water?'

'Fizzy or still?'

'Do you have any Evian?'

She ran her fingers through her flaming red hair and looked at him as if he were a country bumpkin.

'Of course.'

'And a Coca Cola too?'

'Where are you from?'

He paid – ten dollars! – for his bottle of water and his can of Coke and returned to the rows of metal seats. The young girl in the provocative T-shirt was still there shivering, her teeth chattering. Martin handed her his bottle of water, guessing that she was dying of thirst.

'What's your name?'

'Lizzie,' she replied, after drinking nearly half the bottle in one go.

'Do you feel OK?'

'Where are we?' she asked, sobbing.

Martin avoided the question. She was bathed in sweat and shivering all over. Her vulnerability reminded him of Camille, the little girl he'd visited for several years. He gave her the can of Coke and left her for a moment while he went to look in one of the terminal shops.

When he came back, he tossed her a Berkeley University sweatshirt.

'Put that on – you're going to catch cold.'

She pulled on the sweatshirt after nodding meekly at him, which no doubt meant thanks in the language of lost teenagers.

'How old are you?' he asked, sitting down next to her.

'Fourteen.'

'Where do you live?'

'Here in San Francisco, near Pacific Heights.'

'Do you remember the last thing you did before finding yourself here?'

Lizzie wiped away the tears running down her face.

'No. I was at home … I cried a lot and then I swallowed some stuff … Stuff to make me die.'

'What stuff? Pills?'

'No, Mom had locked the medicine cabinet.'

'What then?'

'I went out to the garden shed and swallowed whatever I could find, rat poison and weedkiller.'

Martin was concerned. 'Why did you do that?'

'Because of Cameron.'

'Who's he? Your boyfriend?'

She nodded.

'He doesn't love me any more. And yet we were so happy.'

He looked at her sadly. Whether you were lovesick at fifteen, twenty, forty or seventy-five, it was always the same story: that fucking disease struck down everything in its path, with its moments of fleeting happiness, but at what price?

285

Still, Martin tried to make a joke out of it.

'If you're already trying to kill yourself over boys at fourteen you've got a long way to go!'

But Lizzie could tell that something wasn't right.

'Where are we?' she repeated, terrified.

'I have no idea,' he confessed, getting up, 'but I can tell you we're going to get out of here fast.'

*

He ran.

With the young girl behind him, Martin ran. It didn't matter where this place was, he knew he had to get out and the sooner the better.

This wasn't a dream, it wasn't heaven or hell, you couldn't buy five-dollar cans of Coke in heaven – this was something else.

And it was from this 'something else' that he had to escape.

He decided to trust the signs and followed the ones saying 'Exit – Taxi – Bus'.

These led them to the duty-free area where all the luxury brands from Hermès to Gucci had a retail outlet. Then they crossed a food court with its twenty neon signs clustered around a central atrium offering a huge variety of culinary specialities: hamburgers, salads, sushi, pizzas, couscous, kebabs, seafood …

At regular intervals, Martin turned round to look at Lizzie, to encourage her to quicken her pace.

They took an escalator and then an endless moving walkway like the one at Gare Montparnasse in Paris, except that this one was actually working.

286

The building was long and narrow and comfortingly clean and bright. Several teams of cleaners were busy polishing the picture windows whose surface rippled like water under the changing yellow light.

The crowd was bustling and in holiday mood as they hurried to get away. Hats and scarves, runny noses, gift-wrapped presents: some of them were going to celebrate Christmas. Others looked summery with their Bermuda shorts and surfers' tans.

Martin took Lizzie's hand and began running faster, jostling the people in his path: crumpled-looking executives playing at being businessmen, youngsters drowsily listening to their iPods.

On every wall, clocks were a reminder of time passing.

Staring up at the signs, Martin kept running, guided by a sense of urgency. Soon they were nearing the exit. He pulled Lizzie's arm to make her run even faster.

They arrived in the main departure lounge. For the first time, Martin was aware of the outside world: the noise of traffic, the animated sounds, harshness, life …

Just as they finally reached the sliding doors which led out onto the tarmac there was a violent blast, which deafened them and blurred their vision.

When Martin opened his eyes again, he was facing the same row of metal seats as when he'd first woken up. Behind him was the same souvenir shop and the same Golden Gate Café with the same black waitress with flaming red hair.

He looked at Lizzie apologetically: they'd ended up right where they'd started!

287

'There's no point in trying to find the way out, kid, we're stuck here.'

Martin turned round.

Face calm, eyes sharp, Archibald blew out a cloud of smoke from his Havana cigar. Clearly the airport wasn't a no-smoking zone. So it was true, even God smoked Havana cigars. Maybe getting cancer when you were dead wasn't as bad as getting it when you were still alive.

'This is all your fault,' said Martin, pointing an accusatory finger at him.

'It's as much your fault as it is mine,' Archie corrected. 'If you hadn't tried to be so clever, we'd still be there.'

Archibald was feeling good. The exhaustion, pain and nausea associated with his illness had miraculously disappeared.

'You killed us both,' Martin cried out. 'Because of your inordinate pride.'

'I think you're just as much of an expert in the pride department, kid.'

'Stop calling me "kid"!'

'You're right. I'm sorry, kid. But where you're mistaken is in thinking that we're dead.'

'Think about it for a moment. We fell at least 230 feet into freezing-cold water. Can you imagine the injuries?'

'True,' conceded Archibald with a frown; 'even so, we're not dead. At least not yet.'

'OK, but in that case where are we?'

'Yes, where are we?' insisted Lizzie.

288

Archibald smiled at the teenager and with a movement of his hand gestured to the two of them to follow him.

'I want you to meet somebody.'

'No!' Martin said. 'Not until you tell us where we are.'

Archie shrugged, then, as if stating the obvious, said, 'In a coma.'

*

Martin, Archibald and Lizzie walked through the door marked 'Prayer Zone'. The place consisted of a reception area and a series of small rooms set aside for the various denominations: a chapel, a synagogue, a mosque, a Buddhist and Shinto sanctuary.

It was run by Father Shake Powell, the airport chaplain, a tall black man, built like a wrestler, who wore Nike Air trainers, a pair of baggy trousers, a hooded tracksuit top and a 'Yes We Can' Obama T-shirt.

Shake Powell greeted the visitors in his office, a cosy yet bare room overlooking the runways. Although very busy, the chaplain was more than willing to answer the newcomers' questions. He offered them a cup of coffee and without them asking began telling them about himself.

' Originally from New York, Powell had been visiting his brother in San Francisco when ten months previously he'd been stabbed in the back as he tried to stop a fight between two homeless people. When he'd arrived at the departure lounge, he'd been trained by the former chaplain before he left for distant lands.

He loved his job. Here, he claimed, God was everywhere: in the building, in the light, in the glass ceilings looking up

289

to the sky. He'd even performed marriages and baptisms.

The departure lounge was a frontier, a no man's land, a place conducive to prayer and meditation. In this 'other world', people felt their deepest fears resurface. And when it was time to leave they felt the need to confess. It wasn't Father Powell's place to judge, but to understand. For some people it meant coming to terms with their fear of the unknown, their guilt or their regret. For others this retreat was a wonderful and unexpected opportunity, which allowed them to become better people or to be at peace with themselves.

'In the departure lounge, I've witnessed every aspect of the human soul up close in all its glory as well as its wretchedness,' he explained, finishing his coffee.

Martin had let Shake Powell conclude his account. He'd understood from it that all the passengers in this mysterious airport were in a coma following an accident or a suicide attempt, but there was still one unanswered question:

'You keep talking about the departure lounge,' he began.

'Yes.'

'But departure to *where*?'

Powell studied Martin and then Lizzie and shook his head.

'Look at the planes,' he said, turning towards the window.

Martin looked out at the runway. He could see two parallel strips and two rows of jumbo jets shimmering in the sun, waiting for the signal from the control tower before taking off in opposite directions.

290

'There can only be two destinations,' announced Shake Powell, zipping up his tracksuit top which showed off his impressively muscular body.

'The return to life or the departure towards death,' Martin concluded glumly.

'You've got it, kid,' said Archibald approvingly.

Lizzie looked at the chaplain's two huge hands, the fingers of which were tattooed with the letters L.I.F.E. and D.E.A.T.H.

Stammering, it was she who brought herself to ask, 'But how can we know where we're going?'

'It's printed on your ticket.'

'What ticket?' asked Martin.

'The ticket given to every traveller in the departure lounge,' explained Powell.

'You mean a ticket like this one?' declared Archibald, placing his own boarding pass on the table.

Depart: Departure lounge
Destination: <u>Life</u>
Date: 26 December 2008
Time: 07.05
Seat no: 32F

Martin frowned. He was wearing the same clothes as on the day of the accident: the made-to-measure suit given to him by Mademoiselle Ho and a crumpled shirt which hung outside his trousers. He rummaged in his jacket pocket and found his wallet, his phone and a piece of card which he in turn placed on the table.

Depart: Departure lounge
Destination: <u>Death</u>
Date: 26 December 2008
Time: 09.00
Seat no: 6A

'Bad luck, kid.' Archibald frowned.

And then both men turned towards Lizzie, a quizzical look on their faces.

Lost in her oversized sweatshirt, the young girl had a look of terror on her face.

She fumbled in her jean pockets and finally found her boarding pass folded in half. She opened it with shaking hands. The card bore bad news.

Depart: Departure lounge
Destination: <u>Death</u>
Date: 26 December 2008
Time: 09.00
Seat no: 6B

26

THE BEAUTIFUL THINGS THAT HEAVEN BEARS

Then, for the last time, I saw the earth – an enduring globule of radiant blue, swimming in an eternity of ether. And there I, a fragile flake of soul dust, flickered silently across the void, from the distant blue, into the expanse of the unknown.
William Hope Hodgson

Departure lounge
11.46 p.m.
The Canopy of Heaven was the finest restaurant in the departure lounge.

Thirty or so circular tables with cream-coloured tablecloths were neatly laid out in a large, elegant, modern room. On the wall an amazing luminous curtain made of hundreds of optical fibres bathed the space in a soft light, giving it a warm, stylish feel. In the centre of the room, a modern fireplace added a touch of cosiness to the scene.

Even here, at the gates of heaven, the customers were no different from those you'd find in any luxury establishment: wealthy Russians and Chinese, Middle

Eastern oil magnates. The global elites dripping in Louis Vuitton.

In the middle of this illustrious company Martin and Archibald sat at a table near the huge picture windows which reflected the lights of the runway. Despite the late hour, planes continued to take off relentlessly.

'You look out of sorts, kid,' commented Archibald, who was thoroughly enjoying a plate of roasted calf sweetbreads accompanied by fresh pasta and forest mushrooms.

Martin had only taken a few mouthfuls of his Aveyron lamb.

'It's easy to stuff your face when you know you're going to come out of it alive! I'm going to die, remember.'

'We're all going to die at some time or other,' argued Archibald.

'Yes, but for me that's tomorrow morning!'

'You're right, it's unfair,' admitted the thief. 'I'm twice your age, and I'm the one who dragged you into this mess.'

He poured himself another glass of wine and put the bottle down on the small trolley next to the table. Mouton-Rothschild 1945 and Romanée-Conti 1985: the finest wines for an evening like no other.

'Are you sure you don't want to taste the Burgundy?' insisted Archibald. 'It would be a shame to die without having tasted such magnificence.'

'Fuck you and your Burgundy!' Martin shot back in a weary voice.

Her head resting against his shoulder, Lizzie had fallen asleep on the banquette. In front of her sat the remains of her hamburger royale with extra cheese and bacon.

Archibald took a box of matches from his pocket and fashioned a toothpick with his penknife, an old habit which was out of place in this discreet, sophisticated restaurant.

'I'm wondering whether to be tempted by the pigeon with foie gras before I go on to dessert,' he said, leafing through the menu. 'What do you think?'

This time, Martin chose not to rise to the bait.

Through the window, he looked out at the starry sky. He was particularly fascinated by the bright star he had thought was the moon. Maybe it was Earth, that blue planet floating in the distance with its inhabitants who systematically loved, killed and destroyed one another.

That planet where he'd always felt so alone but which he found difficult to leave.

'We've got to talk about it, kid.'

Martin looked up. Above the crystal glasses, Archibald's eyes burnt with a feverish light. He looked drawn and from the expression on his gaunt face it was clear that he was no longer in the mood for joking.

'And what do you want us to talk about?'

'Gabrielle.'

Martin sighed. 'What do you want to know? What my intentions were?'

'Precisely.'

'My intentions were of the most noble kind possible, but in any case, it's over for me.'

He decided to pour himself a glass of wine before continuing.

'And do you want to know something? Your daughter is a dangerous woman. Like you! She's a lunatic who destroys happiness each time it shows its face.'

A waiter came over to clear their plates. Archibald skipped dessert and imperiously ordered two coffees.

'I've got some good news and some bad news for you this evening, kid.'

Martin sighed. 'The way things are I think I'd prefer to hear the good news first.'

'The good news is that you're the first, the only man she has ever loved.'

'How would you know? You've hardly had anything to do with your daughter for thirty years! You don't know her.'

'That's what you think. But I'm going to tell you something.'

'Go on ...'

'It may seem incredible, but I know Gabrielle better than anyone.'

'Better than I do?'

'Yes, of course, but then that's not difficult.' Seeing Martin's eyes flash with rage, Archie raised his hand in a gesture of appeasement. 'Gabrielle is an extraordinary woman. To your credit, it seems you were able to recognise that even as a very young man.'

Knowing how rare it was to receive a compliment from the older man, Martin felt quite pleased.

'Gabrielle is open, sincere and generous,' Archie went on. 'A little complicated at times, like all women.'

Martin nodded. Men always agreed on that point.

'Gabrielle,' Archie resumed, 'is one in a million, a rare and precious stone, rarer even than the diamond I planned to steal.'

The two espressos came with a small plate of sweetmeats. Archie took one of the sugared figs.

'Gabrielle has character, she has personality, but anyone who bothers to look beneath the surface would realise that she's been scarred by life. Again, you recognised that immediately.'

'Where are you going with this?' demanded Martin impatiently before downing his scalding coffee in one gulp.

'Where am I going? No one could accuse you of being perceptive, could they? Gabrielle doesn't need an immature bloke who is stuck in the past. She doesn't need another man who is going to make her suffer even more than the others. She needs someone who will be everything for her: her friend, her boyfriend, her confidant, her lover and even sometimes her enemy … Do you know what that means?'

'That someone was me, you imbecile. And it would still be me today if you hadn't come along and stuck your oar in.'

Furious, Martin stood up and …

Lenox Hospital
1.09 a.m.
'Dr Giuliani! Wake up!'

The nurse switched on the fluorescent lights in the on-call room. Claire opened her eyes. She hadn't been asleep. She hadn't actually slept properly for years. Each night she snatched little bursts of sleep now and then, bursts of sleep that no longer refreshed her but left her with the constant feeling of being worn out, and with permanent dark circles under her eyes.

'Here are the results of Martin Beaumont's scan. His blood pressure is sky high!'

Claire put on her reading glasses and held the X-ray up to the fluorescent light. This second brain scan was alarming: blood had accumulated between the dura mater and the brain, producing a worryingly large haematoma. Inside the meninges, several branches of one artery must have ruptured all at once to cause such haemorrhaging. The haematoma was compressing the brain inside the skull, and if they didn't intervene immediately the blood vessels would also be compressed, which would starve the cells of oxygen and cause irreversible damage.

Martin would need to be operated on straight away if they were to have any chance of relieving the pressure on his brain, but his body was so weakened that Claire was doubtful that he would survive it.

'Call the anaesthetist, we're going to operate.'

Departure lounge
1.12 a.m.
Archibald pushed open the door of Harry's Bar.

The hushed and cosy atmosphere, the mahogany panelling, old leather Chesterfield armchairs and red velvet benches conjured up a London club, the kind of place where men would meet to smoke cigars and drink brandy before a game of bridge.

298

He crossed the smoking room and joined Martin at the bar, where he was sipping a mojito.

On seeing the young policeman's cocktail, he couldn't help smirking a little. 'That's a bit of a girl's drink, isn't it?'

Martin chose to ignore the remark.

With a connoisseur's eye, Archibald scrutinised the impressive collection of whiskies lined up behind the bar, like old tomes on a bookshelf. His eyes lit up when he spotted a treasure: a Glenfiddich Rare Collection from 1937, the oldest Scotch in the world.

He ordered a glass and looked appreciatively at the precious amber liquid.

'Leave the bottle on the bar, young man!' he told the barman.

Martin was watching him out of the corner of his eye. Now Archie was breathing in the aromas rising from his glass with undisguised relish, enjoying the hints of caramel, chocolate, peach and cinnamon. Then he took a swig of the single malt and savoured the subtle flavours.

He poured out a glass and offered it to Martin. 'Try that, lad! Your tipple isn't a patch on that, you'll see.'

Martin sighed, but Archibald had tickled his curiosity. He took a gulp of the whisky, and, even though he was no expert, he let himself be seduced by the complex flavour of the powerful nectar.

'So? What do you think?'

'Yeah, it certainly packs a punch!' Martin agreed, knocking back more of the Scotch.

'You know, I'm starting to like you! Come on, let's go and sit somewhere quieter,' Archie suggested, taking the bottle of Glenfiddich with him.

Martin hesitated for a moment before following him. He bore Archibald an enormous grudge, but he couldn't stand the thought of spending his last hours alone. And he found he enjoyed the company of his arch-enemy despite his annoyance.

The two men seated themselves on leather sofas arranged around a low table made of varnished acacia and mango wood.

'Can I offer you a cigar?'

Martin declined. 'You do know that there are other pleasures in life apart from drinking, smoking and stealing paintings?'

'I'm not taking any lessons from you, with your cannabis and your Coke Zero. You think that's good for your health?'

Martin frowned. Archie smiled thinly.

'Ah, yes, you see, I do know a bit about you, Martin Beaumont.'

'And what exactly do you know?'

'I know that you are someone who is brave and sincere. I know you're an idealist, that people trust you and that your heart is in the right place.'

'But ...'

'But what?'

'When someone begins with a bunch of compliments, it normally means they're about to criticise you, don't you think?'

Archie widened his eyes. 'Criticise? I can think of a few things if you want me to.'

Martin took up the challenge. 'Go on, don't hold back.'

'For starters, you don't understand women.'

'I don't understand women!'

'No. That is, you see things in them that others don't, but you don't understand them when they talk to you. You can't decode what they're saying.'

'Oh, really? For example?'

Archibald screwed up his eyes as he searched for an example.

'When a woman says *no*, that can often mean *yes, but I'm scared.*'

'Er, right … go on.'

'When she says *perhaps*, that can often mean *no.*'

'And when she says *yes*?'

'When she says *yes*, that means *yes, maybe.*'

'And when she simply wants to say *yes*?'

Archie shrugged his shoulders. 'I'm not sure a straightforward *yes* really exists in a woman's language.'

Martin was sceptical. 'In my opinion, you're a better thief than psychologist.'

'Maybe I am lacking recent experience,' Archibald agreed.

'And what about talking about Gabrielle instead?'

'We were talking about her, lad. I thought you'd grasped that.'

'Why did you try to break us up?'

Archie raised his eyes to heaven.

'You've got it the wrong way round, you idiot! It was me who came looking for you, me who did everything I could to make you pursue me, me who lured you to San Francisco so that you'd find her again, because I knew that she hadn't forgotten you!'

301

The tone was becoming heated.

'And after that?' Martin asked.

'After that, it's true that I got scared and I wanted to test you,' Archibald admitted.

'You ruined everything!'

'No, because without me you wouldn't have had the courage to come and find her! Because that's your problem, Martin Beaumont: you're afraid!'

Martin wasn't sure he'd understood.

Archie pressed the point. 'You know that quote of Mandela's: "It is our light, not our darkness, that most frightens us." What scares you, lad, is not your weaknesses, but your strengths. It's kind of freaky, isn't it, to tell yourself that you've got lots of tricks up your sleeve? Much more reassuring to bathe in your own mediocrity, while cursing the whole world.'

'What are you getting at?'

'I'm trying to give you some advice: put your fears aside and take the risk of being happy.'

Martin stared at Archibald. On his face was no trace of a threat or of animosity, only understanding. For the second time, Martin felt tied to him by some strange bond.

'You said earlier that you had some good news and some bad news.'

'That's exactly what I wanted to come to.'

'What's the bad news?'

Archibald tried to tread carefully, then announced, 'The bad news is that you're the one going back, kid!' He laid down his boarding card as if showing four aces.

Depart: Departure lounge
Destination: <u>Life</u>
Date: 26 December 2008
Time: 07.05
Seat no: 32F

'I don't understand.'

'You thought you'd done with love and all that hassle? Well, nope, it's not that easy. You're going back in my place.'

'A swap?'

'Yep. Boarding cards aren't named. Nothing to stop us exchanging them.'

'Why are you doing this?'

'Oh, don't you go thinking that I'm sacrificing myself. In any case, I have neither the strength nor the opportunity to fulfil my dreams.'

'You're ill?'

'Condemned would be more accurate – a lousy cancer.'

Martin shook his head, his eyes clouded.

'And … why me?'

The bar had by now emptied. Only the barman continued to polish the glasses behind the counter.

'Because it was only you, lad, who knew how to solve the equation – who had the courage to follow me here. Because you were cleverer than the FBI, the Russian mafia and all the police forces in the world combined. Because you use your head and your heart as well. Because you've taken some blows, but you're still standing. Because, in a way, you're just like me, except that you're going to succeed where I failed. You're going to learn how to love.'

McLean poured them each another drink, draining the bottle. They raised their glasses and, as they clinked them, they swapped tickets.

Then Archie looked at his watch and got up from his chair.

'You'll have to excuse me, but I've not got much time left and there's one last thing I want to do before tomorrow morning.'

He pulled on his coat, then, after a moment's hesitation, said, 'You know, about Gabrielle … She can seem complicated, but in fact she's transparent. Don't make her suffer, not even for a minute.'

'It's a promise,' Martin said.

'Right, I'm no good at goodbyes …'

'Good luck.'

'Same to you, kid.'

27

ANYWHERE OUT OF THE WORLD

What have I left, from loving you?
Just my voice, with no sudden echo
Just my fingers, which grasp nothing
Just my skin, which seeks your hands
And above all fear, of loving you still
Tomorrow, almost dead.
Charles Aznavour

Lenox Hospital
3.58 a.m.
For the first time in a long while, Claire Giuliani was genuinely happy. The operation had gone remarkably well. She had opened up Martin's skull in order to drain the haematoma.

The surgery was coming to a close. She looked at the monitor: the vital signs were good. This young French guy had a really strong constitution!

Claire smiled. Her iPod, which was plugged into the speakers, was playing a Bob Marley hit.

Departure lounge
3.59 a.m.
Bob Marley's 'No Woman, No Cry' blared from the airport speakers.

Martin wandered up and down in front of the glass wall overlooking the runways with their landing lights. The airport's parking aprons stretched away into the distance, accommodating dozens of identical aircraft: long-haul double-decker four-engine airliners, whose precise sequence of movements was directed by an immense control tower with bluish sides.

Invested with a renewed confidence and hunger for life, Martin thought back over the events of the last five months: from his first confrontation with Archibald on a bridge in Paris up to this evening's strange discussion in the out-of-the-world bar. Five months during which he had unwittingly undergone a dramatic transformation that had made a man of him. The last conversation with Archibald had freed him from his fears. From that point onwards he had felt empowered – he was on a mission.

In the long corridor bathed in light, his hand gripped the new boarding card Archie had given him: his magic pass, his return ticket to life and love.

In the long corridor bathed in light, he felt an urge to run and to shout out his relief.

In the long corridor bathed in light, he lived again.

Departure lounge
4.21 a.m.
The restaurant was empty. All the chandeliers in the main

dining room were turned off. Lit only by the faint light coming from the skirting boards, it was like a silenced nightclub, deserted by all its dancers.

Huddled up on her banquette, Lizzie tossed and turned in her sleep, strands of hair stuck to her careworn face.

Martin covered her with his jacket before sitting down in an armchair opposite her.

She was fourteen years old; he was pushing thirty-five.

She could have been his daughter.

He'd only known her for a few hours, but he felt a duty towards her.

He lit a cigarette, smoking it silently with his eyes closed.

Childhood.

His own childhood.

Memories surfaced, neither good nor bad. As did an echo that he would have preferred to keep at bay, but which still resounded loudly.

The housing estates, Évry …

The often prison-like atmosphere of the playground.

For his own peace of mind, he'd always come to the defence of the weakest kids, even though he sometimes ran the risk of having to pay a very high price for it: retaliation or being left out, and no thanks from those he'd helped.

But what he did wasn't in any way deserving.

The strongest should protect the weakest, rather than oppressing or neglecting them: that was what he firmly believed; it was part of him.

It was an ideal that he'd always lived by and that had enabled him, even in the darkest hours of his work, to face himself in the mirror without shame.

Departure lounge
4.35 a.m.

Archibald hurried. The floor was silvery and smooth like a mirror.

He had already walked for miles, but wherever he went the airport seemed to be endlessly replicating itself. He had crossed a succession of halls, travelled on a dozen moving walkways, walked through several shopping malls, but to no avail: it was impossible to put any real distance between himself and the immense transparent picture windows that blurred the separation between building, sea and sky.

Like the one in Hong Kong, the airport seemed to emerge from an artificial island. Everything about it was streamlined, modern, too new, like a building awaiting its official opening.

Archie looked at the time on the display screens and clenched his hand round his boarding card. He had just a few hours before departure, but ever since he'd woken up in this out-of-the-world place, one thing had become obvious. Perhaps he was being naïve, perhaps he was mistaken, but he had to pursue his idea to the bitter end. Each time he came across an airport employee – security guard, waiter, shopkeeper, maintenance worker – he would stop to ask the same question. To begin with, he'd drawn a blank, but the shop assistant on the Ladurée macaroon stand had sent him off on another track. And that had given him hope.

He sensed that he was approaching the hour of truth, the moment that could redeem all the others.

After all, in amongst all the woes it offered, life also served you up some great moments. Why should death be any different?

Departure lounge
6.06 a.m.
Lizzie was woken by the smell of cocoa.

As she opened her eyes, day was dawning over the runways. Soon the first rays of sunlight would be beating down from the purplish-pink sky.

Despite a night's sleep, she wasn't looking too good: her clothes were rumpled, her hair tangled, her nails bitten down to the quick.

She rubbed her eyes, took a moment to work out where she was and stared with terror at the clock on the wall, then at the glass screen displaying the departure schedule.

She rummaged through her pocket and pulled out her plane ticket.

Depart: Departure lounge
Destination: <u>Death</u>
Date: 26 December 2008
Time: 09.00
Seat no: 6B

Only three hours. Only three hours before the …

'Greek yogurt, fresh raspberries, lychees, toast and a nice cup of hot chocolate!' Martin said cheerfully, as he placed the breakfast tray on the table.

309

He smiled at her, sat down beside her on the banquette and buttered her some toast.

She drank a mouthful of cocoa before tucking heartily into the slice of toast. One couldn't live off love and fresh air, even in the departure lounge.

'Hey, the postman's been,' he joked, handing her an envelope.

Looking hesitant, she didn't move, holding the envelope in her hands.

'Well, open it then!'

She tore open the envelope to discover a new ticket.

Depart: Departure lounge
Destination: <u>Life</u>
Date: 26 December 2008
Time: 07.05
Seat no: 32F

'The departure time's been brought forward,' Martin explained. 'But it's not the same destination!'

'Does this mean I'm not going to die now?' she asked, full of hope.

'No, Lizzie, you're not going to die now.'

Her lip quivered, her throat tightened.

'But how come …?'

'It was Archibald,' Martin explained. 'The man with us last night. He left his ticket for you.'

'Why did he do that?'

'Because he's very ill and hasn't much time left to live.'

'I haven't even thanked him!'

310

'I thanked him for you,' he reassured her.

Tears welled in the teenager's eyes. 'And what about you?'

'Don't you worry about me,' Martin replied, forcing a smile. 'But I would like you to do me a favour.'

'A favour?' she asked, wiping her eyes on her sleeve.

'Did you say you lived in Pacific Heights?'

'Yes,' she nodded. 'Just behind Lafayette Park.'

'Then, if we really are in a coma, you're going to wake up in Lenox Hospital.'

'That's where they took me when I split my chin open playing basketball!' She pointed to a very delicate scar that started at the corner of her mouth.

'Ouch!' Martin winced. 'Did it hurt?'

'No, I'm a tough nut!' she said, with a certain pride.

He winked at her and explained what he wanted her to do. 'When you're able to talk, you should ask to see a woman called Gabrielle.'

'Is she a doctor?'

'No, she's the woman … she's the woman I love.'

She couldn't contain her curiosity. 'And does she love you?'

'Yes.' He hesitated. 'At least, it's complicated … Hey, you know what it's like.'

'Yeah. Love affairs, always complicated, even when you're a grown-up, right?'

He nodded in agreement. 'Yes, always the same mess. Except that one day it will be the right person at the right time, and then everything will be simple and straightforward.'

She nodded. 'And Gabrielle, is she the right person?'

'Yes,' Martin smiled. 'And this is also the right time.'

'What do I need to tell her?'

Lenox Hospital
6.15 a.m.

'Doctor, we've a problem with our mystery patient!'

Elliott took the liver scan results from the nurse.

Archibald was haemorrhaging around his liver.

Elliott put on his glasses; the wound was deep, causing a lot of bleeding behind the right lobe.

How was this possible? He hadn't suspected any of this during that first operation a few hours earlier.

He would have to be opened up again immediately, even though a new laparotomy might kill him.

Damn it!

Departure lounge
6.56 a.m.

'Hey, Lizzie!'

At gate number six, the queue of passengers was getting shorter as boarding got under way for those lucky enough to be 'going back'.

The young girl turned round. Martin had caught up with her to say one last thing.

'No more of this crap, OK?'

She looked down.

Martin went on. 'Rat poison, weedkiller, slashed wrists, overdoses, you're gonna forget all that, right?'

'Sure,' she said, with a slight smile – the first for a long time.

'And also, don't worry about it all. Love is fabulous, but it's not the only thing that counts in life.'

'Really?' she asked seriously.

Yes, it is the only thing that counts. The only thing that really matters, thought Martin. But he decided to put on a brave face.

'Family, friends, travel, books, music, cinema, that's all pretty good too, don't you think?'

'Yes,' she agreed, with little enthusiasm.

The teenager was now the only one not to have boarded.

'Go on, *bon voyage!*' Martin said, giving her a little tap on the shoulder.

'See you soon?' she asked, giving her boarding pass to the stewardess.

He smiled at her and gave her a final wave.

Then she was gone.

7.06 a.m.
Claire Giuliani stuck her head out of the car window.

'Move it, Grandpa!' she shouted to the driver of a fat saloon car dawdling along in front of her.

Her mauve VW Beetle was stuck in traffic.

'This cannot be happening! Seven a.m. and there's already a traffic jam!' she exploded.

On top of that, it was raining heavily and her old banger wasn't too keen on the wet.

Its smoky interior was filled with the guitar chords of The Doors and Jim Morrison's alcohol-fuelled cool voice belting out a pirated copy of 'LA Woman'.

Right in the middle of the song, a musician had the crazy idea of playing a Mozart air on a harpsichord.

Frowning, Claire stubbed out her cigarette.

That wasn't in the song, no, that was her mobile phone.

At the end of the line was her favourite nurse, with whom she had left instructions to be kept informed of the progress of 'her' two patients.

Clearly, Martin Beaumont's condition had suddenly deteriorated. The scan results showed uncontrolled haemorrhaging around the pancreas. Strange. On the scans from that night, the lesions hadn't seemed so major.

He'd have to be operated on again, but how often could the man's body take such trauma?

Lenox Hospital, intensive care unit
7.11 a.m.
Red cells, white cells, platelets, plasma …

Blood.

The soiled, poisoned blood of a fourteen-year-old girl.

For several hours, the red liquid had been pumped by dialysis machine to rid it of toxins before being pumped back, once purified, into Lizzie's veins. It was a shock

314

treatment, accomplishing in record time what it would take the kidneys two days to do.

Stretched out, eyes closed, the teenager had had her stomach pumped. She'd been given activated carbon and high doses of vitamin K1 to clean her blood, which had been prevented from clotting by the rat poison.

After that, the vital signs on the monitor were good.

After that, there was nothing to stop Lizzie from opening her eyes.

And that's what she did.

Lenox Hospital, emergency room waiting area
7.32 a.m.

Gabrielle slid two coins into the coffee machine.

She hadn't slept for forty-eight hours.

Her ears were buzzing, her legs had turned to jelly, she was shivering, she no longer knew if it was day or night, midday or midnight.

She had spoken to Elliott, whom she'd known for a long time, and to the female surgeon taking care of Martin. Neither medic had given her much hope.

'Are you Gabrielle?'

Confused, she turned to find herself face to face with a man of about the same age as her, whose clothing was just as crumpled, whose face was just as sunken and whose eyes were just as tired, except that they were shining with relief.

'My daughter Lizzie has just come out of a coma after

315

an overdose,' he explained. 'And the first thing she asked for was to see you.'

'I beg your pardon?'

'She claims to have a message for you.'

'There must be some mistake, I don't know anyone called Lizzie,' she replied tersely, still wrapped up in her own pain.

He tried to stop her from going, begging her almost. 'These last three years, since separating from my wife, I don't think I've seen my daughter grow up. In any case, I'm sure that I haven't talked to her enough, or rather haven't listened to her enough. I think we're ready, she and I, to try to talk and trust each other more. She made me promise that I would do everything to bring you to her, so, if you don't mind, I'm going to insist: please, just give her a few minutes.'

Gabrielle made a superhuman effort to rise out of her apathy.

'You say she's got a message for me?'

'Yes, from someone called Martin.'

Lenox Hospital, Theatres 1 and 2
7.36 a.m.
Elliott made a wide incision from the pelvis to the sternum and opened up Archibald's abdomen.

Claire made an incision in Martin's abdominal wall.
Show me you've really got some guts, handsome.

Elliott compressed the liver with both hands, inspecting each lesion and trying to stop the haemorrhaging.

It's bleeding everywhere!
Swabs, haemostasis, draining off: Claire did everything she could to stabilise her patient.

The wound was deep and bled profusely. Elliott pulled it open to cut away the unhealthy tissue, then he used a triple clamp in the hope of being able to stitch the opening with resorbable thread.

Through her surgical glasses, Claire tried to assess the injury and what she saw worried her. She suspected a rupture of the Wirsung duct associated with a duodenal lesion.
You're not having much luck tonight, are you?
For the moment, there wasn't a great deal she could do.
Once he was completely stabilised, he'd have to be opened up for a third time for major intestinal surgery.
But would he still be alive by then?

Elliott got a move on, but he sensed that Archibald wouldn't win his last fight. He'd already been given a lot of blood and he'd withstood far more than a human body could ordinarily stand. Age, illness, multiple injuries, organs giving up left, right and centre ...
When the body reaches its limits, when life is ebbing away, what can you do but let it go?

Lenox Hospital, intensive care unit
7.40 a.m.

'Your father said that you wanted to speak to me?'

'Yes.'

Lizzie's throat was tight and her complexion pallid. She looked at Gabrielle with a mixture of fascination and compassion.

'I was over there, with them,' she began.

'What do you mean "over there"? Who is "them"?' Gabrielle asked coldly.

'I was with Martin and Archibald, in a coma.'

'You were in a coma at the same time as them,' Gabrielle corrected her.

'No,' Lizzie continued forcefully, despite her still feeble voice. 'I was with them. I spoke to them and Martin asked me to give you a message.'

Gabrielle raised her hand to stop her from going on. 'Listen, I'm sorry. You must be really tired and a little distressed by what's happened to you, but I don't believe in those things.'

'I know. Martin warned me that you wouldn't believe me.'

'So?'

'So he made me learn this sentence by heart: *Dear Gabrielle, I just wanted to tell you that I am going back to France tomorrow. I wanted you to know how much the time we spent together meant to me.*'

Gabrielle closed her eyes as an icy shudder ran down her spine. The first sentence from the first letter, the one that had started it all …

318

'Martin told me to tell you that he had changed,' Lizzie went on. 'That he had understood certain things and that your father was a good person.'

However much she wanted to, Gabrielle was still not ready to believe what she was hearing, but she had to face facts: the young girl didn't appear to be making it up.

'Did he say anything else?' she asked, sitting down next to her, on the edge of her bed.

Lizzie was now shivering in her flimsy hospital pyjamas. She closed her eyes to concentrate better.

'He doesn't want you to worry about him.'

In a maternal gesture, Gabrielle pulled up the sheet and pushed back a lock of hair stuck to the girl's face.

'Martin says he's going to find a way to come back.' Lizzie was finding it harder and harder to speak. 'When he shuts his eyes and imagines the two of you later on, he always has the same images in his mind: sunshine, children laughing ...'

Gabrielle had heard enough. She stroked the teenager's forehead to let her know that she could rest now.

Then she got up. Like a sleepwalker, she left the room and went down several corridors before collapsing in a chair, her head buried in her hands.

Through her clouded mind, a voice made itself heard. It was a voice that was both near and far, a voice from the past, reading excerpts from a letter written thirteen years before.

I'm there, Gabrielle, on the other side of the river.
I'm waiting for you.

The bridge that separates us may seem in bad repair, but it's a solid bridge, built with logs from trees that have withstood many storms.

I understand that you're afraid to cross it.

And I know that perhaps you'll never cross it.

But give me some hope.

She got up abruptly. Her face now showed determination instead of fear. If what Lizzie had told her was true, there was perhaps one person who could help Martin and Archibald.

She called the lift to go back to the underground parking lot, where she'd left her car. She waited a few seconds, then impatiently tore down the flights of stairs, her heart pounding.

You'll see, Martin Beaumont, I'm not afraid of crossing that bridge.

You'll see I'm not afraid of coming to find you.

Departure lounge
7.45 a.m.

Archibald continued to push on through the departure lounge.

Faster and faster, further and further.

The further he went, the more dazzling the lounge became: the floor was always more shiny, the windows always more sheer and transparent, the corridors always longer, flooded with a light that made you dizzy.

320

Right now, he knew that this was no longer dangerous territory, for he had passed the tests and evaded the traps.

The lounge was not the place where everything ended, but the place where everything began.

The lounge was not a place of chance, but of meeting.

The lounge was a place where the past, present and future converged.

It was a place where faith replaced rationality.

A place where one moved from fear to love.

8.01 a.m.
Persistent rain, interspersed with thunder and lightning, had been battering the city for several hours now.

Gabrielle had put the roof up on her car, but the force of the storm swamped the windscreen with such a torrent of water that the wipers of the old Ford Mustang were struggling to clear it.

It made little difference that the young woman knew the road by heart, she still had to concentrate on not missing exit 33, which led to a charmless district in the southern suburbs, where various office blocks were located.

She parked the car in the open-air parking lot of a ten-storey greyish building: the Mount Sinery health centre.

In the hall, the receptionist greeted her by her first name and gave her a visitor's badge. Gabrielle thanked her and took the lift to the top floor: the one for patients in long-term care. These movements, repeated once a week for thirteen years, had become mechanical.

321

The last room in the last corridor bore the number 966.

Gabrielle entered the room and went over to the window to pull up the blind, letting in the grey light from outside. Then she turned to the bed.

'Hello, Maman.'

28

I'LL STILL LOVE YOU

When the orchestra stops playing, I will still dance …
When the planes stop flying, I will fly alone …
When time stops, I will still love you …
I don't know where, I don't know how …
But I'll still love you …
'Le temps qui reste'
Written by Jean-Loup Dabadie and sung by Serge
Reggiani

Departure lounge
8.15 a.m.
'Hello, Valentine.'

A pair of secateurs in one hand, a painted metal watering can in the other, Valentine was getting ready to open her shop. Amid the glass partitions and immaculate white walls of the airport, the shopfront looked out of place. It had an old-world charm and cachet, resembling the flower stands found in the Parisian *faubourgs*.

Valentine turned round. She had aged, of course. Her face bore the ravages of time, but her short hair, stylish appearance and the intensity of her gaze were all reminders of the radiant young woman she had been.

Above all, she had retained that magic *je ne sais quoi* which, in Archibald's eyes, made her more elegant than a Michelangelo sculpture, more harmonious than a da Vinci painting, more sensual than a Modigliani model.

As they gazed at each other, they were both overcome with emotion.

'I knew you'd come eventually,' she said, before sinking into his arms.

San Francisco suburbs, Mount Sinery rehabilitation centre
9.01 a.m.

Gabrielle went over to the bed and took her mother's hand in hers. Valentine's face was serene and her breathing even, but her eyes, though wide open, stared desperately into space.

'I'm not doing too well, Maman, I'm losing hope.'

Valentine had sunk into a coma in December 1975, following the stroke she'd suffered giving birth. For thirty-three years, only a tangle of drips and a feeding tube had kept her alive artificially, together with a nurse and a physio who massaged her every day to prevent bedsores from forming.

Gabrielle gently stroked her mother's forehead, pushing away a stray lock, as if tidying up her hair.

'Maman, I know it's not your fault, but I've missed you so much all these years.'

In those first few months following the accident, the doctors had diagnosed a persistent vegetative state. For them, there was no doubt: Valentine was not conscious and there was no chance that she would ever recover.

'I've been feeling alone and abandoned for such a long time now,' Gabrielle confided.

Even if the press hyped up the miraculous cases of people coming out of comas, for the medical profession it was taken as read that if a patient showed no sign of consciousness after a year, his or her chances of recovering brain activity were practically nil.

And yet …

Yet it was so tempting to believe it was still possible.

Valentine had cycles of wakefulness followed by periods of sleep. She breathed unaided, moaned, fidgeted and twitched, even though it was said that these were reflexes and not voluntary movements.

'I don't have the strength to go on alone any more. With no one at my side, living is killing me.'

Gabrielle had read dozens of books, trawled through hundreds of websites. And she'd realised pretty quickly that, even for the experts, a persistent vegetative state remained a mystery. No one really knew what was going on in the heads of those afflicted.

'Maman, there has to be some meaning to all this! You've survived for more than thirty years, enclosed in your silence. If your body has kept going all these years, there must be a reason for it, mustn't there?'

Ten years after the accident, Valentine's mother had been tempted to give up hope. What was the use of going on? What was the use of refusing to mourn her passing? Several times, she had been on the point of giving the go-ahead to stop feeding her daughter and to let her pass away through dehydration, but in the end, she could never reconcile herself to it. In this respect, Elliott Cooper had been a decisive influence. The surgeon had gone to great lengths to monitor Valentine's condition, each year repeating the tests and MRI scans to take advantage of the latest advances in medical imaging.

By studying the white matter of Valentine's brain, Elliott had come to believe that the extensions of the neurons, which had been separated during the stroke, were slowly regenerating, but not enough to bring her out of the coma.

As far as he was concerned, Valentine's brain had not shut down. It was more as if it were on standby, having passed through a number of stages from coma to vegetative state before stabilising in a state of minimal consciousness.

Gabrielle moved closer to her mother. Outside, the storm rumbled on and the rain was torrential, lashing the windows and making the old dilapidated blinds shake.

'If there is any truth in what they say … if you can hear me somehow … if you are there with them too … then you've got to help me!'

Often, she had the sense that her mother was smiling faintly when she came into the room or when she told her something entertaining. She liked to think that her mother's eyes misted over when she told her of her troubles, or that her gaze would inconspicuously follow her when she moved around the room. But did it really, or was it only what she wanted to believe?

'Give me a miracle, Maman!' she begged. 'Find a way to bring Martin back to me. He's the only man I want, the only one I love, and, also, the only one who'll let me become the woman I want to be.'

Departure lounge
8.23 a.m.
In each other's arms, Valentine and Archibald were surrounded by fresh flowers: lavender-hued roses; white pink-tipped birds of paradise; orchids and pearly lilies.

'You see,' Archibald said, 'I've kept my promise that I would come and find you wherever you were, if one day I had to lose you.'

She looked at him tenderly. 'You never lost me, Archie.'

'Yet our happiness was so short-lived! Barely two years.'

'But we never really left each other. Through all these years, I was there for Gabrielle and you, and I've always watched over you both.'

She appeared serene and full of self-belief. Archibald, on the other hand, was tormented, full of remorse and guilt.

'You seem happy,' he declared.

'That's down to you, my love. I've already told you: it's you who cured me. Without you, I wouldn't have had the courage to wait for so long.'

'I've spoilt everything, Valentine, forgive me. I didn't know how to raise our daughter, how to love her, how to help her. For me, life without you, it ... it had no meaning for me.'

She stroked his cheek with her hand.

'I know that you've done your best, Archie. You mustn't think I'm angry with you.'

327

Archibald looked at the finely wrought little clock placed next to the cash register. The minutes slipped quickly by. He'd only just found Valentine again and now he was worried that he'd lose her once more.

'I've got to go,' he explained, getting out his ticket.

A sudden tear ran down his cheek and into his beard. It was the first in thirty-three years.

'I can't stand losing you a second time,' he said, lowering his head.

Valentine opened her mouth to reply, but a furious noise made them turn round.

Without them realising it, the corridor through which Archibald had arrived was now closed off. He was blocked in by a glass wall, upon which a man was hammering, trying to join them.

Martin!

Archibald went over to the wall.

The kid hadn't left!

Of course not. He must have given his ticket to the young girl, but was that really any surprise?

After ramming it with his shoulder, he tried kicking it, still to no avail.

Archibald grabbed one of the metal chairs from the entrance to the shop and hurled it with all his strength at the transparent wall. It came bouncing back like a boomerang. He tried again, with the same result.

He was powerless.

The two men were now opposite each other, separated by just a few feet. So near, yet so far.

They felt the cold hand of death around them.

Why was the departure lounge inflicting this final test on them?

Archibald stared at Valentine, hoping to draw from her some of the wisdom that he lacked.

She too moved towards the wall. She knew that within the departure lounge, just as within each one of us, there were opposing forces engaged in relentless combat.

It was the battle between light and darkness.

The battle between the angel and the demon.

The battle between love and fear.

'Everything stems from a certain logic,' she said, turning to Archibald. 'All our actions have a meaning. And we always have it within us to find the solution.'

On the other side of the glass, Martin had heard everything.

This glass barrier was his fear, he could sense it. It was the fear that he'd never managed to overcome.

If love was the only antidote to fear and if the solution was always to be found within ourselves, then ...

The diamond.

The Paradise Key.

He rummaged through his jacket pocket: the oval diamond was still there, spellbinding, dark blue and gleaming, a symbol of purity and good fortune when not acquired by someone out of greed.

He moved the mythical stone closer to the glass wall.

He might have all the faults in the world, but he wasn't greedy.

And, come to think of it, what had led him to possess the diamond was his love for Gabrielle. An immature, awkward love but one that was so strong and sincere.

He placed the tip of the jewel to the wall and, with a wide sweeping movement, scratched the glass surface to create a circular incision.

Well done, kid! thought Archibald, who then seized the chair and threw it against the glass.

This time, the glass shattered into a thousand pieces, freeing the way for Martin.

'And now, what do we do?' Archibald asked.

'Now, you leave me to talk to him,' Valentine replied.

Departure lounge
8.40 a.m.

A ray of sunlight bounced off the small shopfront, making the external woodwork gleam.

Valentine had invited Martin to sit down with her at a long trestle table outside the shop. The trestle was loaded with vases containing flower arrangements of striking originality and creativity. Wild irises combined with vibrant poppies, brilliant sunflowers, variegated tulips and blood-red carnations.

'I know a lot about you, you know,' Valentine began.

She opened a leather-covered Thermos flask and poured them each a cup of tea, before continuing.

She spoke unhurriedly, as if she were indifferent to the urgency of the situation. 'And he often talked to me about you as well,' she added, indicating her husband.

Archibald, a little way off, near the boarding gate, was getting increasingly agitated. Check-in had begun and a dense, silent crowd obediently pressed forward to take

330

their places inside the plane where the two men also had seats booked.

'Not a week would go by without him giving me some news about "the kid",' Valentine joked.

Martin watched her in fascination: she had the same inflection in her voice as her daughter, the same slightly haughty bearing, the same intense gaze.

'Do you know why Gabrielle didn't come and meet you in New York?'

Martin froze and, for a few seconds, the question that had tormented him for so long hung painfully in the air, before Valentine provided him with the explanation.

'In the autumn of 1995, when Gabrielle's grandmother died, she left her a letter telling her of my existence. Can you imagine: for twenty years, my daughter had believed me to be dead and all the time I was in a coma!'

Martin was visibly shaken. He turned away and gazed distractedly at a colourful floral arrangement in which a moonflower appeared to have been frosted in something translucent.

'Gabrielle found out right at the start of the Christmas vacation,' Valentine went on. 'She was all packed to come and meet you, but she was devastated by the news. To begin with, she spent all her time at the hospital, prostrate at my bedside, begging me to wake up. For three years, she came every day, so sure was she that her presence would help wake me from the coma.'

Over the airport's loudspeakers, a voice urged the final passengers to go to the check-in desks.

Indifferent to the flurry of activity, Valentine sipped her tea before going on. 'You don't have to be afraid, Martin.

331

Gabrielle is exactly as you imagine her: loving and faithful, willing to commit to you. Just as you are prepared to be there for her, she will be there for you.'

'But I can't go back,' Martin explained, showing his ticket.

'Yes, you can,' Valentine assured him, taking from her cardigan pocket a yellowing card pinned with the steel tip of a flower-holder.

Martin examined the document. It was a very old, rather strange plane ticket.

Depart: Departure lounge
Destination: <u>Life</u>
Date:
Time:
Seat no:

'Why is there no return date or time?'

'Because it's an open ticket,' she replied. 'You leave when you like.'

His eyes widened. He wasn't sure that he'd properly understood.

'For thirty-three years you had the chance of coming back? But why didn't you?'

She raised her hand to interrupt him.

'In my coma, Martin, I can hear everything, especially the very gloomy prognoses of the doctors. I would have returned to life, but in what state? After my stroke, my body was frozen by total and irreversible paralysis. I didn't want to be a burden, not to Archibald nor to Gabrielle. By choosing to stay here, I gave myself the role of Sleeping

Beauty – an easier role to play than that of a vegetable with wide-awake eyes. Do you understand?'

He nodded.

'Right now, I need you to do me a favour, Martin.'

'You want me to accept your ticket?'

Valentine looked down. The rays of the rising sun played on the sprigs of lilac in a blue Chinese vase in front of her.

'It's more that I want you to give me your ticket ...'

29

ETERNALLY YOURS

The sound of a kiss is not so loud as that of a cannon,
but its echo lasts a great deal longer.
Oliver Wendell Holmes

Runway no. 1
9 a.m.
The plane taxied to the start of the runway and came to a halt.

'Take-off in one minute,' announced a woman's voice from the flight deck.

The aircraft had wide windows, comfortable seats and illuminated aisles.

Valentine gripped Archibald's hand.

'You know, this is the first time we've taken a plane together.'

'Are you afraid?' he asked.

'With you, never.'

He leant over and kissed her, almost timidly, as if for the first time.

Runway no. 2
9 a.m.

Having reached the runway, the jumbo jet stopped dead,
awaiting clearance for take-off. Its four engines hummed
gently.

Seated next to the window, Martin felt his eyes were
burning. Perhaps it was fatigue? Or the blinding sun
bouncing off the tarmac? Or the build-up of tension over
the last few days? Or was it the great emptiness he felt
in the pit of his stomach, at the end of this journey to the
very depths of himself, which had been as gruelling as it
had been life-saving?

*

Now, the two planes faced each other on parallel runways,
bound for radically different destinations.

They began taxiing at the same moment, making the
tarmac vibrate beneath their wheels.

As they passed each other, interference of some sort
shook both aircraft, reminding the travellers that love and
death were but a hair's breadth apart.

'Now we'll be together for ever,' Valentine declared.

Archibald nodded his head and squeezed his wife's
hand harder still. Since the day he'd first set eyes on her,
he'd never desired anything else.

Only to be with her.

For eternity.

*

Once they reached the end of the runway, the two silver planes reared up gracefully.

As the plane left the ground, Martin felt a sudden pain shoot through every part of his body as if he were on fire.

Then everything went white.

San Francisco, Lenox Hospital
9.01 a.m.

At his friend's bedside, Dr Elliott Cooper stared fixedly at the heart monitor screen and its desperately flat line. At his side, the young intern who was assisting him couldn't understand what was preventing his mentor from pronouncing the time of death.

'Is it over, Doctor?'

Elliott didn't even hear. Archibald was his age. They were of the same generation and had known each other for more than thirty-five years. It was painful to see him go.

'It's over, Doctor, isn't it?' the intern repeated.

Elliott looked at Archibald's face. He seemed at peace, almost serene. The medic decided to hold that image in his mind.

'Time of death 9.02 a.m.,' he announced softly, closing Archibald's eyes.

San Francisco suburbs, Mount Sinery rehabilitation centre
9.01 a.m.

Gabrielle had called in a doctor and a nurse.

Her mother's condition had deteriorated for no apparent reason. After racing violently, her heart was now beginning to fail.

'Charge to two hundred!' the doctor ordered, placing the paddles on Valentine's chest for a second time.

The first electric shock hadn't succeeded in regulating Valentine's heartbeat. Neither did the second attempt. For a moment, the doctor attempted cardiac massage, steadily pumping her chest with the palm of his hand, but he'd realised that the battle was already lost.

Alone with her mother, some time after she had been pronounced dead, Gabrielle saw that her face was so peaceful, so radiant that she drew comfort from this.

'Goodbye, Maman,' she murmured, giving her a final kiss.

San Francisco, Lenox Hospital, staff room
9.02 a.m.

Claire Giuliani pushed two fifty-cent pieces into the coffee machine. She pressed the 'cappuccino' option, but the plastic cup didn't drop down and the creamy liquid spilt over the metal grille before trickling onto her shoes.

This could only happen to me! she despaired.

Furious, she hammered on the change button, as

much to let off steam as in the hope of at least getting some coins back.

Just to make things worse, her bleeper went off, emitting a shrill sound. She left the room and hurried to the intensive care unit.

'It's incredible!' the nurse said as she arrived. 'Your patient's woken up!'

What are you talking about, you stupid woman? How do you think he's gonna wake up with all the anaesthetic we've given him?

She leant over Martin. Immobile and with his eyes closed, he was breathing evenly. Claire took advantage of the moment to check his vital signs, which she found to be pretty satisfactory.

She was about to leave when … Martin opened his eyes.

He looked around slowly, then, desperate to free himself, he ripped out the tubes attached to his throat, nose and arms.

He was back.

EPILOGUE

San Francisco
Six months later
A bright-red Ford Mustang emerged into the pale light of the small hours.

The old convertible pulled up in front of the museum of modern art to the south of the Financial District, a few yards from the spring gardens and fountains of the Yerba Buena Center. A temple of contemporary art, the innovatively designed building resembled a glass cylinder which spurted up from a stack of orange-coloured brick cubes like a light well.

'If it's a girl, I think "Emma" is very pretty. Or maybe "Leopoldine" if we're going for originality,' suggested Martin.

Sitting in the passenger seat, Martin still wore a soft neck brace, a consequence of his accident. It was the first time he'd ventured outside since coming out of the coma, after six months in hospital and rehabilitation.

'Leopoldine! You sure you're feeling OK? I should remind you that you've got to conceive the child first before choosing its name. And frankly, this morning, we've other fish to fry.'

With grace and suppleness, Gabrielle bounded onto the sidewalk. That Sunday morning, the street was deserted, still bathed in the freshness and calm of dawn.

339

Martin extricated himself from the car with difficulty, leaning on his walnut walking stick with its twisted handle.

Gabrielle couldn't help teasing him. 'You look very sexy like that, honey. Just like Dr House!'

He shrugged his shoulders and leant over to undo the strap holding three wooden packing cases wedged in the back of the Mustang.

'Let me do it,' Gabrielle cried, grabbing the first one, which had the deconstructed face of a Picasso canvas sticking out of it.

These cases contained treasures stolen by Archibald over the course of the last twenty years or so. They were his favourite paintings, for which he'd never demanded a ransom: legendary canvases by Ingres, Matisse, Klimt and Goya, which would soon be returned to their rightful places in different museums around the world.

During their painful, yet life-affirming discussion at the little San Simeon cove, Archibald had given his daughter the secret address where the paintings were kept. It was his legacy to her. In three return trips and less than two minutes, Gabrielle had placed all the boxes in front of the entrance to the famous museum.

When she came back to the car, she commented that there was still one canvas, half hidden behind the seats: the self-portrait of Van Gogh, on a turquoise background, with the painter's wild gaze and his fiery hair and beard.

'Maybe we could keep that one,' Martin ventured.

'You're joking, I hope!'

'Go on! Just one!' he went on. 'In memory of your father. The painting of our first encounter on Pont Neuf!'

'Not a chance! We've chosen the straight and narrow and we've got to stick to it right to the end!'

But Martin was not ready to give in. 'You've got to admit that it would look pretty amazing in our apartment! It would give a classy edge to our sitting room. I've nothing against your IKEA furniture, but—'

'My furniture is very nice,' she interjected.

'Hmmm, depends on your point of view.'

With a touch of regret, he resolved to hand the masterpiece back. Limping, he in turn walked over to the museum to leave the painting *Man with Severed Ear*.

Then he got back into the car and it sped off.

*

The Ford Mustang went down Van Ness Avenue then turned into Lombard Street.

The rising sun bathed the city in an intense pinkish light that changed tone every minute, while the sea breeze brought the summery smell of the ocean to the south.

In the distance, veiled in a fine milky haze, the immense, familiar silhouette of the Golden Gate Bridge stood out as it was greeted by an incessant chorus of foghorns from the ferries and yachts.

Gabrielle took the slip road onto the bridge and stopped in the right-hand lane at the exact place where Martin and Archibald had held their final duel.

'Your turn now!' she said.

Just as he had done six months earlier, Martin slammed the door and straddled the blocks separating off the cycle lane.

He leant over apprehensively and saw the foaming waves breaking against the pillars firmly embedded in the ocean. His face battered by the wind, Martin took stock of his amazing luck in still being alive.

He put his hand in his pocket and touched the facets of the diamond, rolling it between his fingers.

'Make a wish!' Gabrielle shouted to him.

He took his hand out of his pocket and opened his fist to the wind. In his palm, the Paradise Key sparkled like a thousand suns.

To see it shine like that, no one would have suspected that it had brought bad luck to most of those who had possessed it.

It was out of the question to keep it, out of the question to give it back to the finance company it belonged to, who incidentally, had not dared demand its return.

So Martin looked at the precious gem one last time then with all his strength hurled it into the Pacific.

From the 'kid', he mused, directing a silent thought to Archibald.

Interview with Guillaume Musso, by Anna Brown
30th November 2010

Mention Guillaume Musso's name in France and it's not long before people start talking in numbers. Quite large numbers, in fact. It's hardly surprising when you learn that this economics teacher turned writer has sold eight million books in less than seven years. Or that his latest work to be published in English, *Where Would I Be Without You?*, sold one million copies in France alone. Or that, at the age of only thirty-six, he's writing his eighth novel, continuing the mélange of thriller, romance and the supernatural that has won him readers in thirty-three countries.

His success has surprised Musso himself. But it's not his place in the best-seller lists that pre-occupies him. The readers are his primary motivation. 'If I didn't have a readership, I don't think I would write,' he says. 'I write first and foremost for my readers.'

By all accounts, literary stardom has changed Musso very little. He still lives in his birthplace, Antibes, in south-eastern France, close to friends and family. 'I don't live the high life or go out partying,' he says. 'I'm very conscientious about work; I'm up early, to bed late.'

Gallic Books caught up with Guillaume Musso on the phone one morning to discuss his newly translated novel *Where Would I Be Without You?* in which he presents a young woman with a cruel dilemma – pitting her loyalty for her father, a notorious art thief, against her love for Martin, a dogged young detective.

Q: Why did you choose such a dilemma as the focus for the novel?

A: I wanted to try to take a female character and to confront her with two men, her father and her former lover. I wanted to explore the consequences arising from her loyalty for her father and her love for Martin. That was the main theme of the novel: to create a triangular relationship with this woman torn between her father and the man she loves. So it's about the choices we have to make in life, the difficulties we have in making these choices, especially when love seems to contradict the loyalty one has to a family member. For some critics in the French newspapers, this theme has hints of [the French seventeenth-century dramatist] Corneille about it, when one is torn between love and family loyalty.

Q: Your previous books were all set in the US, while this one takes place both in San Francisco and Paris. Why this change of location?

A: For a long time I've wanted to write a novel set in Paris, and my readers have been keen for me to do this. And it's true that quite a lot of people in France have struggled to understand why so much of my work has been set in the US, especially New York. So this time, I really wanted to talk about the Paris I love: the booksellers, the culture, the museums, the banks of the Seine. It coincided with a time when the woman I loved (and still love, incidentally!) was living in Paris, so I was constantly travelling back and forth between south-eastern France and Paris – a week here, a week there. It was the first time I'd really had the chance to live in Paris. It also made me want to create a French male protagonist – Martin. It was the first time that I'd wanted to create a protagonist who resembles me so closely.

Q: So for instance, you included elements of your life such as spending a few months in the US when you were younger.

A: Yes, that's right, when I was nineteen, I went to work in the US for four months. I did odd jobs, selling ice creams, working in hotels, washing cars. That way, I got to know New York and Manhattan. I go back there at least two or three times a year and also to San Francisco. They're places I know well, and for some reason, I don't know why, my imagination for writing is really fired up by being in a place that is not part of my usual universe.

Q: There's also your experience at the age of twenty-four, when you were lucky to survive a very serious car accident. How did that influence your writing?

A: Having so narrowly escaped being killed at the age of twenty-four made me very aware of just how fragile life is. It affected the themes I wrote about in my first book *Et Après* [which was made into a film *Afterwards*]. Elements of the same thought process are in this book too, particularly in the third part, when three of the characters are in a coma. It reminds us that life hangs by a very thin thread and that we're not immortal. Having the accident made me re-evaluate what was important in my life. I made an effort only to worry about things that really mattered, not to fret about things over which I had no control.

Q: So would you say that you and Martin just share similar life events, or do you have characteristics or emotions in common?

A: A bit of both, I think. Martin is born practically the same day as me, in the same year. He has some of the same sensitivities as I do. It's true that there was

345

a time when I was younger, right at the start of my studies, when I was on the cusp of sitting the exam to become a police officer. Maybe my life could have been similar to Martin's had I not become a writer.

Q: Another theme that runs through the novel is that of getting a second chance in life. Why does this fascinate you?

A: It is a strong theme in my work; it crops up a lot in my earlier novels. I've always been fascinated by a person's resilience, by the capacity to pick oneself up after a major trauma and bounce back or rebuild oneself. A bit like in Nietzsche's famous phrase: 'that which does not kill us makes us stronger.' Also, it's important for me to write books that have some hope or optimism. At the start, my characters are people who have been scarred by life and have experienced some major problems, but they finally overcome these things and bounce back. I'm reassured by this theme and I see from the correspondence I get from readers that it's important for them. I'm more comfortable writing books that are not completely dark or cynical.

Q: Something very striking in your book is the way you depict scenes and locations, particularly your use of colour. How do you capture this?

A: For practically every setting in the book, I've visited the place first-hand. I take photos, I talk to local people, I document the area before I write. But of all that preparatory work, I probably only look back at maybe 0.01 per cent of what I've collected, just a tiny fragment of it. I need to immerse myself in the place but at the same time I don't want to be drawn into writing great long descriptions. So I've trained myself to focus on two or three salient details.

I hope that in doing so, the reader can then recreate the image in their own mind.

My mother is a librarian and so from a very early age, I was immersed in literature and read through the classics when quite young. Later in adolescence, and as a young adult, I discovered cinema, cartoon strips, TV drama. The innovative narratives and incredible pace of some TV series and films have influenced the style of all my novels. It's very visual, it cuts from one scene to another, quite film-like. I'm at the crossroads of two cultures: that of the written word and that of the image.

Q: How would you describe your works so far for an English readership yet to discover the other Musso novels?
A: I would say that most of my other books, like this one, are a mixture of several types of genre: love stories, thrillers, and the supernatural. These three dimensions often come together. In this book, I use the supernatural in the third section to discuss more serious subjects like death, mortality, grief. The idea of using the supernatural this way came to me after watching films from the 1940s, like *The Ghost and Mrs Muir* by Joseph Mankiewicz or *Heaven Can Wait* by Ernst Lubitsch. There, ghosts are used in a light-hearted way to explore themes such as ageing or grief. Similarly my books aren't just entertainent, they have wider themes that can be read at a different level.

Q: You've said before that you write each book as if it were your last. What did you mean by that?
A: It means that each time I write, there is an enormous amount of work, for more than a year. It demands all my energy. Each time, I get a feeling that it's going to be

347

the last. I get a feeling that I'll never manage to create another book, that I never want to leave the characters I've created. It's quite strange because I do love writing – I've been writing since I was fourteen. I get a lot of pleasure from writing but at the same time it's very painful. On one hand, it's the greatest joy, to create something, to write stories, to have readers all over the world, it's like a dream. But at the same time, it's painful to write: there is the anxiety and stress that comes with success, with the pressure to come up with something new for the readers, who are eager for the next book. Each time, I push the bar a little higher and I just hope I can clear it.

Q: How would you characterise your relationship with your readership?
A: It is the most important relationship for me. I write first and foremost for my readers. If I didn't have a readership, I don't think I would write. I'm completely focused on the reader. I do lots of meetings, book signings, dedications. I read correspondence from readers for about an hour a day. There's something a little bit magical about having readers in so many countries. The country where my books sell the most after France is South Korea. So my stories are striking a chord in a country with a totally different culture from that of France. I find that exciting and kind of inexplicable.

Q: You've had an enormous success with your books, from quite early on in your writing career. What has this success enabled you to do as a writer that you couldn't do before?
A: It's enabled me to stop work as an economics teacher and dedicate myself totally to writing. I really am quite

assiduous. I don't live the high life or go out partying. I'm very conscientious about work; I'm up early, to bed late.

Success has enabled me to spend my whole day within my imaginary universe, with my characters, within my narrative. In fact, the theme of my latest book [*La Fille de Papier*] just published here in France is that of a writer who lives the life of one of his protagonists. The idea came to me one day when I realised that I spend more time in my imagined life than in my own real life.